ETERNAL NIGHT
A VAMPIRE ANTHOLOGY

EDITED BY
ANTHONY GIANGREGORIO

OTHER LIVING DEAD PRESS BOOKS

JUST BEFORE NIGHT: A ZOMBIE ANTHOLOGY
THE WAR AGAINST THEM: A ZOMBIE NOVEL
BLOOD RAGE & DEAD RAGE (BOOK 1& 2 OF THE RAGE VIRUS SERIES)
DEAD MOURNING: A ZOMBIE HORROR STORY
BOOK OF THE DEAD: A ZOMBIE ANTHOLOGY
LOVE IS DEAD: A ZOMBIE ANTHOLOGY
BOOK OF THE DEAD 2: NOT DEAD YET
DEAD HISTORY: A ZOMBIE ANTHOLOGY
END OF DAYS: AN APOCALYPTIC ANTHOLOGY VOLUME 1 & 2
DEAD HOUSE: A ZOMBIE GHOST STORY
THE ZOMBIE IN THE BASEMENT (FOR ALL AGES)
THE LAZARUS CULTURE: A ZOMBIE NOVEL
DEAD WORLDS: UNDEAD STORIES VOLUMES 1, 2, 3, 4 & 5
FAMILY OF THE DEAD, REVOLUTION OF THE DEAD
RANDY AND WALTER: PORTRAIT OF TWO KILLERS
KINGDOM OF THE DEAD
THE MONSTER UNDER THE BED
DEAD TALES: SHORT STORIES TO DIE FOR
ROAD KILL: A ZOMBIE TALE
DEADFREEZE, DEADFALL, DARK PLACES
SOUL EATER, THE DARK, RISE OF THE DEAD
DEAD END: A ZOMBIE NOVEL, VISIONS OF THE DEAD
THE CHRONICLES OF JACK PRIMUS

THE DEADWATER SERIES

DEADWATER
DEADWATER: Expanded Edition
DEADRAIN, DEADCITY, DEADWAVE, DEAD HARVEST
DEAD UNION, DEAD VALLEY
DEAD TOWN, DEAD SALVATION
DEAD ARMY (coming soon)

COMING SOON

BOOK OF THE DEAD 4: DEAD RISING
THE BOOK OF CANNIBALS VOLUME 1 & 2
END OF DAYS: AN APOCALYPTIC ANTHOLOGY VOLUME 3
CHILDREN OF THE VOID (FOR ALL AGES)

ETERNAL NIGHT: A VAMPIRE ANTHOLOGY

Table of Contents

A LIGHT TO STARVE

AXEL TAIARI

The starving tore us apart. It began with a few rumbles over who would drink who and when. The arguments turned to grudges, feuds, claw fights, gang battles and then bloomed into a full-blown civil war. The more organized clans traded clean humans like rare diamonds, keeping them chained in underground lairs and milking them like your average bovine. They fed them rich meals, kept them healthy and drained their blood bit by bit every week, filling vials with their juices and selling the vials to buy more humans. Every clean human death became a miniature tragedy. The loners like me, we morphed from hunters into buyers. One night you're emptying a schoolgirl's tasty veins, blood gushing from your lips, a grin etched on your face, and the week after that you're breaking into flats and stealing jewelry to pay for your next hit.

We laughed at the mentalists when their struggle started. The hum of electricity was a minor annoyance. After that, radios gave them headaches or made them puke. Then the television revolution, the tide of cell phones and the wireless internet boom brought forth a new invisible Hell. Mentalists taking the train at night would randomly shriek when the meat-sack next to them would get a call from his lover. Humans swamped the air. The mentalists, they shied away from cities, fearful of the signals. Silence became their haven. They retreated to the forests and the deserts, fighting over territory with the werewolves. Most of them starved, went insane or were murdered and pissed on by the shape-shifters. The more desperate ones would try to walk back into the cities despite the pain and maybe they'd get too close to an antenna, and their brains would gloriously erupt into flesh fireworks before splash-painting the pavement. The humans couldn't ignore the super-natural anymore and blood and mind-suckers alike became public knowledge. Still we laughed at the mentalists while we kept drinking. Then the vaccine was invented, and we didn't laugh so hard anymore.

The Paris sidewalks gleam with evaporating rain. Saturday night in the starless city. Walk past the Saint Michel fountain as street dancers sweat and pop joints beneath chest-thumping bass lines. Nudge myself between dumb tourists and dumber teenagers, their savory warmth blasting a constellation of shotgun holes through my stomach. The street lights unveil the dancers' perfect bodies, heartbeats and frantic blood flow compelling their veins to stand out. Saliva rushes into my mouth and I descend into the Latin Quarter's stinky alleyways before my mind breaks into smithereens. I slither past endless waves of potential meals as they clog their arteries with gyros and trade jokes in foreign tongues. Get the hell out of the cramped streets, head for the river banks. The Seine's flat surface soothes me. Every few minutes, bateaux mouches drift past, the passengers throw waves my way and I wave back thinking, you're nothing to me. I hide under a bridge, fuse with the shadows and ignite a cigarette to relieve the hunger. I stay still as the minutes race by and the ripening hours cocoon the city to sleep. Not too long after I finish my pack, I see her walking along the river. Alone.

She doesn't walk straight, drunk or high. Curly blond locks that cascade down to her waist and legs that stretch on for miles. She approaches the underpass while I shrink further back into the dark. Her scent reaches me before her. Once she's close enough, I step out and wrap my hands around her neck. She lets out a yelp of shock. I dig my nose into her skin and inhale. She smells so dense and lovely I have to bite my tongue to shreds. Force her to turn around and face me. Her green eyes lock on my fangs and she relaxes under my grip.

"You...you can't hurt me," she says. "I got the shot."

"I can still kill you," I hiss. "Unwrap your guts and dump you in the Seine. Don't have to drink you."

"Oh, God. What do you want?"

Moments later I ride the metro, her wallet in my pockets, along with her phone and music player, rings and necklace. Reduced to a scavenger. I choked her and left the body under the bridge as a present for the others to find. Give it twenty-four hours and the area will be infested with hunters, courtesy of the government.

Vampires starve the same way humans do: slowly. We're not so much dead as caught between life and the casket. Our nerves still work. Pain is very, very real. Stick a stethoscope to my chest and behold my heart morse-coding messages of life through my torso. Mucus and tears, sweat and hair growth—our bodies mimic life. But spend enough weeks without a hint of blood and your fat and muscle flutter away, black bags pop out from under your eyes and your skin turns chalk white. You lose control of your extremities, your reflexes as torpid as underwater uppercuts, rot resuming its march and jet-lagging your neural circuits from beyond the grave. It takes months to die of starvation, but the more you look, react and smell like the corpse you are, the more likely people will spot you. What works: stake through the heart or brain, silver bullets blessed with Mesopotamian prayers, severing our heads off, fire, losing too much blood from our wounds. What makes us laugh: holy water, crosses, prayers, religion in general, begging for mercy, delusional Goth kids idolizing our lives. The sun? An itching annoyance, the equivalent of walking butt-naked through poison ivy.

I get off at Charonne and embrace the streets. A few months back, Chateau d'Eau would have been my destination, but the Ames Perdues got exterminated. Hunters blew up the reinforced steel doors and burst into their hotel, machine gunned the Perdues down with silver bullets. Fourteen brothers and sisters gone. They freed the few humans kept in the cellar, then torched the place with a healthy dose of gasoline and ruthless arms nursing flame-throwers. They let the hotel burn into the night as a warning, the inferno licking the skyline while they watched and patted each others on the back. A shame, but the Ames Perdues were running greedy and failed to deliver a few vials of blood to other clans. No doubt the competition got pissed and informed the authorities of their location.

I stroll the barren streets in a hurry, the hunger tracing throbbing glyphs in my insides. Fresh propaganda clings to brick walls, depicting a man looming over a city shrouded in darkness. He exhibits cartoonish fangs, along with a face smeared with white powder and ketchup-like blood splatters. Beneath him you can read, **IS YOUR NEIGHBOR A BLOODSUCKER? ALERT YOUR NEAREST CHURCH FOR A HANDSOME REWARD**, followed by two phone numbers: the first for the Church's help line, the other for the police's supernatural department.

I reach David's place and knock on the door five times, pause, then three more times. He unlocks a myriad of bolts, opens up, takes one whiff at me and says, "Shit, you don't look so alive."

David haunts a crummy studio he bought back in the late forties. He was a salesman, a damn good one–if not the best. Now one of the last independent blood dealers in Paris, for those of us who don't want to, or can't, deal with clans. He uses his grandfather's name to fake his way through official paperwork and does it well. A horde of candles garrison the place, fashioning restless shadows all around us. No electricity or internet. No television or radio. Old habits die hard: his ex was a mentalist. A pretty redheaded thing, small and thin, but strongly attuned to the static. The girl could liquify bones with the bat of an eyelash, unbind molecules with a sneeze. She went berserk when all the white noise cajoled her away from sanity, heard the angels' voices heralding the Rapture and she tried to kill her lover for a front-row seat in Heaven. David never talked about what he did to her then, but the fight must have been brutal: multiple reddish scars deep as craters landscape his face, mangled flesh like strips of raw meat dangle loose where his right ear used to be. He inserted a blizzard-white prosthesis in his vacated eye socket.

He invites me to sit down on the stained avocado couch. He offers me a cup of jet-black coffee he heated up using a pot placed over a portable butane stove.

"I'd rather have something thicker," I say.

"No can do," says David. He slides a hand over his shaved skull and shakes his head.

"What the hell do you mean?"

"I'm out of blood. More busts in the suburbs, haven't you heard."

"Shit. What are you running on?"

"Nothing," he says, his scars writhing with each facial expression. "No shipments anymore. Last meal was a couple of days ago. Found an untreated bum while I was making enquiries up north. So completely desperate I risked it, wasn't sure if I were going to die or not. Tasted like crap but hey, you take what you get. And they're getting rare. You?"

"I can't remember the last time I ate."

He sighs and offers me a look dripping with empathy.

"David, I got money." I whip out the cash, jewelry and gadgets.

"Brother," he says, not even looking at the goods. "I know you're trustworthy. I just don't have anything for you or anyone else."

"What am I supposed to do?"

David lights up a cigarette and doesn't offer me one. He looks away for a short spell before saying, "Maybe we ought to leave town."

"And go where?"

"I don't know," he shrugs. "Migrate with the others to some of those third world countries I can't even pronounce the name of. Shitholes with governments in ruins and limited access to the vaccine. I'm gonna go soon I think."

"How long will that last?" I say. "Few years, maybe a couple of decades before they catch up and the rest of the world makes the vaccine mandatory all over the planet. Then you're back to basics, except you're in the middle of fuckin' nowhere."

"Maybe, but it's a few years of peace."

"I'm not coming, I say. Paris is my home."

"Alright, alright. You want a cigarette?"

"No. Tell me where I can find some blood, man."

"I don't know."

"Come on, there has to be something somewhere."

David sucks on his smoke for a long while after that, blowing unstable rings toward the ceiling. "There's this rumor going around, okay?"

"I'm all ears."

"Hunters."

"What about them?"

"They don't vaccine themselves."

"Where did you hear this bullshit?"

"The Pure. They captured a hunter and had one of their offspring taste his blood. Then they tortured him for a while and got the truth out of him."

"The Pure are insane. They drink each other, for fuck's sake. You believe this crap?"

David thinks for a moment. "Maybe. Part of the Church's code. Something about, if you're weak enough to get your blood sucked, maybe you deserve to die anyway."

"Jesus."

"So now you know. All I can offer."

Dawn will drag Paris out of its slumber in a couple of hours. Before heading home, I stop by Porte d'Orléans, on the edge of town. Stride for a while beneath the drizzle, hidden under the hood of my sweatshirt.

The house sits alone on a lost street where detritus litter the gutter and the city's persistent roar turns into a muffled growl. A coat of dust and dirt blindfolds the windows. Frail light strains to shine through, a weak sign of life from inside. Now and again, a phantom wanders past the windows, looks outside for visitors, for painful memories to resurface, step on the porch and say hello. The ghost doesn't notice me, lurking in the trees on the other side of the street. I watch it pace back and forth for a fistful of minutes. When it doesn't reappear and the house falls prey to blackness, I climb down, light a cigarette, and head home.

I know this house. I bought it a lifetime ago. I have watched over it thousands of nights. Or rather, I have watched over the woman inside.

I was born in the heat of World War Two, in the south of France. Years later, growing up on the farm, my father would tailor epic tales of being part of the French Resistance, stories of my mother raising me and my sisters while Dad was off slitting Nazi throats and smuggling goods and missives to nearby villages. After his smoking and drinking forced his heart to yield, my mother confided he had never fought. I was the kid that saved him from the war, the fourth child allowing him to legally take care of the family. He was gone at night because he scavenged empty houses, bringing back hidden jewelry and squirreling away money to keep us fed. Half a century later, I picture a frightened man rummaging through war-torn hovels for his family's survival, and I remember his lies with fondness.

Cell phone's alarm chirps at seven-thirty-two p.m., nineteen minutes after the sun disappears. Home: a rapidly collapsing hotel in Pigalle, where rooms are rented by the hour unless you punctuate your sentences with threat-laced words or promises of money and drugs. My last victim's MP3 player paid for this week's bill. At any given hour, women with voices eroded by tobacco manufacture gasps of pleasure or pain that slash through the thin walls. Drug dealers and pimps exchange knife wounds on a monthly basis. The receptionist greets you with a loaded hunting carbine. The police never comes here: the French mafia control the area. Five hundred meters uphill, naive tourists saturate camera rolls with pictures of Paris from atop the Sacré Coeur, minds and hearts ablaze with awe for the most romantic city in the world.

When I step out of bed I trip over my own feet and nearly kiss the ground. I barely slept, shockwaves in my intestines kept me twisting and turning. A mouth drier than bleached bones crafted nightmarish images, fountains of blood geysering out of bottomless wounds found on the bodies of dying beauties. I lean against the wall for a while, praying for the pulsing headache to evaporate and the hallucinatory locust to scatter out of view. A long cold shower and an entire bar of soap refuse to banish the stink escaping from my pores. I put on clean clothes and head off into the night.

The plan for tonight is to mug more people, and try to barter with other clans. I'm a well known loner, but not a betrayer, and that may grant me access to a fresh vial assuming I can pay the price.

Sunday night turns this city into a ghost town. I sit alone in the metro and stare at my skeletal reflection, then shy away from it. Before my nightly routine, I decide to take an early detour by Porte d'Orléans. I need to see her, if only for an ephemeral second.

Out of the metro and another cigarette keeps me company. I reach the empty street, and stop in front of the house. A flickering lamppost trickles yellowish light on the pavement. The house itself is pitch black, its windows empty of life. I crouch and wait, hoping. But no light appears. This isn't normal. There's a talon hooked in my guts, but not from hunger. For more than thirty years, the house lights have been on at night, every single day of every year. When she was out–trying to rebuild a life I had ripped away from her–the light was still on. During power outages and storms, candles would replace bulbs.

This isn't normal.

More minutes stutter by as the worry grows within me.

Then for a nanosecond, the blackness ruptures, replaced by a blue ray zooming by inside the house–a flashlight. I dash across the street, rogue fangs exploding out of my gums, a swarm of anger abuzz in my every muscle. Into the garden and up the stairs, silent as a thief I kick the door in, blowing apart the joints, the frame slamming against the hallway wall. Crash dive past the kitchen, where the cupboards and drawers lay wide open, papers, letters, silverware and dishes strewn about, and into the living room, where a crouching man waits for me, pointing a flashlight in my face with one hand, holding a gun in the other.

The shot goes off and I dodge over the couch, roll behind it as more gunshots rip through the fabric but fail to reach me. One, two, three, soundless seconds and I jump over the couch again, another shot goes off, an arctic cold stab radiating through my shoulder, meaningless and fleeting. I'm on the intruder, my hand smacking his gun away, shouting, "Where is she, where is she?" While I dig claws into his chest, blood spilling out. He screams, then hurls a legion of wild punches at my head. I grab his arm, break it, and laugh at the crackling harmony of snapping bones, pin him to the floor harder then prepare myself to feed.

Get my mouth close to his neck, can't stop myself, way past the loss of control, the thirst insatiable, never ending. Lips pressed against his skin, the fat vein there waiting for me, but then the bullet hole in my shoulder blossoms into something more, an unbearable torment driving me to shriek as it leeches away all my strength. I slap at it in a frenzy, cursing the internal conflagration scorching my nerves, but it spreads through me and I'm on the floor, rolling and writhing, fighting back my body's impending shutdown, unable to comprehend. The intruder jumps on me and simply smiles, overpowering me with ease now, and a tattooed cross on his forehead tells me all I need to know.

A hunter.

His useless right arm dangles by his side, but with the left arm he digs inside his jacket with a grin. I slam the back of my head onto the wooden floor, summoning consciousness with more pain as a galaxy of sunspot flares implode beneath my skin. While he's sitting on me, I knee him in the crotch then reach for his throat with one hand, choking him, speed jabbing him with the other. We roll on the floor and I'm on him again, as I break his other arm. No laughter this time, my pixilated vision crashing then rebooting itself while he screeches his lungs out, a desperate cry aborted within a split second because I'm still choking him, crushing his windpipe. Air soon expires, his puffed up eyes roll back, and he's out.

Six minutes later and he's still unconscious, naked and gagged with duct tape, bound tight with power cables taken from various appliances. I'm on the couch, leaking precious blood I can't afford to lose. Look at the wound: dark-red, overflowing, thin ribbons of putrid smoke unwrapping themselves, the enchanted silver bullet dissolving then corrupting the nearby flesh a necrotized black.

Leave the projectile lodged there for too long, and the dying tissue will propagate to the rest of my body. I unsheathe my claws, bite my tongue and dig into the wound. Head submerged in a thickening fog but I persist, digging around, deeper, deeper until I feel the silver's combustive lips nibble at my fingertips, charring the calluses. I let out a growl and fish the bullet out in one swift move, toss it across the room and then tear a cushion apart, wrap the ruined cloth around the wound. I rest on the couch until I manage to shiver off the chaos. I do my best to get up to take care of the hunter, but the effort shatters my balance, and before I can ease back down a total eclipse drags me away from the world and engulfs my brain in darkness.

I met Lucille on the 6th of May, 1968. The students were striking and rioting all over Paris, burning trash cans, crusading for their rights. More than six hundred students and three hundred policemen were hurt during the ensuing fights while I fell in love in the deepest bowels of a noisome bar called l'Alchémiste.

We were both enrolled in the university, but had ditched classes for the past semester in search of something more. I was a painter, a self-proclaimed struggling artist. She studied languages, Spanish and Latin, quit school when she became fluent in both and decided to spend her days reading instead. Mutual friends introduced us. Eight hours and an untold number of pints later, she was dry humping me outside the bar while I sat against a building door. She kissed me as dawn rose over the shattered city.

She followed me home.

Six years later, I left a letter on our shared bed that ended with, I'm unable to love you anymore, and abandoned our house forever. Thirty-four years later, I still remember how it felt to hold her while petals of time withered around our bed.

Cognizance washes over me in arrhythmic rip tides. An ocean of petrol first, then distant waves of my own breathing carrying me closer to reality's shores. But my consciousness begs for more sleep, for it all to stop, and I pass out again, until my blackout shipwrecks itself upon the jagged reefs of suffering still chanting in my shoulder. My eyes trudge open and I puzzle the world back together, connect the dots, the house, the fight; the hunger and the danger jump start my fight-or-flight instinct, glands dispatching a blistering blast of adrenaline that torpedoes through my veins and propels me from the couch.

A bucket of freezing cold water slaps the hunter awake. Blood pours down his destroyed face and leaks from unseen wounds seep beneath his torn black t-shirt. He can scarcely keep his eyes open. The broken arms and injuries he suffered would send a common man into shock. I crouch in front of him, rip off the duct tape.

"Where is she?"

He drools. I grab him by the cheeks then use one of my claws to puncture his leg, the sudden pain unhinging his eyelids, fleshy curtains unraveling rolled over eyeballs.

"Where is she?" I repeat. Every muscle in my system rattles from the adrenaline, each spasm and twitch making me more aware, more alive. Angrier.

The hunter stays mute, so my claw goes deeper into his leg until it tickles bone. He clenches his teeth and sweat pearls emerge on his skin, his conscience crawling back into focus.

"The woman who lives here. Where is she?"

"Gone," the hunter says with a shaky voice.

"Gone where? What are you doing here?"

The son of a bitch actually forces himself to smile and this is my cue to break his little finger. A moan escapes from his throat.

"You have nine more of those. You also have toes, a penis, and various orifices I can play with for days on end. Where is she?"

"I was left behind to look for more evidence. Piss-easy job, right? Low priority. Night shift," he laughs. "Shit shift. The...others took her earlier tonight."

"Her? Why?"

"Why do you care, vamp? She your grandma or something?"

His thumb snaps in half. More screaming.

"Eight left. It's impressive training you got, holy man. But crack another joke and I'll crack another finger. Why did your people take her?"

The hunter should be in no condition to handle more damage. He looks deader than I do. He groans and whispers, "Associating...with vampires."

"Bullshit, she's been living alone for years. She doesn't even have human friends, much less vampires."

The hunter looks around, his head lolling but his senses still tethered to his surroundings, scampering to find a possible way out. I grab his cheeks again and force him to stare at me. "Talk," I say.

"She...she kept strange hours...new neighbors reported her, she never slept at night and we paid a visit. Found a diary in her room. Fang-banger in her youth, was in love with one of you animals. You believe that?" He grins, revealing crimson enameled gums and pulverized teeth.

"Where did you take her?"

He spits in my face, a mixture of saliva and blood, the red nectar so fresh my belly immediately rumbles and I can feel my bowels contracting.

"Hungry, vamp?" he laughs, blood snail-trailing down his chin. "Have a taste; I'm dying one way or the other, anyway."

Another finger gone, then another one, then another one, a rapid fire chain of crunches as easy as breaking twigs. His entire left arm and hand now useless. He's weeping and mumbling, half delirious from the agony, stumbling through a prayer that goes, "Though I walk through the valley of the shadow of death, I will fear no evil, for thou art with me."

"I was born Catholic, so spare me," I tell him. "Time is of the essence. Let's move on to other parts of your body. Where do we start?"

I tried, for a few weeks. I snuck out at night, fed, then came back to our bed. I went out in the sun, coating my skin with hydrating lotions and creams. A well-fed vampire can fake everything. Dinner involved stuffing food I couldn't taste down my throat. Life carried on for her as if nothing had happened, while each tick of the clock made me more aware of the decay inside me.

And how do you tell the woman you want to grow old with that you never will? That you have changed, someone has cursed you with a gift you never wanted. You're nothing but an animal, damned to spend the rest of his existence sucking the life out of others. How do you stay young for eternity while she ages by your side? What of children? Vampire-human offspring die inside the womb, or come into the world as ghoulish mutants, freaks doomed to turn summer sky-blue within hours of childbirth. How do you hide everything about what you are, and pretend you are who you were? How do you tell her that when you're making love, you're plagued by horrible fantasies where you bite into one of her arteries and suck her dry?

You don't.

You pack your bags, chew off those plastic wings, and toss your mock halo in the mud. You leave with a heart so full of guilt it very well may rot, and give her a chance to be happy with anyone, anything, but you.

Half past eleven under a rusted full moon and I'm throwing up bile in the gutter. Being so close to so much blood has taken its toll on me, every inch of my flesh commandeering me to go back in and slurp up the leftover gore. When I'm done, I wipe the sick away with a sleeve and light up a cigarette. Then I call David. He has no phone in his house—part of the old habits, but always hears the public pay phone right below his window. A series of boring tones until he finally picks up, not pronouncing a word, just listening.

"David, it's me. I need your help."

"Told you I got no blood, brother."

"They have her. They have Lucille. Meet me at Tolbiac. Get any help you can. If what you told me about the hunters is true, then you and whoever you bring can feed as much as you want."

David grunts and hangs up.

I left the hunter's body in the bathtub, mutilated and dislocated. Only took a couple of hours to break him down. Burrow deep under a man's flesh and secrets will come flowing out, too many of them to remember, spectral memories haunting the limbs and begging to be exorcized. He confessed his sins, sexual acts, fantasies about succubi, throwing stones at helpless toads by a pond when he was a boy, and I let the words hum past me and only retained an address of where they are holding her. Temporary confinement while they look further into her past and decide her fate. Meaning a simple apartment, not a Church outpost. Low security, a couple of hunters at least, and possibly a chipped mentalist, one of many Judases who traded their freedom for the ability to live in cities again, in exchange for a control chip implanted smack dab in the middle of their oversensitive cortex.

So yes, I left his body in the bathtub—but still alive. After he told me what I needed to hear, I made sure to smash his cell phone to guarantee myself a few hours of peace. Either he will slowly bleed out in the tub, or his brothers will find him and finish the job before they track me down. When he understood what I was doing, he began thrashing around in his own juices, blabbering nonsense, sobbing and moaning like an infant between bouts of, "Finish it, finish it! Oh, God don't leave me here, they'll kill me, they'll kill me, they..."

But I slammed the door and left the house, muting his cries for help and sealing his fate. Whatever the Church has in store for him is worse than I could ever offer.

During the long two hours spent investigating his nerve endings, every second meant locking horns with my demons. My psyche and digestive system banded together, hijacking my common sense and mouth, whispering, "You know he's right, and David told you hunters aren't vaccinated. Drink him. It's been so long."

The only thing pulling me back from the abyss was the thought of Lucille. If I tasted the hunter's blood and David's potential fact turned out to be anything but, I would be left hemorrhaging on the floor while she was left alone, kilometers away. I owe her too much to give in to my hunger. So I saw my gruesome work to completion, and tied a knot in my guts until I could finally leave.

The years waltzed by after I left Lucille. A garbled strand of seasons where I learned about myself, my kind. Clans ruled the nights. Werewolves and warlocks were our only terror. We raided forests and sewers to win a war that never ended.

I met David. Made friends. Lost friends, too many to count. Some clans offered to take me in, but I had no desire for this kind of family. Drank blood every day, sometimes more than once. Consumed myself with guilt, then learned to conceal it underneath my ribcage.

And each night found me dropping by our house to watch over her. The light she left on became my anchor. Through the windows I saw her cry into the telephone, stare at the television set with vacant eyes, break vases and silverware in fits of rage. She tried to forge a new life, eventually. Met a man. He seemed nice. They spent their evenings having fiery sex while I bawled and clenched my fists so hard my palms squirted blood. Still the lights came on every night while he snored. She appeared to be happy for a time, until he backhanded her one whiskey-fueled night. She came out in the garden, sat among the azaleas in the starlight, displaying herself. Her ravishing face glowed purple with bruises. Dawn found the man's wasted corpse breezing down the Seine, veins hollowed out and an infinity of knife wounds emblazoned on his flesh. After that, she seemed to give up on the idea of finding love again. Friends stopped coming around, Lucille's heartbreak too heavy to witness. And still the light beckoned me every night while her youth deserted her.

I purchase another pack of cigs, chain-smoke outside of Tolbiac station, one step away from Paris' very own Chinatown. On Avenue d'Italie, a perpetual flurry of cars flash by below an oily night sky made of stark black clouds. A deluge of neon lights from endless fast food chains waging civil war flood my eyes. The long avenue is a telltale sign of the twenty-first century: fast food, temp agency, fast food, hip clothing store, bank, temp agency, fast food, pharmacy, fast food, unemployment agency. Repeat ad nauseam until the avenue takes you to the périphérique and out of the city.

I discreetly check my shoulder wound by patting it through my jacket. Still hurts, but not anywhere close to what it was earlier. David shows up twenty minutes later sporting a heavy black duffel coat that makes him look as nimble as a tank. Two young ones follow in his footsteps, wearing hooded sweatshirts and skinny black jeans saran wrapping their legs. The both of them can't be older than twenty, but they reek of worm food.

David nods at me and says, "This here's Abel and Cain."

"You've gotta be shitting me," I say.

"Hey, man," says the one on the left. "I'm Abel." Smaller than the other, rail thin, greasy black hair in a ponytail, crooked teeth and a pretty boyish face. "You got a few cigarettes for us?"

"Where you gonna store them," I reply. "Those jeans don't even let you walk properly."

"Hey, dude," says the other, built like a golem, buzz cut, obviously the alpha male. "We're here to help, okay?"

"Who the fuck are these clowns, David? I tell you to bring help and you get me children with nicknames. It's adorable, but these kids are gonna die tonight."

Cain and Abel look at each other, grinning.

David moves closer to me and says, "You think any clan would try to take on any hunter's nest? Please. Plus half of them probably have deals with the government. It's either them or no one."

I drag David a bit further away, while Cain and Abel step inside a bar to buy smokes, giggling to themselves. "I'm not taking them with me."

David laughs, rolling his one good eye. "They're hungry and young, armed and dumb, and they think they're invincible. If you don't take them, they'll follow you anyway."

"What about you, David, why are you coming?"

"Just testing my theory. No one will believe the Pure's rumors, bunch of crazy cannibalistic bastards they are. But assuming these kids taste hunters tonight and survive, then a new market opens up for me. Hunter's blood would be a big thing, especially if it has any special property."

I reply, "This wouldn't have anything to do with the mentalist they may have with them?"

David lights up a Camel, inhales, says nothing, so we bathe in the silence and let the smoke uncoil around us.

"What are you going to do about Lucille?" he asks.

"I don't know."

"She's untreated, isn't she? No vaccine?"

"Either you or those boys try to touch her, and you'll feel my wrath."

David says, "I know what she means to you, don't worry. Boys might be a problem, though I doubt it. I guaranteed them the hunters were drinkable."

I take one last drag of the cigarette then toss it at my feet before it hits me. "Shit," I tell David, "these kids are your sacrificial lambs. Food tasters and meat shields?"

He looks up at the herds of clouds trotting past the obsidian sky and says, "Oh, the things we do for survival."

How I was turned into a vampire is meaningless. It was a random act of violence on a drunken weekend, no different from the incessant rapes and murders that occupy the evening news. I stumbled out of the bar after a night out with my friends, my throat stupefied to numbness from too many tequila shots. I was headed home to Lucille, until someone grabbed me in a lightless alley. Never really saw his face. I could smell death on him, and he giggled as he stole my life away. Then the fucker made me drink his blood, gashed his wrist open and held it over my mouth. He let it drip down my throat, like feeding a newborn. He cradled me while singing a lullaby. He planted a goodbye kiss on my lips, whispered merci and vanished. I awoke in the gutter at sunrise, morning dew clinging to my skin. I went home feeling ashamed of my drunken antics, not really remembering much. I was annoyed at what I believed to be a severe hangover, and Lucille laughed it off. Nightmares came to me a few days after that, bearing shards of memories from that lost night. My usual breakfast cereals and milk left me unimpressed. Later on I walked by a butcher's shop. I stopped and found myself drooling and panting at plump slabs of bloody meat. My skin wouldn't stop tingling. I knew something was wrong, then.

The address divulged by the hunter lays only ten minutes away, down a rotten street devoid of parked cars. The four of us stand in front of the five-story building, facing a coded door.

"Which floor?" asks Cain.

"Fifth."

"Got the code?"

I nod.

David unbuttons his coat and hands me a gun, a six shot older than the both of us, and says, "At the end of the day, they're only humans. Toss it aside when it's empty."

Abel and Cain hug each other for a brief instant, then remove Uzis from their respective zip-up hoodies. "We're ready," they say in unison.

I enter the code, and we're in.

Up the stairs, not speaking, walking fast on feline soles and soon enough we face the door. Press my ear against the wood, faraway chatter echoing through.

I nod to David. The brothers stand back. David removes a shotgun from his coat and calmly blasts away the lock, the first shot of the night head-splitting loud, and we both kick the door in, light from inside inundating the hallway. Abel and Cain rush past us like wraiths, and we follow. From down the hall on the left, a voice warns, "We got vamps, send back up, hurr..."

But the sound of his voice gets cut off by a streak of gunshots barking from everywhere in the flat. I run past the kitchen while David stomps into the living room, a vague form waiting for him there, but he can handle himself. I open doors, peer inside, empty, move on to the next one. From another room, Abel screams, "Fuck you!" while Cain laughs at the percussion of gunfire. Last door in the hallway is locked but I destroy the goddamn thing with a furious slam and I'm into the room. And there she is, tied up on a chair, looking at me in her nightgown but something, someone, blindsides me and I bounce against the wall on my hurt shoulder, crying out as I do so. Cold metal pokes my temple but I duck, weave to the side and drill a solid punch into the hunter's kidney, robbing the wind from him. I grab his wrist while his shot goes off then with my other hand place my own weapon against his thorax, pulling the trigger three times. He stumbles back all blood and blank confusion, then crumples to the floor. I rush over to Lucille, her eyes still fixated on me. I kneel next to her while the dissonance of violence swells up in the other rooms.

"Are you okay?" I ask, fumbling behind her and failing to break the cuffs.

"It's you," she says.

"I can't undo the cuffs. I need to find the key. Where is it?"

"It's you," she repeats, about to burst into tears.

I stop, calm down, look at her. Place a gentle palm on her face, a gesture my muscles never forgot. "It's me," I say.

Time has scrambled her features into a patchwork of wrinkles, the decrepit ruin of old age unable to avoid but her eyes have never changed–a loving blue a man could build a dream on.

Then Cain screams, "No!" at the top of his lungs, his yell tailgated by several fat blasts from David's shotgun. I rise up and sprint out, shouting out their names and enter the living room. Spare a slice of a second to take in the scene: Abel kneeling and crying over his murdered brother, his hands bathed crimson. A dead hunter lies discarded near them, body freckled with tiny bullet holes all slobbering red. Umpteen shells grace the linoleum as if they had just hailed from a murderous sky. The flavor of copper and sugar waft heavy in the air. Cain's head has been obliterated to a chunky stew, his beyond damaged body resting on the floor. In the corner, a shotgun-less David wrestles against someone and begs for help. I jump past Abel, yell for David to move away, which he manages to do and I fire the leftover bullets at the man–clearly not a hunter by his attire, and wait for his inevitable collapse.

The man stands still, rips his gaze away from David and turns his head in my direction. Two meters tall, spiked blond hair, twice my weight but all muscles. His eyes shine a nuclear-green and his mouth offers a smirk. The bullets I fired his way hang in the air, as if frozen in time.

David, out of breath, mutters, "Guess why I dropped the shotgun?"

Behind us, Abel's mournful wails never cease.

The hovering bullets spin around slowly, now aimed in my direction. David gasps then charges into me as both of us go wrecking into the coffee table while the bullets soar past us, missing by centimeters. We rise up side by side, I toss the gun away then pounce on the mentalist with David. We pummel him, two versus one but something's wrong. Knuckles brush by my face and the skin splits open canyon-wide. I throw everything I have behind heavy fists but an electrical crackle deflects each hit, air and static braiding an ethereal wall I can't break. The mentalist has a shield up. An interminable succession of blows and parries compose the sickening melody of dragged-out primal fights while Abel's cries reach a new level of misery. I keep punching, kicking and biting while my body crepitates and tries to dismantle itself. My tongue stings and I gurgle pure high voltage, then my mouth overflows with boiling blood and I think this is it, end of the ride.

David pulls away, about to succumb or so I fear, leaving me to deal with the bastard by myself which I do pitifully, by now my skin singing, a burning meat smell invading my nostrils, my whole perception flaring a sparkling blue until I see the mentalist's cocky grin switches to a confused frown. Do a one-eighty and David removes something big and squarish from under his huge coat, presses a button and the mentalist tries to back away but it's too late: a gorgeous crescendo of classical music blasts forth. David grabs his portable radio like a brick in his palm and slams it against the mentalist's skull, his nose spraying blood straightaway, the frequencies too strong for the chip in his head to handle, and this is my cue to move in. I dig my claws directly into the mentalist's eyes, through them as violins and cellos screech and he falls to the ground, David and I both tumbling over him while he struggles and shrieks, trying to protect himself. Mad sprites detonate all around the room, arcing branches of lightning searing the walls. I get back up. The mentalist froths at the mouth, a rabid seizure trapping him to the floor, the walls of his mind caving in at the sound of his own requiem. I lift my foot up and stomp on his head. Again, and again, and again, flesh, veins, bones and gray matter squashed to a messy oblivion.

I help David back up and realize the extent of his injuries for the first time. Blisters cover most of his still-smoking baked face. Dime-sized smothering holes flourish on his coat. David can barely stand up by himself. He drops the radio to the floor, removes and throws away his coat with a whimper. He feels his face with a cautious hand. In the corner, Abel rocks back and forth, holding Cain's body, whispering useless comforting words where his brother's ear used to be.

David limps over to him and crouches. He says, "I'm sorry. I'm so sorry." But Abel doesn't hear him.

Glittering shades glissade around in my vision but I beat them away with blinks, every inch of me shuddering, my body trying to heal itself but me starving slows the process.

David turns around and eyeballs the dead hunter. He squats near the body floating in its pool of blood. He stares at Abel, says nothing. Then dives a finger into the blood and smells it.

"No, don't," I tell him.

But he simply nods and replies, "I changed my mind. That kid already lost a brother tonight. I'd rather not have another death on my hands," and he licks his finger.

I await, ready to see him convulse and howl. David breathes in and out, waits. Abel, still holding Cain, looks at David, too.

David's eye expands like a blast of fireworks, colors shifting, and he digs his head into the unvaccinated blood, licking it up like a starved dog, slurping noises followed by grunts of pleasure. Abel gets up, placing his brother's corpse on the floor in silence, and joins David in his feeding.

I leave them to it, in spite of everything.

Back to the room where they kept Lucille. She gasps when I enter, relief inundating her features. The other hunter's body is still here, his walkie-talkie working and emitting warnings. They'll be here soon—backup, more hunters, more mentalists, the police. We have minutes left to slip away, if we're lucky. I dig through the hunter's pockets and find what I need. I reach behind Lucille and unlock her cuffs. She falls on me, embraces me so tight despite how frail she looks, her perfume the same as it was all those years ago but I can't hold her up, I'm too weak, and her smell is so perfect I might just have myself a nervous breakdown.

"Are you hurt?" I croak.

She whispers, "I knew you'd come, all those nights. I guessed what you were, when the news told everyone about...you know. I waited and waited and..."

"We have to go," I tell her. "We'll talk at home." But a thought slaps me: where is home now?

Black and white still-frames assail my head: a new life together, me by her side, young and perfect while she exhales her last breath in a piss-stained hospital bed. We have no future together, there is no point in lying to myself. But in this instant, it doesn't matter. It doesn't matter.

She gets up. I try to do the same but can't. A warm migraine inflates within my cranium, the pain, exhaustion and starvation too much to take. I'm bleeding so much I must be running on empty. Lucille sees this, then helps me up without a word, my wounds staining her velvet nightgown. Her iceberg blue eyes look at the dead hunter. The walkie-talkie keeps repeating that backup is on the way. I calmly stagger to the corpse and kneel. Every joint in my body broadcasts hysterical distress signals, my famished stomach amok from such a long starving. I turn back to her and she nods, blind approval for who I am, what I need.

I bend over the still warm cadaver, drown my parched lips in blood, and as she watches over me, I feast.

GOAT SUCKER BLUES

CHRIS DEAL

The two vaqueros rode out into the southern field as the sun decided to make its morning appearance. They traveled the low, sloping hills, over grass eaten down beneath the hooves of their conveyance by the cattle they moved between. Each bull, cow and calf bore the Cole brand, but the rich man rarely came out to the ranch from the city, and neither vaquero had even seen him astride a horse, much less riding the land. The only time Tobin ever thought of the heir was when he took his monthly pay. Mel had never met the boss.

Mel was seasonal, an indígenas, and would go home to Atarjea, Guanajuato in the winter. Tobin was there year round. He was always glad to see Mel come back in the spring, fat from his wife's cooking, full of stories about his children, while Tobin spent the winter, Christmas, with the other hands at the ranch.

"We could have waited for the huevos," Mel said.

"Could have, but then the sun would be out."

"Could have slept a little longer."

"Could have, then we'd be out of a job."

They kept riding, the conversation silenced, drinking the remains of the morning's coffee. Mel watched as Tobin poured out tobacco from his pouch into an open paper, his cup balanced in the hand that held his reins. He licked the cigarette and closed it tight. He placed it between his lips and lit a match on the saddle, inhaling and letting out a filament of smoke that rolled and found the currents of wind, and left them to go down towards Mexico.

"You'll need to teach me that someday," Mel said.

"Can't teach a stray dog no tricks."

Four miles from the ranch, towards the river where the land got rockier and the grass grew sparse, they were past the herd, save for some stragglers. The two men pushed their horses to the edge of the river and followed it to the west. After ten minutes, with a smell on the air, they found what they were looking for. A bull lay on the ground, a few feet from the river, covered in flies and early maggots, lying before God, the morning sun, and the two vaqueros.

"Ese es un gran toro," Mel said.

"Yep," Tobin replied.

"No coyote'd go after one that big."

"I don't doubt that."

"Los lobos?"

"Ain't no damn wolves around here."

"Could be a stray. La unica."

"Could be."

"Probably not, though."

"Probably not."

"Mi padre told me once that when he was a little gordo, un lobo came to the farms of his little village, down from the mountains, and it started killing goats and chickens, perros y vacas. The men of the village were worried it would soon start going after los niños. So, mi padre went out one night, just after la medianoche with mi abuelo, mi padre carrying the rifle. They went out to the field and found a good place, favor del viento, and they waited for hours. Mi padre was asleep when mi abuelo took the rifle from him, and he took aim. Mi padre saw el lobo among the cattle, going slow, very low to the ground. It was crouched, and just about to jump a vaca. Mi abuelo, Dios lo bendiga, he pulled the trigger and boom," Mel said, making the motion of the firing gun with his hands, "and mi padre swears he heard el lobo scream. When mi abuelo y mi padre went to where el lobo was, it was gone, no blood anywhere, and mi abuelo knows his padre shot it. The bullet was sitting on the ground where it was."

"Bullshit," Tobin said, spitting coffee grounds to the dirt.

"It's true. La mano de Dios," Mel said, his hand in the air.

"You're from Atarjea. Ain't no damn mountains in Atarjea. Ain't no damn little village, either."

"You calling mi padre mentiroso?"

"I'm calling you mentiroso."

"I never said I wasn't."

"Neither did I." Tobin put the empty cup in his saddlebag, and got down from the horse. His feet on the earth, he gave the reins to Mel, who stayed atop his mount. Tobin took his knife from his belt and the sun struck the blade, scattering the morning's light out to the field.

He approached the beast slowly, carefully, with the reverence the thing deserved on its deathbed of clean, trampled grass. He crouched down on his knees above the animal's throat. It had been torn out. Tobin poked into the wound with the knife, moving the growing maggots out of the way. He then took the knife and dug it into the bull's chest. Nothing came out.

"No sangre?" Mel asked.

"Nope."

"Could be caimán."

"Could be, except there ain't no damn alligators up in this river. Ain't nothing but cow shit."

"Could be el chupacabra."

"Ain't no damn such thing as chupacabra."

"How many does that make?"

"Seventh bull this month."

"Could be more."

"How's that?"

"Coyotes may have taken some bodies. Could be more we're not finding."

"Could be, but on those we've found, there ain't no sign of coyotes. This one's been here since last night, I'd say. They'd have been eating the damn thing soon as it fell. Coyotes don't want nothing to do with whatever's been doing this. Ain't even a damn vulture around," Tobin said, looking to the sky, holding his hat to block the sun rising in the east.

"Smells bad out here. Extraño."

"That it does."

"Why ain't the coyotes been here?"

"Don't know."

"Could be el chupacabra."

"Ain't no damn chupacabra." Tobin stood to his full height and put the knife back in his belt. He took the reins back from Mel, put his foot in the stirrup and got back on the horse. "Let's get back."

"Huevos are going to be cold," Mel said as they started back to the ranch.

"Probably." Tobin rolled another cigarette, lit it and exhaled the smoke. The wind had shifted, took the smoke out over the river.

"Nothing worse than cold huevos."

"Well, you didn't have to come out with me."

"You told me to."

"You could have stayed in bed a bit longer."

"I don't like you sometimes."

"Yeah, well, at least you didn't miss out on any time with me."

"Rather spend the time with el chupacabra."

* * *

When they got back to the ranch house, Mel went to the kitchen to scoop up the cold, leftover eggs, and Tobin went to the office, where Teresa, Cole's sister—the owner—and the only member of his family that wanted anything to do with the ranch was doing her paper work.

"What say you, Tobin?" she said when he knocked on the door.

"Another bull out by the river, ma'am."

"Damn. Sixth one this month?"

"Seventh."

"Damn. We can't afford to be losing them like this."

"At this rate, we'll be out of cattle in a month."

"Maybe," she said, laughing. "What do you thinks doing it?"

"Don't know. No coyote could take down a bull the size of this one."

"A wolf, maybe."

"Doubt it, ma'am. Aren't any wolves around these parts anymore?"

"Guess not. What do you think we should do?"

"I'm going to go out by the river tonight. See if I can figure out what's happening."

"All right. See if Melquiades will go with you."

"Yes, ma'am."

"And be careful out there."

"Yes, ma'am." Tobin stood for a moment, about to say something more. Teresa waited, the thought in her mind that she knew what he was going to say, but he nodded, and left the office, to go outside, to the porch. He sat in an old rocking chair and rolled a cigarette, using both hands this time, finishing the job faster than on the horse. He sat smoking, looking out over the land he worked. There were clouds out, past the river. He crushed the first smoke under his boot and rolled another. Mel came out from the kitchen, holding a sopping tortilla wrapped around his eggs. He chewed slowly, and watched the clouds with Tobin.

"What'd she say?"

"That you're a damn idiot and you're getting a pay cut."

"Mámalo."

"Figures you'd say that."

"We going out there tonight?"

"I am. You can come if you want."

"I got a say in it?"

"Yeah, you do."

"I'll come out."

"You really do deserve that pay cut."

"Güey. Bring a bottle with you."

"Will do."

"When do you want to go out?"

"After supper."

"Trabajo?"

"Trabajo."

*   *   *

The day moved as if under the apathetic eye of a sleeping god. Tobin, Mel and the other hands were out in the fields. A fence to the north needed mending. The horses needed feeding. The cattle needed to be looked after. By lunch, Tobin had forgotten the morning's dead bull. All hands came to the kitchen for their daily tortas. Tobin sat at the end of the long table, his back to the window brimming with sunlight, warming his back. He took a big bite from the torta de lengua, a sip of his horchata, and he thought only of the food, the drink, the present. Mel got himself a sandwich and drink and joined him at the table, sitting across from him.

"Guillermo and Hugo were out in the southern field."

"Were they?" Tobin asked after a swallow of horchata.

"Down by the river."

"We need to have someone go get that bull."

"That's why they were there."

"They get the bull?"

"Dos."

"What?"

"And the calf."

"What?"

"They were maybe five hundred feet from the first, just by the river."

"Three last night."

"Guillermo said there were footprints around the bull. It was barely out of the water."

"We need to run a fence to block that river."

"He said that the footprints looked almost human."

"Christ."

"There was no sangre. None at all."

"Christ Almighty."

"You know what I think it is."

"Don't you say it." Tobin took the last bite of his torta and swallowed it down with some horchata. He stood up, took his plate and cup to the washbasin. He went out to the porch again, sat in a rocking chair and rolled a cigarette. He didn't want to say it, especially not to Melquiades, but a part of him was beginning to humor the man's idea.

When Tobin rolled and lit up his third smoke, Mel came out onto the porch with a cup of coffee and sat in the rocking chair to Tobin's left. Mel put the cup on the ground beside him, and took a cigarillo from his shirt pocket.

"Tienes una cerilla?" Tobin handed him the matchbook, and Mel took his time selecting the perfect stick. He struck his match and lit his cigarillo, holding the smoke in for a few moments, savoring it. "I was thinking," Mel said, his voice filled with a dangerous tone.

"Now you know we don't pay you to think."

"Es malo."

"We tried letting you think once, you know."

"I know."

"You thought it would be a good idea to try raising llamas out here."

"Shut up."

"This place ain't going to make no damn money on llamas."

"I was thinking, maybe we need to take some bait with us when we go out there tonight."

"Bait."

"Si, some bait."

"What sort of bait were you thinking?"

"Cabra, of course."

"Cabra. You want to take a damn goat out there."

"Thinking it's only right."

"It's only right. How is that?"

"We keep las cabras so close, that's why el chupacabra goes after los toros y vacas. It really wants them cabras."

"You're a damn idiot sometimes, Mel."

"You going to tell me you weren't thinking it? What the hell else is going to be drinking the blood of them ganado."

"It sure as hell ain't a chupacabra. Ain't no such thing as a damn chupacabra."

"You know, when I was a boy, I didn't think there was such a thing as gringos. You sure changed my mind on that."

"You ever stopped to think that the answer is obvious."

"The answer."

"It makes perfect sense, you just stop to think on it."

"Que es?"

"Aliens."

"Chinga usted."

"No, listen, it's true. Aliens came down and abducted them cattle. Ran some tests on them, checked whether or not they'd make a good food source, found them not to be quite right for the need, then checked to see if maybe they could breed with them, then drained the blood to fuel their space ships, and dropped them back down, then went to your bunk while you were sleeping and shat in your pants."

"Hijo de puta," Mel said with a laugh, coughing on his cigarillo.

"Makes about as much sense as a damn chupacabra."

"You're right. It's silly."

"Still, it's a good idea. We'll go out there with a goat. See if that can lure whatever-the-hell is doing this into our sights, and then we blow it away. If it happens to be a chupacabra, you and me will take it out on the freak show circuit; make us some real walking around money."

"Sounds like a plan."

"That it does. Just don't let me catch you thinking no more."

"Puta."

* * *

Tobin had supper with Teresa, in her office. They kept the door closed. None of the other hands, not even Mel, said a thing about it. Tobin had been there the longest of them all, since before Michael Cole, the old man's heir, had taken control and left his sister, Teresa, in charge of the day to day matters. Cole went to the city to spend all the money he made off the cattle. Even before the old man had died, the younger Cole was a rare sight on the land. Teresa had been raised up among the horses and cattle. Tobin had been a young man, new to the Texas sky, when he taught Teresa how to ride the mare her father gifted to her. There was no need for talk of the time they spent together. Old man Cole had thought highly of the Okie. He had always been a good worker, the best on the ranch. There was talk from the old man that he would sell the ranch to Tobin one day, but the old man's son had raised a stink about it, about how the ranch was his inheritance, that it was only right it came to him when the old man decided it was time to give up control. When the old man's health took a turn, Michael Cole signed the papers and the ranch was his, but he gave his sister the position as manager to placate her. He came by maybe once a year to make sure it was running its best to keep his bank account full to the brim.

Tobin had a bunk out with the other hands, in the cabin old man Cole had built, with a television and showers and enough beds for ten men, but he spent most nights in the main house with Teresa. The younger Cole may not be the most loved of bosses, but Teresa was fair, and Tobin was a respected elder, though he could still do all he needed and had no issues throwing a few punches when necessary if the need arose.

No one talked about the time they spent together. There was no need.

After having their suppertime in the office, Tobin went out to help Mel put together what they needed for the night. Canteens of water, a bundle of tortillas and beans, the goat and the bottle Tobin had conceded, their rifles, and a bedroll for each. Teresa gave Tobin a peck on the cheek, and not a hand there so much as snickered. Mel was up on his horse and looked away, out to the southern field. Tobin nodded at her, put his foot in the stirrup, and lifted himself up to the saddle. The two vaqueros were off with out a word into the dying light, their horses moving without a hurry through the standing cattle.

In the northern sky, stars began opening their eyes to the lonesome men, watching with interest as they rode towards the clouded night. In the south, a cord of blue light cracked through, out over Mel's homeland, and some moments later a rumble came out over the land, into the heart of each man, a reverberation that rattled their ribs as the evening wind blew coldly over them, bringing the smell of cattle droppings to their nose, a smell familiar and comforting to each. The moon rose like a black eye in the east. The cows murmured in their slumber. The goat trailed behind them, it's rope tied to Mel's horse.

The low, childlike gurgle of the thirsty river met them after an hour's travel. From his saddle pouch, Tobin drew forth a flashlight, and as they went along the river, he shinned it like a searchlight until he found what he was hoping not to.

"Un toro," Mel said, looking at another dead bull awash in the halo of light, less than five feet from the river.

Tobin got down from his horse, as did his compatriot. Both men crouched down low on their knees over the deceased. The wound on the animal's neck was still steaming in the cool night, and he didn't have to, but Tobin put his hand to the beast's chest. "Still warm." He stood back up and shined the light over the surrounding sand. A trail of tracks led to the bull and back to the water. The air smelled of shit.

"What do you think?"

"Seems whatever did this is across the river."

"Si."

"Come on. Let's cross here."

"Here?"

"The river's barely a foot or two deep. Get your lazy ass back up on that horse."

"Pajero." Mel went and got back on his horse, and Tobin picked up the goat and handed it up to him.

The river was fifteen feet wide and came up to their horse's knees. They crossed slowly, keeping the animals calm, each man mindful of loose rocks. The foul stink in the air became heavier when they reached the other side, and the horses started to behave skittishly, jumping at the wind in the brush, the water running by. The two horses were tied to a low tree. Tobin found a thick stick, two feet long, and started whittling a point on the end. Satisfied, he pushed it deep into the ground, and tied the goat's leash to it. The animal went to the end of the leash and began eating the fresh grass.

The two vaqueros sat at the base of a tree and waited, a rifle across each lap. After an hour of silence, Mel took out the bundle of tortillas and beans.

"Frijoles están fríos."

"What you want me to do about that?"

"Get a fire going."

"Give it an hour."

"Tengo hambre."

"Eat them cold, then. Let's wait and see what we see before we start up a fire." Mel put the food back in the bundle and set it to the side.

"What do you think that smell is?"

"Cow shit."

"Don't smell like no cow shit I've ever smelled before."

"You a connoisseur of cow shit now?"

"You know what I mean."

"Yeah."

"Ever been this side of the river?"

"Maybe once or twice. We never kept nothing out this far."

"We're not all that far from the border."

"Nope, we're not. Be quiet."

"Could be anything out here. Narcos."

"Ain't no narcos out here. We've never had a problem with any-one crossing the land. Be quiet."

"I don't like it out here."

"Shut up."

"Extraño."

"I mean it, shut up. Did you hear that?" he asked, standing to his feet, clutching the rifle. Mel mirrored him. They stood stock still, watching the outer dark, listening. There was a sound like breathing, quieter than the horses, the goat. Tobin lit up the flash-light and shined it out over the surrounding brush.

A flash of movement, and something like a growl came from the north.

Quick footsteps away and the two vaqueros were following, away from the horses, the bait. After a minute, Tobin stopped, and Mel almost ran into his back. The sound of the pursuit had gone quiet.

"What was it?" Mel whispered. Tobin swept the light from side to side, all around him. The breathing was still there, just outside of sight. It was heavier, winded.

"Don't know. Looked white."

"White? Un gringo?"

"Don't know. It was low to the ground. A wolf, maybe."

"Thought you said there were no lobos out here."

"Quiet." Tobin extinguished the light and put it in his back pocket. He held the rifle like a soldier, stepped softly, avoiding twigs or rocks. Mel took his lead.

There was a rustle to their left.

Tobin turned and fired at the sound. The explosion kept any-thing else from reaching their ears.

The older hand took the light back out, shined it where the bul-let had gone.

A drop of blood on the dirt.

A trail of red leading away from the river.

They followed the markings through the brush, direct for fifty feet to a small cave made from two boulders. The outside was littered with the bodies of small animals: squirrels, rats, rabbits and bats.

Not a drop of blood anywhere to be seen.

"I told you. El chupacabra."

"Shut up."

Tobin shined the light into the opening of the cave. The dark was stronger than the light, refused to give any ground.

"Come on," he said.

"In there?"

"In there."

"Mierda."

Stepping inside, they found the cave to be deeper, going into the ground, like a burrow. They heard the breathing, louder, echoing off the walls. It was harsher. Whatever the source, it was in pain. Something like a whimpering came to the two.

"You hit it."

"Yeah."

Ten feet in, there was a rustle of movement. The flashlight illuminated crude designs on the dirt walls, shapes like bulls, buffalo, and something like a person, more animalistic. The drawings looked to be made in blood.

They went towards the sound, deeper underground. The walls got closer, more claustrophobic. The light save for their torch grew darker. The air thicker. The smell fouler, shit and sulfur and decomposition. More animal corpses lined the walls.

The tunnel opened up into a small den, ten feet wide. A nest of twigs and scraps of cloth was in the center. A body rested there. The source of the breathing.

It looked like a man. Emaciated, with not an ounce of fat under the pale, luminescent skin. Thick fibers of muscle. Hair long and dreaded with dirt. A patchy, black beard crusted with blood. The thing's eyes were the color of the sky by the horizon, twisted with hate and pain. It growled, not the sound of a man, but a cornered animal. The bullet had hit its shoulder, gone straight through. Thin rivers of blood on its chest and back.

The thing got to its legs. They trembled at first, but grew steady. Tobin raised his rifle, took the thing's head in his sight.

With an obscene screech it threw itself at Tobin. He didn't hesitate with the trigger. The explosion was louder in the close walls of the burrow. The thing fell to the ground in a pink mist.

Tobin waited for his breathing to steady, for the hearing to come back to his ears. "Told you weren't no damn chupacabra."

Mel didn't respond.

Tobin turned slowly, making sure another bullet was in the rifle's chamber.

Mel was on the ground, another thing on top of him, its broken yellow teeth in the man's neck.

Mel tried to speak, only a bubble of blood came out.

Three more things stood between Tobin and the exit. He fired, once, twice, until the cartridge was empty.

The things kept coming.

SYLVANIA'S BEST

TONY SCHAAB

Trent opened one eye and looked around cautiously.

He realized that he was face-down on the floor; which was a good sign. That means that last night's party must have gone well, right?

He slowly got to his feet, brushed off the front of his shirt, and looked around his apartment. It was a total disaster area: empty pizza boxes and beer bottles covered every inch of his coffee table and both end tables, the recliner was on its side with the footrest up, the couch cushions were spread throughout the apartment and nowhere near the actual couch, and the kitchen table was covered with various empty hard liquor and wine bottles.

Trent smiled widely. Even though he had a throbbing headache and couldn't remember much of it, the party must have been awesome. His first year as a PolySci student at the University of Pittsburgh hadn't gone exactly as he had planned; between studying hard to make sure he earned the grades he needed to keep his scholarship and working part-time to pay the rest of his bills, he certainly didn't have any time for socializing or making close friends. A few weeks ago, he finally decided he'd had enough of feeling lonely and invited every classmate and casual acquaintance he knew to a party he was throwing. A promise of providing all the beer and booze anyone wanted, for free, had ensured that plenty of people showed up for the big event last night.

Even though his memory was a bit muddled through the haze of his hangover, he was confident that he had made friends and collected a lot of phone numbers and e-mails, which was exactly what he wanted to happen.

A hot shower and a few aspirins later, he was ready to start cleaning up the apartment. Starting in the living room, he unfurled two huge trash bags and began piling the empty pizza boxes and beer bottles from the tables into the big black bags. After gathering up the trash there, he moved into the kitchen, where the table was full of more beer bottles, used shot glasses, and an assortment of liquor bottles, most of which were totally empty.

As Trent dropped the beer bottles into the trash bags one-by-one, he thought absent-mindedly about keeping the empty liquor bottles, perhaps displaying them somewhere as a sign to others that he was a guy who knew how to party, and as a reminder that last night had actually happened. He had been to the apartments and rented houses of other students and seen rows of bottles prominently displayed, almost like a notice to others that said, 'Hey...we *party*,' so why couldn't he do it, too?

He might have to take them down when his parents came to visit, but that would be a small price to pay.

He grabbed the bottles by the necks, three or four at a time, and took them to the sink to wash out prior to displaying. As he grabbed the last few bottles, he stopped and looked at one bottle in particular that he didn't recognize. It was a wine bottle made out of dark brown glass with a small, nondescript white label on the front. Printed in a large bold font at the top of the label were the words **SYLVANIA'S BEST**.

Beneath that, in smaller letters, were two more lines that read **Bottled 2002** and the initials **B.A.T.**

Frowning slightly, Trent turned the bottle to look at the back side. There was no UPC code, ingredients list, or bottler information listed anywhere. He didn't remember buying this bottle, so he assumed that one of his guests must have brought it.

He then suddenly noticed that the bottle was corked, and there was still some liquid left in it. He grabbed a clean glass from the cupboard and put it on the table. He uncorked the bottle, putting it under his nose and taking a sniff. The liquid inside had a sweet aroma, a little like rusted metal mixed with the smell of salty seawater. He poured a little bit of liquid into the glass. It was dark red and thick, much thicker than the average liquor, making for a slow pour and pooling quietly in the glass.

He put the bottle down and lifted the glass to eye level, visually inspecting the syrupy liquid. He cautiously lifted the glass to his lips, ready to taste it, when he was interrupted by the sound of *Don't Stop Believin'*, the ring tone on his cell phone. He put the glass down and quickly scrambled around the apartment to find his phone, finding it under his bed. He'd just flipped the phone open when the call stopped.

Every time, he thought as he looked at the caller ID of the missed call: Unknown Caller. He shrugged, tossed the phone on the bed, and went back into the kitchen.

He picked up the bottle and stared at the brackish liquid inside. After a moment of silent debate, he picked it up and carefully poured the contents of the glass back inside. He re-corked the bottle, put it on the far side of the kitchen counter, and went back to cleaning his apartment.

Twenty minutes later, Trent sat on the reconstructed couch, trying to watch Sports Center. He found that he couldn't focus on the show, however, as he was still thinking about the strange bottle in the kitchen. Who could have brought it to the party last night? Someone with the initials B.A.T., maybe? He mentally ran through the list of party guests he remembered seeing last night, trying to come up with a match. He sat upright on the couch when it suddenly came to him: Brandon Taylor.

A classmate of his from this semester's Geopolitics class, Brandon had definitely been at the party last night, and Trent vaguely recalled him bringing a brown paper bag with him.

It was as good a lead as any, and Trent found the urge to know about the origins of the bottle growing by the minute. Even though Trent didn't know him very well, Brandon was his friend on Facebook.

A quick moment on his laptop revealed that Brandon, in addition to being a Pitt student, worked as a blood drive coordinator for the Red Cross.

After a few moments of internal debate, Trent decided it couldn't hurt to at least pay Brandon a visit and ask some innocent questions about the nature of the bottle and its contents. He grabbed the bottle and put it in his backpack. After a quick phone conversation with a gentleman at the Red Cross office, Trent discovered that Brandon only worked nights, and would be in to work this evening.

Trent spent most of the afternoon plodding around the apartment, going back into the kitchen to inspect the bottle every so often. He wasn't sure what about it was so enchanting to him, but he knew he had to have more information about it.

After what felt like an eternity, evening came. Trent grabbed his backpack and his car keys and braved the chill of the late-fall air. Even as he drove across town, his thoughts constantly meandered to the bottle inside his backpack.

Pulling into the parking lot of the office complex, he found a parking spot for his Honda Civic, turned off the car, and sat blankly for a moment with his hands on the steering wheel. His eyes shifted down to his backpack, sitting upright on the passenger seat next to him. Inside it was the bottle with the strange liquid that had somehow propelled him into action, and now he was about to go question one of his semi-friends with the very good chance that he had no idea about the origin of the drink.

Being this proactive was very uncharacteristic for him and he wasn't entirely sure he was feeling right in the head.

Before he could talk himself out of it, Trent grabbed the backpack and headed into the office building. He checked the directory in the lobby and headed up to the third floor, where the Red Cross office was located. He entered the office, and walked down a long hallway and cautiously entered the first room he came to. A young woman looked up at him from a desk just inside the door and with a smile said, "Hi there, can I help you?"

Upon entering and looking around, Trent noticed that Brandon was sitting at another desk in the far corner of the room, chatting on the phone. When Brandon recognized Trent, he hung up the phone and waved to him. "Hey, Trent, what's up? Come on over."

Trent smiled at the young woman, pointed to Brandon, and made his way across the room to Brandon's desk.

Brandon, who didn't get up, reached out and shook his hand. "How's it going, man? Wicked party last night, I'm surprised you're up and mobile today."

Trent smiled, sat down, and stifled a yawn. "Yeah, well, you gotta do what you gotta do, know what I mean? Fortunately today is a rare Saturday off of work for me, so I figured it wouldn't kill me to get up at the crack of noon, especially after last night's shindig."

Brandon laughed slightly as he reclined in his desk chair, propping his feet up on the end of the desk. "I hear ya. So, what's going on? What brings you to this neck of the woods today? Feeling the need to donate and 'give back?' After all the brain cells we killed last night, you may want to think twice about letting any more cells leave your body." He winked at Trent.

Eh, Trent thought, *the guy probably doesn't get much opportunity to throw around blood-related jokes, let him enjoy his moment.* Trent laughed half-heartedly as he looked absent-mindedly around the room. "Good call, man! But no, not here to donate or anything." He continued speaking as he unzipped his backpack: "I came by to see if you might be able to shed some light on this." He pulled the bottle out of the bag and placed it lightly on the desk.

The smile slowly faded from Brandon's face as he fixated on the bottle. Without averting his gaze, he said, "Sarah, will you excuse us for a moment, please?"

Trent swiveled in his chair. Sarah, the girl sitting at the desk by the door, stared at Brandon for a moment. Then she nodded silently, got up from her desk, and left the room. Trent turned back to Brandon to see his face had suddenly become very serious.

"I suppose you figured out what's inside?" he asked Trent calmly.

Trent, confused and a little embarrassed at the prospect of admitting that he had no idea what the liquid actually was, decided it was best to answer with a vague, semi-lie instead. "Well, it wasn't that hard, really...pour it into a glass, have a quick taste, it's pretty clear that it isn't just your average wine in a bottle, y'know?"

Brandon quirked an eyebrow. "You tasted it? Really..." He sighed and spoke next in a low voice that sounded almost wistful. "I wondered where I had left that bottle. Very careless of me. But I suppose that's one of the dangers of going to a party and mixing alcohol and blood."

Trent frowned slightly. *Was that another 'blood' joke? If so, I don't get it.* Trent pressed on, his odd need to know more about the bottle and its contents still holding sway over him now more than ever. "So, you bottle this stuff yourself, obviously. How do you do it?"

Brandon took his feet off the desk and folded his hands on the desktop. He looked directly at Trent as he spoke. "Well, I learned how to bottle it in the old country, Romania, where I grew up. My parents taught me, more out of necessity than any passion for it, obviously. Once I came here to America, I really wanted to have easy access to blood without physically harming anyone; working as a blood drive coordinator was the easy solution. I fudge the reporting numbers, a couple of gallons go unaccounted each week, and nobody gets hurt." His gaze was piercing now. "I'm not a monster, Trent."

The gears in Trent's brain had been slowly turning while Brandon was talking, and suddenly everything clicked. His mouth gaped as, for the first time, he realized the full scope of the truth. "Oh my God," Trent said breathlessly. "That's blood in the bottle! Are you a *vampire*?" He said it as a joke, but when he saw the shock of discovery on Brandon's face, in his eyes, the impossible suddenly didn't seem so impossible.

Brandon's face shifted and he stared at Trent with a look of confusion. "Wait a second, you didn't know that when you came in here? You're just now figuring that out?" He sat back in his seat and laughed as he continued. "Jesus, Trent, what the hell did you come over here for? Because you found a shiny bottle in your apartment and wanted to know more about it? I'm surprised you could even figure out that it belonged to me."

Trent was at a loss for words. He couldn't believe that he had missed all the signs pointing him to the obvious answer, though improbable as it was.

Of course you missed the signs, he thought to himself angrily. You were just thinking logically. Vampires aren't supposed to exist!

Brandon continued speaking as he chuckled. "Oh, my, you aren't exactly the brightest Panther here at Pitt, are you? I wish I would have known when you came in here, I wouldn't have shared so much information with you." He abruptly took on a very serious tone. "Unfortunately, I did share a little too much with you, and I have to be honest with you, Trent, I don't know you that well, and I don't think I can let you leave with all of your newfound knowledge."

Trent's mind kicked into overdrive. *Jesus, this shit is real! And that sounded like a threat! Okay, time to stop letting this guy intimidate me.*

He raised his eyebrows in what he hoped was a look of defiance. "And what are you going to do about it, off me?" He mentally winced as he immediately regretted the use of such a stupid phrase as *off me*, but it was far too late now. "I thought you said you didn't want to hurt anybody? That you're not a monster?"

Brandon rose out of his chair, and Trent quickly stood up as well. Brandon came around the desk slowly as he spoke, with Trent backing slowly towards the door at the same time.

"I don't want to hurt anyone, Trent. But I do have a duty to protect myself and my people's integrity. We've worked hard to keep our existence a secret, and despite the rash of stories over the years that have found their way into 'pop culture' and the various forms of fictionalized media, we don't need anyone else running around and trying to prove that we're real. Fortunately, you won't be missed. You and I both know that you're too much of a loner for anyone to really notice that you've stopped showing up to class or stopped calling home for a few months. By the time someone finds your body in Allegheny State Park in the spring, they'll just assume you decided to kill yourself." Brandon's eyes seemed to blaze with a hidden fire. "They probably won't even question the lack of blood in your system."

Trent was trying hard not to freeze up in absolute terror. During Brandon's speech, the two of them had backed themselves across the room and Trent was now standing next to Sarah's desk. He was only a few feet from the door. Trent wasn't comfortable with or willing to rely on his limited athletic skills to bolt out the door and simply outrun Brandon, so in a moment of pure panic, he decided to make his stand.

He quickly grabbed for a sharp object he noticed on Sarah's desk and brandished it in front of him. "I may not be able to outfight you, but I do know one key fact about vampires, a stake through the heart can mortally wound you!"

Chuckling, Brandon couldn't hide the look of bemusement on his face as he replied, "A few key points for you, Bram Stoker. First, a stake through the heart will kill just about any living thing, as the heart is the center of your circulatory system. Second, that's not a stake you're holding, it's a letter opener. And third, there's another key fact about vampires that you may not be aware of." Brandon's smile grew wider. "We almost always travel in pairs."

Even though he had been a little slow to realize many important things today, it didn't take Trent more than a second to understand what Brandon was saying. Unfortunately, Trent didn't have a second to spare before he felt Sarah's hand on his shoulder.

Then he felt her fangs sink into his neck.

Paralyzed with more than just fear, he felt his body become rigid and his motor functions cease to reply to his commands. He dropped to the floor awkwardly, his consciousness fading fast. Above him, the two vampires looked down on him as Sarah licked her lips.

"I'll set him up with an IV to get all his blood before I put him in the freezer," Brandon said, looking down at Trent. "I think I can fill an entire cask of 'Sylvania's Best' without mixing his blood with anyone else's; that will be an amazing pure yield."

"Mmm," Sarah murmured halfheartedly as she licked Trent's blood from her lips, as if she wasn't really listening. "Before you put him in the freezer, be sure and cut out his kidneys. You know it's your father's favorite body part, and I think it would be a nice gift for him when he visits next month for the holidays."

"Will do, my dear." As Brandon stooped down over the near-lifeless body, he flashed a toothy smile as he said to Trent, "I never really thanked you for hosting the party last night. It's too bad that this is where we are now; I think we could have been good friends."

As his consciousness faded for good, Trent could only think one thought that summed up what had easily been the worst experience of his life.

Making friends is hard. I should have stuck to being a loner.

SURF ETERNAL

KELLY M. HUDSON

He glided in on the back of a wave, his surfboard cutting the water effortlessly, as the moon shone down its glistening beams, sparking the surface of the water and making it look like it was coated with thousands of tiny diamonds. His hair flew in the wind, the blonde locks long and stringy with salt water and seaweed. He must have come from far out but he didn't look tired. Indeed, he looked more alive than any person Hilly had ever seen.

That it was quarter past midnight didn't seem odd to her. She had heard about surfers so enamored with their craft that they would practice any time of the day or night and this fine specimen of maleness was surely of that kind of tribe. No, what bothered her is that she had come to the beach to be alone, to think on the things that had brought her to Kauai in the first place, and to do so without the pandering of her current lover, Evan. Instead, she had come to the beach and found herself mesmerized by an Adonis on a surfboard.

It was almost enough to distract her from her dilemma.

Hilly and Evan took a vacation to Kauai in a bid to get away from their friends and families, all of who were prying and pressuring them to get married and have babies.

"You're the perfect couple," they all said. "You're a match made in Heaven," they said. And on and on it went, day after day, until Evan had bought into the hype and Hilly suddenly felt very alone.

She liked Evan; he was a nice, sexy guy. She wasn't sure what the problem was but she couldn't quite connect to him the way he'd done to her. He was smart, funny, had loads of money, and was romantic to the bone. He fancied himself a poet and truth be told, he wasn't half bad; but none of this was enough to convince her that Evan was the one. Her friends certainly thought so, as did his, but she remained unsure; and she was hoping this trip would help her to sort it all out.

Evan had done the right thing at the beginning. He stayed quiet and was loving and kind and never pushy. For the first couple of days. After that, his patience was at an end. He needed her, he'd said, and needed her to love him as much as he loved her. Why didn't she? She assured him that she did, but the coldness in her heart must have seeped through somehow because he never seemed convinced by her words. It had been two weeks since they'd had sex, and she kept holding out, even on this trip. He'd made his moves, tried getting her drunk, and even pleaded with her, but Hilly found she could not bring herself to touch him in any way. It was becoming clearer by the day that whatever feelings he had for her was not going to be reciprocated.

So to the beach she'd come, after Evan had fallen asleep, victim of too big a dinner and too deep a beer mug. She came knowing that the moon was full and hoping that maybe the ocean would whisper some ancient secret to her that would help in her quandary. Instead, she found herself staring at a blonde god, riding the waves like he had wings and the water was made of air. He was an eagle with its head up and its regal body buffeted by winds that did not hurt, but instead caressed, bowing to his royalty. This man on the surfboard demanded her full attention and she was helpless and happy to give it.

He surfed in until the wave died and then dropped into the water, turned around, and paddled back out to find another treasure. Hilly watched, taking in his body and absorbing every detail. He was naked except for a tiny pair of trunks and his lithe, muscled body was not tan but instead almost deathly pale. If the moon that hung high in the air had come down and taken human form, then its skin would be only marginally whiter than that of the blonde surfer that was just now catching another wave and riding it in. He was tall and a natural on the board, wielding it not as a weapon but as an extension of himself. She had read somewhere about the spiritual aspects of surfing, and how those that rode the waves claimed to become one with the ocean, but she had never seen it. Now she was, but more than that, she was feeling it, as well. Her heart hurt as she watched him ride the wave he was on until he got closer to the shore and then turned and paddled out again. She was torn; she wanted him to keep surfing, to keep giving off those good vibrations, but she also wanted him to come ashore and pad over next to her so that she could talk to him. After another three turns, she got her wish.

It was on the last wave, the biggest, that he spotted her on the shore. She was a single, solitary black dot against the white sands until he got closer and saw her, sitting and watching him with an intense gaze. Hilly could feel him watching her watch him, like she was experiencing it through his eyes. Once their eyes did meet, there was nothing that could break the connection.

He rode in and immediately got out of the water, shook his head to knock some of the wetness from him, and tucked his board under his arm. He carried it with no problem; he was much stronger than he looked. His dark eyes held hers and she did not dare break the embrace. He walked across the sand, stopped, and stared down at her. She could not speak, her heart was beating much too rapidly and her breathing was shallow. She felt like a schoolgirl with her first crush on an older boy. She was a weak swimmer caught up in a riptide, only this one would carry her either to a great treasure or to certain death. Either way, she was thrilled.

"What's up?" he said, his voice betraying a southern California tinge.

She shrugged, her tongue caught on the roof of her mouth like she had just eaten a spoonful of peanut butter.

"You got a name?" he asked, flashing a winning grin.

"Hilly," she found herself saying.

"Cool," he said. "Is that short for Hildebrandt?"

Her mouth fell open. No one had ever been able to get that connection. He was the first. Almost everyone guessed that it was Hillary. She nodded slowly.

"That's awesome! I haven't heard that name in a long, long time," he said, still smiling. He plopped down onto the sand next to her.

"Don't you have to worry about sunburns?" she blurted, pointing at his pale skin.

"Nope. Not me," he said, laughing. "I stay out of the sun. I only surf at night."

"Why?"

"Less people, more space," he said and a sad sigh slipped from between his lips.

"What's your name?" she asked, her voice quavering. She looked up into his eyes and froze as a chill came over her body, raising goosebumps and causing the small hairs on the back of her neck to stand at attention. His eyes were black, darker than the space between the stars.

"It's Billy," he said. He thrust out his hand for her to shake. Still hypnotized by his eyes, she reached out like a zombie, taking his hand in hers. It was cold, but it pulsed with a surge of mighty strength. When their fingers touched, an electrical shock went through her. She almost pulled her hand away but he held it firmly. "I used to go by William, but that's a square name, you know? So I went with something cooler."

"It's nice," she whispered, caught up in his magnetic power.

"Hilly, I'm Billy," he said, laughing casually again. He threw his head back and let loose with a stream of giggles, his long blonde hair hanging down his back. Despite her trepidations and her awe of him, she found herself laughing along.

"That's funny," she snorted. She hadn't snorted in years.

"Hilly and Billy, sitting in a tree…" he went on, suddenly so overcome by laughter that he couldn't finish. Billy's head fell forward and his hair dumped over, obscuring his face. Hilly didn't care; she was too busy laughing herself.

After a few moments, their mirth subsided and she found herself staring at his face again.

"So," he said. "What're you out here for?"

"Vacation," she sighed.

"Not having much fun?"

"Oh, you don't want to hear about it," she said.

"Yeah, I do," he replied.

The story poured out of her about Evan and their relationship, and although she was bored with the narrative, Billy seemed riveted, soaking up all the details and following along like a child at story time. When she finished, he looked at her and nodded sagely.

"Bummer," he said, standing to his feet. "I hope it all works out for you." He picked up his surf board and turned towards the ocean.

"Wait. You're not leaving, are you?" Hilly asked, suddenly afraid.

Billy turned and grinned, his canines flashing in the moonlight.

"The waves are calling me, babe." He trotted out to the ocean and jumped in, paddling out to sea and then catching the next big wave to come along.

She sat on the beach for a long time, watching Billy surf. She was rooted to her spot, floored by her encounter.

After a while, Billy swam out so far that he disappeared and didn't come back. Hilly, disappointed, got up and went back to her hotel room.

The next day dragged by.

She and Evan visited a couple of tourist spots, with Evan chattering on and on about the natural beauty of the island. She hardly heard him; she could not get her mind off of her encounter with the mysterious Billy. As the day wore on, she decided to go back out to the beach later, hoping to see him again. It was the only thing that kept her sane through the long day.

Evan agitated her well into the evening and she could barely stand his company. While they were at dinner, she encouraged him to drink up, and her strategy worked, because they were barely back in their room for half an hour before he fell into a deep sleep. She crept out, taking a beach towel and wearing her sexiest bikini.

She went out by the same spot, at the same time, but Billy was nowhere to be seen. Her heart dropped and despair throbbed in her veins, but she wasn't ready to give up yet. She waited an hour before she spotted him, far away, riding a big wave. She waved but didn't receive a response.

Billy glided on the wave until it came to shore. He stopped, grabbed his board, and stood in the crashing waves, staring at her. He seemed unsure of what to do. When Hilly waved a second time, he waved back and then turned to the ocean, paddling out and disappearing like the night before.

Hilly watched him go, disappointment scorching her heart. Then a mad plan came to her mind and she grinned, sure it would work.

She walked into the water and swam after him.

He quickly outpaced her, going farther and farther from the shore, never looking back, unaware she was swimming after him. But she didn't care; she had to catch up and make him see how much she needed him. She didn't understand where this compulsion came from but it stroked her mind and emotions and she was helpless in its thrall. She had to catch up to Billy and be with him.

After a bit, Billy turned and saw her. He paddled over to her and floated by her side as she put her hands on his board to rest.

"Yo, what up?" he said.

She gasped for air. She was breathing hard and out of control.

"Please, stay with me a while," she finally said.

"No way, brah," he said, turning away from her. "You should go back to shore. You don't want to get involved with me." And with that, Billy paddled back out to sea.

She cried out and swam after him, but he was quick, putting distance between the two of them with a casual ease. Hilly tried her best to keep up, but her arms and legs grew tired. After a bit, she gave up as he disappeared on the horizon.

Turning around, treading water, she realized to her horror that she had lost sight of the coast. Before her and behind her lay only the dark ocean, its currents swirling and swelling. Panic surged in her chest. In her single-minded pursuit of her blonde surfing god, she hadn't kept track of where she was or where she was going. Instead, she drifted, lost and alone and very, very frightened.

She told herself to calm down. There had to be an easy answer to this dilemma. She looked up at the stars and found them burning brightly in the night sky. What had she heard about the North Star? Wasn't it in the handle of the Big Dipper? But what if it wasn't? What if the North Star was really in the Little Dipper, or some other constellation? Her breath quickened and the panic pulsed through her veins. What would she do?

Looking around, searching for any help, Hilly spotted something sticking out of the water and heading her way, just twenty yards off to her right. She squinted, trying to make out what it was. When it got closer and she could see what it was, cold fear poured through her body.

It was the fin of a shark, and it was heading straight for her.

She screamed and frantically swam away from it. The shark closed in, its long, primitive body sliding effortlessly through the water as it honed in on her, its eyes rolling into the back of its head.

And then, as if by a miracle, appearing just behind the shark, Billy rode in on a wave, slicing and dicing through the water, his face filled with sheer determination as he bore down on the ocean predator.

Billy leapt from the surfboard, arcing through the air and landing right on top of the shark. He grabbed it by its fins and somehow spun it so that it was upside down and Billy was underwater. The shark struggled at first and then seemed stunned into submission once it was on its back. All of this happened in the blink of an eye as Billy swam up from beneath it, careful to keep his hands on the fins so that the shark stayed upside down. His surfboard glided to a stop just behind him, as if he controlled it with his mind.

"Are you okay?" he asked. Hilly, treading water and shivering uncontrollably, shook her head. Billy flashed his winning smile and she saw them again, glinting in the moonlight: his long canines. "Don't worry, babe, I'll take care of this bad boy."

He roared and launched himself on top of the flipped-over shark. He thrust his head down into the area just below its jaw and bit, hard, tearing through the tough membrane with his teeth until he hit the softer tissue underneath. The shark squirmed then and tried to get away, but it was too late. Billy gorged himself on it, biting and tearing and gnashing away until he'd chewed a giant, bleeding hole in the shark's flesh. He drank deeply of its blood, relishing every drop. By the time he was satisfied, he looked up at Hilly, his face smeared scarlet, his expression like a kid who'd won a cherry pie eating contest.

And suddenly, as hard as it was to believe, she knew why he surfed alone at night.

"You know what?" he asked with bits of shark flesh caught in his teeth.

"You're a vampire," Hilly said. When Billy nodded, the world spun wildly around and she passed out, slipping into the water. As everything went dark, the last thing she saw was the body of the dead shark, floating away and drifting down, swallowed by the shadowy depths of the ocean.

She awoke in a cave with a campfire burning brightly beside her. Billy sat on the other side of it, studying the flames. Hilly stared at him as the reflections of the fire danced on his face, and for a moment she thought she may have died and gone to Hell.

"You're awake," he said.

"You're a vampire," she said.

Billy smiled and showed his teeth, long and gleaming in the firelight.

"You got it, babe."

"How...how is that possible?"

"Vampires don't exist, huh? Well, guess what? They do, and I'm unliving proof," he said with a laugh.

Hilly sat up and studied his features, looking for some sort of insight into how any of this could be possible.

"I know what you're thinking, babe, and you're so right. This is messed up but, hah! That's the way it is." He got to his feet, the mirth never leaving his expression.

"How did it happen?"

"How do you think?" he asked.

Hilly felt immediately foolish and wanted to slink off back into the darkness. She had come to Kauai to sort out her troubles with Evan and it had led to this, her in a cave somewhere with a vampire! What a strange world it was. But that wasn't he worst of it. No, the worst was that she realized right then and there that she didn't care if Billy was a vampire or not. She was in love.

"Sorry," she muttered, casting her gaze to the floor of the cave.

"It's okay; I get that all the time. Well, I don't talk to people much anymore, but when I do..." He rolled his eyes. "What can you expect?"

"I guess," Hilly said, wishing that somehow she had reacted differently, more uniquely, so that he would understand she was different than the others.

"So I'll give you the short of it," he said. "I came out here on vacation thirty years ago and went on a hike to the Na Pali coast and one night, this old man came out of the woods and bit me. I woke up the next night craving blood. I put two and two together when I tried to go out in the sun the next morning and nearly burned up."

"How horrible!" she said. The thought of Billy on fire hurt her heart. "What did you do?"

"Ah, babe, can I tell you how much it sucks to be a vampire in Hawaii? I mean, come on! It's, like, sunshine all the time, brah, and so hot!" Billy was pacing now, really getting into what he was saying. This thrilled her, knowing she had gotten to him somehow and made him excited. She felt good inside.

"That's terrible. I couldn't imagine," she said.

"Yeah, so, I was stuck here and I didn't have much to do. I couldn't drink too much blood 'cause there wasn't that many people around back then, so I tried doing it to animals, and you know something? It worked just fine," he said, smiling to himself. "Most animals don't taste half bad, but pig, wow, pig blood is just nasty!" His face screwed up with distaste. "And you're talking to a man who used to love his bacon."

Hilly nodded, enthralled with his tale. She wanted this night to go on forever.

"But that wasn't the worst of it," he said.

"What was?" she asked, hanging on his every word. Her heart was swelling inside of her with admiration and lust.

"Those animals I bit, they came back, too, and next thing I knew, there was a bunch of vampire dogs and cats and stuff running around at night, trying to suck the blood of other animals. Man, it got to be too much." He rolled his eyes.

"So what happened next?"

Billy looked down at her, his black eyes turning even darker. "The other animals, the normal ones, they came for them. It was weird, like, they knew somehow and banded together. I got really worried, you know, 'cause I didn't want something like that to happen to me. I thought maybe it was a species thing or something, like the humans would get wind of me and it would be like one of those Frankenstein movies, all burning pitchforks and stuff."

Hilly was confused. "I don't know what you mean."

"You know, villagers and pitchforks and torches and stuff like that. But nothing like that ever happened."

"What about the vampire animals?" she asked.

"They all got killed by the others, torn apart. I was there the night it happened. The normal animals hunted them down and herded them near this cave, where I make my home now, and shredded them. There was nothing left by the time they got done but bits of fur and blood," he said, shuddering.

She could feel the fear in his memory and wanted to hug him tight and let her warmth nurture him and chase the shadows away. She wanted to rub her body against his until they fell to the floor of the cave in a frenzy of lust and abandonment.

At that moment, Hilly knew she was forever through with Evan and totally devoted, heart, mind, and soul to Billy. The thought scared her and turned her on at the same time.

This must be what love feels like, she thought.

"And then, the animals all turned and looked at me like they were going to do the same thing to me. I took off but they didn't follow, and I realized they were just warning me to knock it off."

Billy paced silently, lost in his memories. After a few moments, Hilly piped up, hoping not to draw his derision again but to earn his approval.

"I thought it took a stake through the heart to kill a vampire," she said quietly.

He stopped his pacing and looked at her. She couldn't tell if it was pity or lust in his dark, glittering eyes.

"Nah. I thought the same thing, but it isn't true. Bodily dismemberment will do it. All those old stories are just folk tales and stuff. The only thing that's for sure is sunlight. That will do it," he said. "Those vampire animals, they were torn up so bad, they couldn't heal by morning, so when the sun rose and its rays hit their shredded bodies...*poof*!"

"So how do you eat now?" she asked.

"I drink the blood of animals, but now I snap their necks when I'm done and leave them out where the sun will get them," he explained. He sat back down by the fire and kept looking at her. "What about you? Why did you try to follow me? That was a pretty dangerous thing to do."

Hilly took a deep breath and tried to put her best foot forward. She didn't want to blow this now that she was so close.

"I love you," she blurted out and then turned a deep crimson red. She was such a fool! But she couldn't stop herself; the words cascaded from her mouth, clean and new like a waterfall after a fresh rain. "I don't love Evan and I never did. I love you and now that I know the truth about you, I love you even more!"

Billy did a cruel thing then. He laughed at her. It was the most horrible sound she'd ever heard in her life, much worse than fingernails on a chalkboard or the high-pitched squeal of a kicked puppy. The laughter tore through her chest more surely than any blade ever could.

"Why, why would you do that?" she asked, deeply hurt.

"You're a fool, babe," he said, rising to his feet again. He stood there, the shadows from the fire dancing on his naked body, and he looked like an ancient pagan god, mad with desire. "I could never love you. Don't you get that?"

Her world came crashing down upon her. As Billy spoke, she remembered having the same thoughts directed towards Evan, even though he didn't know it. Had she been as cruel to Evan as Billy was being to her?

He smiled, baring his fangs.

"My love is the sea, babe. It's the ocean. I love to surf and it's all I care about. You…You're nothing in the face of that."

Hilly's gaze dropped to the floor of the cave. She would go back to Evan, beg his forgiveness, and marry him. Having someone adore you was much better than being treated like this.

Billy jumped over the fire, landing right in front of her, his naked body gyrating inches away from her face. He laughed again.

"Bet you want a piece of this, huh? That's just the glamour talking, babe. I give it off and can't help it. Just part of being a vampire," he said as he grinned, mocking her with his dance.

"Please, don't be so cruel," she begged him. He stopped dancing and looked down at her, sadness now entering his eyes. Sadness and pity.

"Don't worry, babe, it'll all be over soon."

What did he mean by that? she wondered.

Billy lunged forward, burying his fangs deep into her neck and slamming her onto her back. She was pinned, helpless under his assault, and within moments felt her life swimming away, following a current that led out of her body, into his mouth, and then to his beating, undead heart. As she died, Hilly felt bad for how she'd treated Evan, and sad she had done so little with her life.

After those thoughts, she had no more.

Billy gorged himself on her, filling his belly with her rich, human blood. The animal blood would do, but this stuff was the very best. It was a delicacy and he intended to enjoy himself.

He stayed in his cave through the day, alternately napping and drinking what was left of her blood. When night fell, he snapped her neck and carried the body out into the cool air. He slung her over his right shoulder and carried his surfboard under his left. Since he lived close to the ocean, it only took him a few minutes to pad out to the shore and hit the waves.

He glided out over the sea with an almost supernatural ease, Hilly's dead body cradled in his arms. When he reached a mile or so out, he looked down at her dead face, Hilly's eyes still frozen open in fear and regret.

"Sorry, babe," he smiled as he let her go. Hilly's body smacked down on the rough waves and disappeared, soon to be fish food.

As she sunk, the shark that Billy had killed the night before surfaced. It looked up at him with its soulless eyes and they both knew they had a new friend. Billy whistled and kicked up and rode a big wave in, the vampire shark cruising at his side like an obedient dog.

"I think I'm gonna call you Fido," Billy said.

He looked up into the night sky, staring at the stars and feeling the rhythm of the ocean beneath his feet. There was nothing finer in the world than being out on the sea, his board beneath him, and the water sloshing his sides.

He had all eternity to surf, and as he thought that, a broad smile split his face.

Behind him, a big wave was coming. He paddled out and met it, getting on with his night.

AMIKO

SIMON WEST-BULFORD

Ethan lowered his slender frame into the armchair, his long coat layering the dark leather like shed reptile skin. He touched the glass to his lips, purposely revealing a hint of sharpened tooth against the rim as he took a sip of wine. He viewed the dark liquid with a moment of disdain and set the glass down on the table next to him.

"You still don't believe me, do you, Matt?"

"It's difficult... You're actually telling me there's still one left?"

"Of course."

"Alive?"

"Absolutely," Ethan winked.

"And he's here in this house?"

"He's a she, and yes, she's in this house although she isn't exactly..."

"A female donor, after all these years?"

"You sound surprised."

"I am. I thought all the volunteers had been accounted for and rehabilitated into society."

"So naïve. Why did you think I brought you here if I wasn't telling you the truth?"

Matt Wells shifted in his seat, and tried to ignore the fact that all natural light had been blocked from the study by thick drapes. Candles lit the cherry walls, thick tomes lined antique bookcases and glowing coals crackled warmth from an old hearth. In any other house the atmosphere might have been considered cozy. But this was not any other house, and this was not just an ordinary man he was talking to. To sit in the home of a vampire—or hemophile as the scientific community had labeled them—was more than just a novelty; it was a dangerous thrill ride for a bored detective with more questions than sense. The hemophiles had been living in isolation for almost a hundred years now, protected and hidden under society's nose by a frightened government after a long and secret war. Only after the vampires had announced their discovery did a nervous truce eventually form; a synthetic compound to replace their need for blood would take a full ten years to develop and produce in bulk, then the war would be over. But deals with vampires are never made easily and they demanded hundreds of volunteers; willing victims to sate their needs until the compound was ready. But who would answer such a call? Who would give their lives to become drinking vessels for the enemy?

Ethan slapped a foolscap folder onto the table, opened the cover.

"Take a look through the files," he said, gulping the last of his wine with a grimace. "These are the legal documents for the volunteers that have been released back into the civilian population."

Wells leaned over, examined the jaundiced paper and studied the black and white photograph of a bespectacled man with graying hair. Two paragraphs of small print, a stamp, and several signatures lay underneath.

"That's William Backhouse isn't it?" Wells asked. "I recognize his face from some of the other files I've seen in my investigations. He was the very first of the donors."

"Spot on. Feel free to browse through, won't you?" Ethan twirled a hand.

Wells turned each page over, studying every face, hoping for a glimpse of their characters through the grainy prints, fascinated to understand how they could have volunteered for such a terrible fate knowing that the vast majority of the world would never even learn of the sacrifice they had made for them. "What exactly am I looking for?"

"Take a closer look at the signatures and tell me if you notice anything odd."

Wells peered at the inked text, ran his index finger over the soft etching in the paper. The grooves were deep, written by a heavy grip, probably slowly, and—Wells deduced from the subtle style of loops and lines—by the same hand.

"Fakes," Wells said, still turning each page, still staring at each face.

"Spot on," Ethan said, pouring himself another glass of wine from an unlabelled bottle. "Want to know why?"

"Enlighten me." Still staring at the faces. Something wasn't right about them.

Between sips from his glass, Ethan recounted his story, explaining how the synthetic compound had encountered setbacks in its development, how the vampire community had bargained to keep the donors for longer than ten years, and how several of those donors–graciously willing to extend the length of their sacrifice– had sadly died for... one reason or another.

"...of course, it had to be covered up," he went on. "If it was found out that some of the donors had actually died, the deal would be off quicker than you could say "bite me". So we faked the documents showing they'd been released, bribed certain people in powerful positions and buried the whole thing...until now that is."

Wells listened, but was only vaguely aware of Ethan as he strode around the study, weaving his tale. He knew that the vampire wasn't telling him everything, but the photographs in the files still had him transfixed. And then it came to him. Every pair of eyes of every volunteer had slightly dilated pupils. Drugs perhaps?

Wells looked up. "I still don't understand why you're telling me all this. If this information gets out you'll lose more than your donors, you'll most likely start the war up all over again. You won't be safe. None of you will."

"Come on, Matt. You're in the FBI. Don't they teach you anything there about human nature? Of course we don't want this to get out, but some of us do have principles, you know. I... want to do the right thing. Clear my conscience, so to speak."

It was on the tip of Wells' tongue to point out that Ethan was not exactly human, but he resisted. "So why wait so long to tell anyone. Why now? Why me?"

Ethan looked away, drained his second glass from the table and examined the dregs, again with the same look of disapproval. "Perhaps it's better if you actually see her."

"You'll do that? You'll let me see her? Just like that?"

"If you can handle it."

"Of course I can handle it–I just didn't expect this to happen so soon."

Ethan stared for a moment with his dark hypnotic pupils trained on Wells, offering his guest the door to the hall with a broad but humorless smile. Wells paused for several long seconds before getting out of his seat, suddenly aware how hard he'd been gripping the arms, conscious of his heart swelling with anxiety at the thought of delving deeper into the unknown.

He could turn back now, leave it all behind and go back to the safety of his apartment, but even before he realized he'd made his decision Wells was following the vampire without comment. Pangs of uncertainty surfaced as he started down two claustrophobic corridors, the sense of trust he felt before today, so absolute, so real, now sliding away like the after-effects of deep anesthesia, like thin paint dripping from a wall to reveal a mosaic of obscene imagery. What was he doing here?

Wells hesitated, tried to suppress his uneasiness.

"There's nothing to fear," Ethan said, turning and fixing Wells with those eyes. Eyes as inescapable as black holes. And the fear melted away again. It was what Ethan said the first time they met. The vampire had befriended him three months ago in a bar – told him secrets about the vampire community that would have taken Wells a lifetime to find out on his own. Wells had been on an investigation, following up on a call from a relative of one of the more recent donors, but he had gotten nowhere. After weeks of hitting dead ends, tight-lipped witnesses and chasing false leads, Ethan's appearance was a godsend, and at the promise of revealing the darkest secrets of the vampire community, Wells hurried this new contact back to his apartment to learn more. Memories of that night were unclear. The exchange was brief but intense and almost overnight, through a fog of dream and dark passion, the trust between them ran as deep as an African river. At least it did until he entered Ethan's home.

Wells felt the lining of his coat.

No gun.

He remembered leaving it on his desk. Nothing to fear.

He didn't need one did he? He trusted Ethan. Felt safe around this man, didn't he? His other hand searched his pocket for his cell phone.

No cell phone.

He'd left that on his desk, too. He didn't need it. But he always carried his mobile, didn't he? There'd be no reason to leave it behind, would there?

Wells stopped, blinked heavily. He stared at the carpet, idly following the patterns as if they would help him clear his head.

"Is something the matter?" Ethan asked, his hand on the doorknob at the end of the corridor. "You're quite sure you want to see her?"

"Of...course."

Ethan opened the door and Wells followed him down some steps into a stone-walled basement area, layers of deception peeling away with each slow step, the fog lifting from his thoughts with every breath. They went through another room filled with racks of wine and discarded portraits, and then stopped in front of the final barrier: an arched door, so old it looked like it had been lifted from an Arthurian castle. The buzz of flies from behind the wooden frame warned Wells of death within, and the rank stench of butchery rode the wake of the door as Ethan dragged it open. Wells stepped into cold hell and steadied himself against the doorframe.

"Oh, God!"

"I warned you, Matt."

"God!" Wells covered his nose and mouth.

The remains of a woman breathed at the centre of the room. Something ugly, raw and bestial lay pulsing beneath her.

Ethan walked slowly toward the woman and traced the point of his nail across her pale cheek, allowing the razor edge to split the skin and weep its precious blood. Alive with little else but madness, the woman's bulging eyes watched his hand withdraw slowly back to his mouth and press the ruby-red drop against his cracked lips.

"I thought you said you could handle it," Ethan said.

Wells blinked tears away as he stared at the victim, took a tentative step forward. "She...volunteered...for this?" Wells asked.

"Oh, yes. She knew exactly what she was getting into... She's dying now, of course."

The bastards had hung her on a rack of wooden slats, leather straps around her wrists and ankles, stretching her at an impossible angle. Underneath the slats was the *gore*, a bloated creature that kept its host alive indefinitely, pumping the nervous system full of enzymes and chemicals that caused the human heart to pound at almost six hundred times a minute, and elevated levels of erythropoietin that would cause the bone marrow to produce twenty times its usual quantities of hemoglobin–plenty of blood for the vampiric connoisseur. She had become a vintage, a rare delicacy to be supped upon for special occasions.

Wells coughed, averted his eyes as the woman turned her insane gaze on him. Looking away would make no difference now though; the image of that poor wretch crucified above that fleshy maw would never leave him. He would remember each raw tongue leaching under her skin, gulping the ever replenishing life from what little pulp remained. And as he squeezed his eyes shut against the tears, the rancid stench of the parasite's breath, hot and acrid, would forever linger in his nostrils. Wells fought for the composure to speak again as the slurping of juices filled his ears, bringing another wave of nausea. He thought about all the things Ethan had told him in the past few weeks.

"That... thing is keeping her alive so you can keep feeding off her?"

"Correct."

"But... you told me she was dying."

"I didn't mean a literal death, Matt. The parasite...the gore...will keep her alive for eternity as long as she continues to feed it. And so as long as we continue to feed her every once in a while, they'll have a wonderful relationship that will never end. No, when I said she is dying, I meant that her spirit is failing...it...uh...how should I put it... cheapens the flavor–ruins the bouquet."

"I never believed it," Wells breathed. "Never believed even your kind could do this to someone. Didn't know..."

"Didn't know it was like this?" Ethan's top lip curled in a sneer as his tongue searched for a last morsel of flavor on his fangs. "But the world believed that vampires had found a substitute for blood. You believed the volunteers were cared for, nurtured. You didn't care what was really going on, did you? You just wanted us to leave the rest of you alone. Isn't that right, Matt?"

Wells paused, forced himself to look at the woman. "Yes."

"Why? After so many brutal years of war between us, why did you people think you could trust us?"

Wells considered his answer, thought about the brutality of the conflict, the amount that must have been lost on both sides in the past. The truth is that they were tired. To go on fighting, to wipe out the bloodsuckers would take an age, and few were ready to go the distance not knowing if one day they would wake up and find themselves on the other side, a new recruit to the vampires' cause. The vampire solution was simple, easy, convenient. Lie or not, it was easier to swallow it than to shed any more blood. The war had ended quickly, almost overnight, and the last few million vampires huddled together in their isolated communities, privately drinking from the hemo-substitute they'd created. But Wells realized now that there was no blood substitute—there never would be. The truth was ugly. The truth was right in front of him now.

Wells glanced around him, feeling the walls of the crypt close in on him as the harsh facts congealed into sickening reality. Two unshaded light bulbs hung from the curved ceiling, their pendulum swing making slow, swaying shadows out of the broken-down furniture littered around them. A rotting chair, a cobwebbed wardrobe, an old gramophone in pieces on a crooked, oak table. It seemed all the more disgusting and ironic that this woman, who once agreed to provide sustenance for a town of refugee vampires, should be held in a room that had become a dumping ground for discarded antiques. The charcoal bricks were slick with condensation, their cold surfaces soaking up the violent heat of the woman's body and the breath of the beast. How could she willingly submit to this?

"Does she have a name?" Wells asked.

Ethan chewed his bottom lip, as if considering his answer.

"Why don't you ask her yourself?"

Wells felt snakes in his gut. Shame too. He had been so revolted by what he'd seen, so fearful, that the idea of talking to the woman filled him with cold dread. But he knew he had to. He stepped forward, looked into her eyes. The glassy stare that had characterized the other donors he'd seen in the photos was not there now.

"You don't have to stay here anymore," he told her. "We're going to get you out of here, okay? What's your name?"

She fixed him with the same manic stare that shocked him earlier. Her lips parted and trembled. Her eyes bulged, the bloodshot whites glistening in the shifting light as she strained her head forward. A tortured moan was all she could manage.

"As I said. She's fading, Matt. The mind is a fragile thing, you know."

Wells shook his head.

"She doesn't say much anymore," Ethan said. "Not that she ever spoke much anyway, but every day she managed to tell us... her name. Now she hardly even opens her mouth."

The woman's lips parted again but this time a single word gargled up through her pain, each quiet syllable stretched out in an almost incomprehensible groan.

"*Amiko.*"

"Amiko? Your name is Amiko?"

"*Amiko,*" she repeated, her eyes pleading.

Wells looked at the straps on her wrists. There were no locks, just buckles holding her in place.

"Why didn't you just release her? Why did you need my help?"

"Help?" Ethan laughed the word as he placed a strong hand on Wells" shoulder. "Who said anything about help? I asked you if you wanted to see. And see you have."

Wells felt the fingers squeeze his shoulder as he shook his head to clear his thoughts, the snakes in his stomach released their venom as realization dawned, the mesmerizing hold on him finally gone.

"*Amiko,*" the woman whispered.

"That's not her name, is it?" Wells asked. "None of the donors volunteered, did they? You...drugged them...hypnotized them."

"You got me," Ethan admitted with a slow smile and his hands up.

A rush of pain came like hot metal as the creature lanced Wells' leg with a bony appendage. Then another in his arm and another on his neck. Joints and gristle popped and crackled as the thing drew Wells closer.

"*Amiko!*" the woman screamed, and Ethan began to unfasten the buckles.

"Certainly," he said as the woman collapsed to the hard stone floor, her skin wrinkling like the flesh of a peach engulfed by fire. "There, I've let you go."

Wells felt the creature twist and writhe beneath him as it discarded her and latched on to him. His heart quickened as a rush of enzymes and blood coursed through his body at speeds that brought blinding agony. His muscles ached as thousands of tiny tendrils wriggled under his skin and into his arteries draining fresh blood. Ethan leaned across him, examining him, black eyes wide with greed and lust.

"Let me go!" Wells cried. "Ethan, please!"

"I'm afraid not, Matt. You're far too valuable. Amiko here has become stale, we needed a new donor."

Ethan ducked down for a moment, leaving Wells' field of vision.

"Let me go! I'll kill you!"

Ethan returned with glass in hand, crimson liquid swirling as he lifted it to his smiling lips. "Cheers...and, oh...good health, my friend."

FROM THE GRIME BELOW

JESSY MARIE ROBERTS

*N*ovember, 2010

Chapin, Nebraska

Marty lost his breath when Gina fell atop him, her cheerleading skirt bunched up around her hips, her green and gold sweater glittering in the dim light.

"Um, Gina, I don't think this is a good idea," Marty said, twisting his neck to the side to avoid her open-mouthed kisses.

"Stop being such a baby, Marty," Gina begged in a husky growl, nipping playfully down his neck and sweeping her wriggling fingers under his football jersey. "I promised you a special surprise if we took State—and we did!"

He giggled, the nervous titter echoing through the dank, dirt-floored basement. "It's not like I did anything. I sat on the bench the whole game," he said, shrieking as her green-tipped fingernails scratched across his hairless chest. "I sit on the bench *every* game."

"You're being too hard on yourself," she whispered.

"No, really, I'm not. I mean, I'm not any good at football. I only joined the team for a P.E. credit because the golf team was full."

Gina groaned and cradled his smooth cheeks between her searing palms. "Just shut up already, Marty. This is supposed to be a special night."

Marty gulped, the awkward sound of his swallowing traveling through the cavernous room beneath Gina's parents' old Victorian house. It was a nice house, two stories tall, with ornate detail along the original wood, complementing its high peaks. It boasted two porches, a small balcony, and was perched atop the only hill in town. It was the oldest remaining structure in Chapin, Nebraska. The rest of the town had burned in 1910, with over half of the residents burning to death in the raging fire.

Gina swooped her face down for a kiss and Marty slid his hand over his mouth before she could make contact. "Seriously, Gina, I'm not comfortable with any of this," he said, the words muffled against his fingers. "We barely even know each other."

"Jesus, Marty," Gina sighed, falling onto her back on the dirt floor next to him. "And here I thought we were going to do things the easy way."

Marty lay silent for a moment, his heaving breath the only sound in the creepy, drafty basement. "So, I think I'm gonna take off," he finally said, sitting up. "Um, thanks for the offer." His voice cracked slightly.

She sat up, too. "I wish things didn't have to be like this, Marty. I'm sorry."

"Sorry?" Marty asked nervously. "About what?"

Gina moved suddenly, sweeping her arm above her head. Marty screamed, catching a glimpse of metal in the dust-laden light filtering into the dark, earthy room through the oak floorboards. He jumped to his feet, smashing his head into a rafter. Dizzy, he fell to his knees and crawled through the dirt toward the door.

The back of his ankle exploded in agony as the sharp blade sliced through his Achilles tendon, splashing blood onto the floor. The metallic smell of blood permeated the air, overwhelming the rotting stench of mildew and dead mice. "Help!" Marty shouted, hoping Gina's parents could hear his cries of distress through the ceiling. "Help me!"

There was a loud thumping from above, followed by, "Keep it down! I'm watching *Survivor*!"

Another flash of blinding hot pain swept through his lower leg as Gina slid her knife through his calf, the metal edge of the blade grinding to a halt where it met his shin bone. "Oh my God, stop it, Gina," he groaned in a pleading whine. "Fine, we can do it. Just stop hurting me!"

Gina laughed. "Shut up, Marty. I was never going to *do it* with you. I just...need...your...blood," she panted, accentuating each word with a downward thrust of the five-inch long blade.

The knife plunged in and out of his legs, thick, hot blood erupting out of the deep wounds. The dirt floor became muddy, the dirt combined with the ruddy moisture of his blood. Marty dug his fingers into the dirt, attempted to pull himself to the exit, desperate to ignore the blistering fire scalding his legs after each stab of steel slid through his skin. Exhausted, on the verge of unconsciousness, he slumped into a wailing heap. "Put me out of my misery, Gina. Just kill me quickly."

Gina smiled, the light filtering from upstairs glistening off her white teeth. "It doesn't work like that. They need you alive."

"They?" Marty slurred, his speech impaired by his loss of blood.

Clawed fingers shot up through the saturated soil around him, the earth trembling as *something* within climbed to the surface. The scream died on his tongue when an angular head darted out of the floor, covered in dirt, followed by shoulders and a skinny torso—he was too shocked, too terrified to cry for help.

The first resurrected body was followed by three more, and the shadowy figures rose to their feet, their bony shoulders hunched as they leaned over his prone body. The first *thing* dipped his long, crooked finger into the blood swirling around Marty's thigh and brought it to his lips. "So it is true. You are he."

"I'm who?" Marty gasped, trying to inch away from the imposing creature.

"The descendant," the beast hissed, then turned to face Gina, who stood next to Marty, the dripping knife still clutched in her hand. "And you? Are you she who brought him for our revival?"

Gina dropped to one knee, her head bowed. "Yes, Immortal One. I found the ancient text hidden in this basement and I found the descendant, the one whose blood could reanimate you. I worship you."

"Of course you do," the Immortal One whispered maliciously. "You have served your purpose." He turned to his companions. "Feed."

Marty watched, unable to turn away despite his disgust, as the three forced Gina to the floor and sunk their long, peaked fangs into her veins—one at her jugular, one latched on to the interior of her thigh, the third suckling from her wrist. The slurping moans resounded through the basement, the Immortal One watching with leering bloodlust shining in his cold, demonic eyes.

When Gina had been sucked dry, the three discarded her ashen form and moved with preternatural grace to stand behind their master. The immortal one crouched next to Marty, cradling the teenager's brown-haired head in his lap, and traced the pad of his index finger along his neck until it stopped at the juncture of neck and shoulder. "Your pulse is pounding," the arisen creature said, not unkindly. "You have nothing to fear from me. You are the descendant."

"I don't understand," Marty whispered, oddly comforted by the chilled finger pressed against his throat.

"You are of my bloodline," the Immortal One crooned. "I was not always a creature of the night. Prior to my transformation, I had a wife who bore me ten children. You are the product of my seed and her womb, my lifeline to the mortal world. As long as you live, so shall I, as it was your blood that triggered my reawakening."

"And if I die?" Marty asked, running his hand over his mangled, mutilated legs.

"Then we seek the dirt until another descendant spills his blood over our graves."

"Oh," Marty said, his eyes rolling up into his head, certain he was about to succumb to death. "Then I guess you better start digging."

*　*　*

Marty awoke, the glaring sunlight blinding him. He was in his bedroom, lying on a twin bed, his five-year-old superhero comforter pulled up beneath his chin. Hesitantly, he wiggled his toes, expecting to feel pain, and was surprised when he felt none. He whipped the blanket from his body and stared down at his long, spindly white legs peeking out from his white briefs.

His legs were intact, not a scratch or a bruise to mar their fair complexion.

Confused, Marty leaned over and examined his thighs, and knees, tracing his fingers through his coarse leg hair. "What the hell?" he muttered, wrinkling his brow, looking for evidence of the stab wounds Gina had inflicted.

Nothing.

It must have been a dream. A sick, stupid dream. There's no way Gina Simmons, the head cheerleader, tried to seduce me.

Relieved, Marty fell against the pillows and closed his eyes, determined to enjoy the weekend.

"Marty, dear! Time to get ready for school!" his mother called.

Marty frowned, and looked at the oversized alarm clock on his nightstand as he read the date, shocked when he saw the clock confirmed his mother's early morning wake-up call.

It was Monday. The football game, and the horrifying events in Gina's basement, had been on Friday.

What happened to Saturday and Sunday? he wondered, panicked.

A loud knock banged against his closed bedroom door. "Marty? Did you hear me? Time to get up!" his mother shouted.

"Coming, Mom!" Marty yelled, hopping out of bed and pulling a pair of jeans from the top bureau drawer. He swung open his closet door to pluck a shirt from the clothes hanger as he zipped up his pants. Something bunched up in the corner of the closet caught his eye, and he investigated, pulling the shredded, grimy, blood-stained jeans out.

A sick knowing flooded through his body—he had been attacked in Gina's basement, the Immortal One and his fiendish friends had slithered through the dirt floor, and worst of all, Gina was bloodless, discarded and dead.

"*Marty!*" his mother yelled again, her irritated yowl blistering his eardrums. "Do I have to come in there and dress you?"

He tossed the jeans back into the closet, over his torn jersey, and slammed the door shut. "I said I'm coming!" Marty hollered back, grabbing a pair of socks and racing out of his bedroom.

* * *

"Mom?" Marty asked around a mouthful of cereal.

"What is it, dear?" his mother asked, setting a small glass of orange juice in front of him, then filling another one and putting it in front of his father. His dad, as usual, munched on dry whole-wheat toast, his nose buried in a newspaper, gold-rimmed spectacles resting on its crooked tip.

"Well, I have a class project. I need to do a report on my genealogy."

His father narrowed his eyes and set down his newspaper. "You know your mother was adopted. Why would you bring up such a painful subject?"

"It's okay, Don," his mother said. "It's only natural to want to know where you came from. I, of all people, know that. I can't tell you anything about my birth family, honey. I can ask your grandma and grandpa about their family, if you'd like. My adopted family tree should suffice for your school project."

Marty dropped his spoon into his cereal bowl, frustrated. He turned to his father. "What about your side of the family, Dad? You weren't adopted."

"Nope," his father said. "But I don't know anything."

"Does Aunt Fran?" Marty asked, hoping his father's sister would know more about their lineage.

"Nope. We didn't talk about things like that."

"You don't even know your grandparents name? That's weird, Dad."

"I know their names, sure," his father said, "but that's as far back as I can go."

"Well, give me their names and I'll do some research down at the courthouse. Our family has lived in Chapin for generations—you said so yourself. Maybe I can find some old birth records or something."

His mother laughed. "Well, I've never seen you so eager to write a school paper before. That's wonderful, dear."

"You're not going to find anything," his father said, standing up from the table, grabbing his jacket, and sliding it over his telephone serviceman's uniform. "All of the town's records were burned in the big fire in 1910. Looks like you're going to have do your paper on your mom's adopted family."

* * *

"You look like shit," Spencer said, giving Marty a once-over with his wide-set brown eyes. "Have you showered since the football game?"

"I don't know," Marty answered, sipping on a cafeteria carton of chocolate milk.

Spencer rolled his eyes. "So no? That's gross, dude. You should skip next period and go shower in the locker room. You seriously stink."

Marty lifted his arm over his head and stuck his nose in his armpit, taking a deep whiff, then blanching at the odor. "I can't believe you waited until lunch to tell me I'm the smelly kid in class. As if I don't already have enough going against me."

"It's obvious, dude. I shouldn't have to tell you that you reek." Spencer shrugged, then tossed his red apple into the air before buffing it to a shine with his t-shirt. "So, you didn't show at the big party after the game Friday night. Did you go home and hit on your mom?"

Marty slugged Spencer in the shoulder. "Shut up."

"Did you hear about the four homeless guys found dead at the park? I read they were mauled by animals."

Marty's breath caught in his throat. He knew very well what sort of animal was capable of tearing apart a group of men. "No. Maybe the police should put out a curfew and warn people."

"Jesus, you're such an alarmist. Well, out with it—where were you this weekend? You didn't return any of my phone calls."

"I was out. Hey, have you seen Gina Simmons today?"

"Nope. She didn't show for first period. Missed the final test on *Macbeth*. She's in big trouble."

"I doubt she cares."

Spencer glanced sideways at Marty. "Dude, what is wrong with you?"

"I'm the descendant."

"The descendant of what?" Spencer asked.

"You don't want to know."

* * *

"What're we doing here again?" Spencer asked, crouched beside Marty in a thick bush outside of the Simmons' Victorian home, each of them holding a flashlight. The sun had set an hour ago, and other than the moonlight and the sparse streetlamps, it was dark. "Since when did you have a crush on Gina Simmons?"

"I don't, you moron. You said you wanted to know where I was this weekend. Well, the last thing I remember is being in *that* basement, vampires coming out of the ground, and then Gina Simmons dead. Do your hear me? D-e-a-d. *Dead.*"

Spencer sighed. "You're so full of shit, Marty."

"I'm serious, Spence! I'm going to prove it to you, too. Follow me." Marty skulked out from the bush and skittered across the wide lawn until he reached the back gate secured with a flimsy, metal latch. He freed the gate and slipped through, Spencer behind him.

Sprinting to the side of the house, their backs scraping against the yellow stucco siding, they reached the rickety wooden staircase leading down into the doom-inspiring basement. Marty felt freezing fingers of dread dance up his spine and shivered. He reached out and pushed against the basement door, letting out a high-pitched yelp of fear as it squeaked open. He was instantly assaulted by the repugnant stench of rotting flesh intermingled with the odor of moist mildew and blood.

"Holy shit!" Spencer choked, waving his hand in front of his nose. "What is that smell? It's like your dirty armpits times a million!"

"Shut up, Spence. I said I'd shower after I showed you this. Now, come on." Marty clicked on his flashlight and motioned for Spencer to follow him. They crept through the low-ceilinged basement, their bright beams of light searching the crevices of the unfinished basement.

"This place looks like the gateway to Hell," Spencer whispered, waving his flashlight around the large, damp space.

The two teenagers jumped as the flashlight beam illuminated the vacant, clouded gaze of the cheerleading captain. Without a word, Spencer scanned the flashlight over Gina's punctured neck, the wounds crusted with dirt and coagulated blood, then trailed over her wrist and inner thigh, which showed similar markings.

"I told you she was dead," Marty said, swallowing a mouthful of bile.

"We need to get out of here, Marty. We need to tell someone about this!" Spencer said, spinning around and shining the light in between he and his friend, showcasing their terrified faces. "We should tell her parents. Scratch that, let's tell the *police!*"

"Tell them what, Spence? That I saw friggin' vampires sit up from their graves and drain Gina of her blood? They'll think I'm crazy! They'll think I did this! I'm not going to jail because that crazy bitch tried to hack off my legs and my blood brought on about some kind of vampiric apocalypse?" Marty started speaking in a soft whisper, but his tone escalated through his rant until he was shouting at Spencer at the top of his lungs.

A familiar pounding shook the floor above their heads, dusting bits of clumped dirt over their heads. "Keep it down!"

"Calm down," Spencer hissed. "Oh, Jesus, let's just get the hell out of here!"

They scurried across the dirt floor, their flashlights aimed at the old door. Just as they reached it, it flung open, and a tall, lanky form stood blocking their path. Marty gasped and fell backward as Spencer slammed against the vampire's chest.

The flashlights fell to the ground, skidding to a muted halt on the dirt floor. The extra moonlight filtering in through the open door helped Marty make out the features of the Immortal One. Though still quite pale and withered, he looked healthier than he had the previous evening. His gaunt cheeks were tinged with red, the blush probably a result of recent feeding. Behind him, more angular visages craned around their master's shoulders, Marty made out three fiendish faces.

Marty realized, with terrible certainty, which side of his family the vampire came from. The Immortal One looked eerily similar to his father, though twenty pounds lighter, ten years younger, and without glasses.

"You have returned to us, my descendant? To bring us an offering, perhaps?" the Immortal One smiled, exposing his wickedly sharp canine teeth. His fangs curved slightly inward, more like a viper than a wolf. He leaned down and pulled Spencer to his feet, though the teenage boy fell back to the floor, unable to support his weight with his quivering legs.

"Leave him alone!" Marty screamed. He squatted, grabbed his best friend's wrists, and pulled him away from the vampire. "Just let us leave!"

Spencer slowly made his way to his feet, then stood, his chest pressed against Marty's back, his teeth chattering.

The Immortal One clucked his tongue against the roof of his mouth. "So soon? It's been...ages...since we've entertained company." The vampire laughed, the sound more menacing than joyful.

Marty looked at the door, then at his ancestor looming in the doorway, hesitating. Finally, he asked, "How am I healed? You didn't turn me into a vampire, did you?"

The Immortal Once chuckled. "Hardly. I already told you, our survival is dependent upon yours. Though we walk and feed, we are dead."

"Then why don't I have any stab wounds?"

The vampire tilted his head from side to side, the odd mannerism making Marty's skin crawl. "I covered you with my blood. I didn't have much, after one hundred years, but I spared what I could," he admitted. "As you are my descendant, my blood has the power to heal you. You did not drink any of my blood, which would have turned you into one of us."

One hundred years, Marty thought. *The same time of the big fire.*

"Let us pass," Marty demanded, walking toward the four vampires lurking in the exit. "You can't harm me. I'm not afraid of you."

"I am," Spencer whispered in Marty's ear.

"Shut up, Spence!" Marty whispered over his shoulder. "So, stand aside!" he yelled at the vampires, taking another step forward.

To his amazement, the vampires parted, two on each side of the door. The Immortal One made a sweeping gesture with his arm. "As you wish, descendant."

With excruciatingly slow strides, Marty walked through the path the vampires created with their bodies, pulling Spencer behind him. He released a deep sigh of relief when they were out of the basement and walking up the rickety wooden steps leading to the Simmons' backyard, the moonlight shining down on them. With a huge grin, Marty turned around, walking up the steps backward. "That was freaky, dude," he said to Spencer.

"Fuck you, Marty. I want to go home."

"You're mad?" Marty reached the top of the staircase. "You're seriously mad? I told you what happened. You should have believed me."

"You're an ass..." Spencer's words were cut short as clawed hands wrapped around his midriff and pulled him back into the basement.

"Spence?" Marty screamed, barreling down the steps and hurling himself through the basement entrance. He smashed into the Immortal One and fell to the floor in a heap.

The vampire leaned over him, his fanged mouth inches from Marty's face, and hissed, "Don't bring anyone else to my lair. While you may be safe from us, your friends are not. Now, run!"

Marty jumped to his feet, tears streaking down his face, ashamed he had led his best friend into danger—and even more so because he was too scared to fight for his safety. He heard a horrific cry come from the basement as he raced up the steps, followed by a deafening silence.

Spencer's dead, Marty thought as he ran through the back fence and across the lawn. *I killed my best friend.*

He sprinted past the bush they had waited in, watching the house for any sign of Gina's parents. He kept up his furious pace until he reached his house. He flew through the front door and slammed it shut behind him, panting and heaving and crying.

"Marty?" his mother asked, walking from the living room into the foyer, a concerned look etched in the small wrinkles around her blue eyes. "What is it, dear?"

Marty wiped his eyes with the back of his hands. "Uh, nothing, Mom. It's just really cold out there."

She frowned and put the back of her hand against his forehead, checking his temperature. "You don't feel hot, but you're so flushed. Are you feeling well?"

"I'm fine, Mom, really," he said, brushing past her to walk up the flight of stairs to his room.

His mother sniffed as he went by, her lips curling with disgust. "You smell like a dumpster, young man. Straight into the shower with you!" she said, pinching her nostrils shut and pointing at the bathroom.

Without another word, Marty marched into the bathroom to rid himself of the stench of death.

* * *

The next morning, Marty feigned sick until his father left for work and his mother went to the natural food co-op for her volunteer shift. He had all afternoon to figure out a course of action, a plan to rid his small town of the vampires his blood had resurrected.

He pulled a Vikings' purple beanie over his head as he headed out the front door for the three block walk to the courthouse. There had to be something in the old records to help him fight the Immortal One and his three emaciated cohorts.

Pulling fifty cents from his pocket, he dumped the two quarters into the newspaper stand slot, jimmied open the plastic lid, and extracted the morning paper.

The headline read **TEN DEAD, TWO MISSING.**

Standing on the front steps of the courthouse, Marty scanned the article, dread seeping into the pit of his stomach. Six more people had been found deceased, victims of the same peculiar animal attacks. Two high school students, Gina Simmons and Spencer McLain, were missing. Anyone with any information was asked to call the police department. The number was splashed on the page, the bold digits searing into Marty's mind.

He glanced at the payphone, then back at the emergency tip number.

Maybe I should call anonymously, he thought, taking a step toward the phone booth. He envisioned a Kevlar-clad S.W.A.T. team busting down the wooden basement door at the Simmons' Victorian and blowing away the evil pack of vampires. Then the vision changed and Marty imagined the police officers taken down and drained of their bodily fluids by the bloodsuckers.

No, reporting the supernatural beings to the police wasn't the answer. He would find another way.

Three hours later, after studying the newspaper articles from right after the fire of 1910, Marty had a plan.

* * *

The internet was full of clever ways to make homemade bombs, and Marty smirked as he carefully lined the cherry red children's wagon with Molotov cocktails. He had raided the recycle bin, pilfered his father's empty beer bottles, and then raided the cleaning supplies from the laundry room. His shoes, devoid of their laces, were piled next to his bed, their shoestrings now used as wicks for the dozen, fluid-filled bottles.

He slipped a box of long kitchen matches into his jacket pocket and lifted the wagon, careful not to jostle its contents, and gingerly made his way down the steps and out the front door. Tuesdays was his parents' night out, and Marty knew they wouldn't return from his neighbor's house for hours. They had left early to dine out at their favorite Mexican restaurant before returning next door to play cards.

The sun was teetering in the sky when Marty stepped out of his house. He had about half an hour until sundown.

Marty ran to the garage and grabbed the plastic, five gallon gasoline jug for the lawn mower. After filling the beer bottles, it was still half full. More than enough to do the trick, he decided, as he hefted the heavy jug in one hand, and carted the wagon behind him with the other. He trudged along the sidewalk, toting his precious cargo, until he reached the Simmons' Victorian.

The shadows of dusk made the house seem sinister, the bare-leaved trees bristling in the soft breeze. Leaving his wagon by his previous hiding bush, Marty uncorked the gasoline jug and ran around the circumference of the house. He let himself through the back gate and shook the rest of the volatile fluid in a straight line across the backyard until the fuel-circle was complete.

He threw the gasoline jug at the basement door, then scampered back to his wagon. He wished Spencer was with him. Marty wanted to share his brilliant plan with his best friend, to have help extraditing the demon-like vampires straight into Hell. After reading the newspaper articles at the courthouse, Marty knew why Chapin had burned in 1910—the town had been infested with some sort of animal, one that stalked the citizens at night and went dormant during the day, one that mauled necks and inner thighs, draining the victims of blood.

Vampires.

The Immortal One and his three undead cronies had been awakened a hundred years ago in Chapin, probably through the blood of Marty's great-great-grandfather, and wreaked havoc through the small Midwestern town until some of its inhabitants fought back with torches and flame.

Marty pulled his cell phone out of his pocket and dialed the Simmons' residence. When Gina's father answered, Marty deepened his voice and spoke gruffly into the phone. "Mr. Simmons? Detective Stanton here. We have news about Gina. We need you to come to the police station immediately, both you and your wife."

He hung up the phone before Mr. Simmons could ask any questions. Moments later, the front door banged open and Mr. and Mrs. Simmons dashed to their car and peeled out of their driveway.

Marty felt guilty giving the grieving couple false hope about their daughter, but he figured it was better than lighting their house on fire while they were still inside.

Once the Simmons' taillights had faded into the burgeoning darkness, Marty looked at the sun hovering over the horizon.

"It's now or never," he muttered, pulling the box of matches from his pocket and striking a sulphured-tip against the coarse igniting strip. A plume of smoke drifted into the crisp air as the match ignited. Marty tossed it into the stream of gasoline and watched as glowing red flames sputtered to life, licking up to the sky.

He grabbed his wagon and pulled it to the edge of the ring of fire just as nightfall descended over Chapin, Nebraska. With bated breath, he waited until he saw the wooden door of the basement creak open, the Immortal One peeking out. A harsh hiss caressed Marty's ears, the satisfying sound of the vampire coming face-to-face with fire.

Without hesitation, Marty swiped another match, lit a shoestring wick on one of the bottles, and flung the bomb at the basement door. The glass shattered, the contents igniting. He hooted, waving his arms above his head when he saw the fire begin to eat through the antique door.

Marty lit the remaining eleven bottles and hurled them at the house, determined to bring the entire structure down upon the vampires with scalding fury. He heard the whine of the fire whistle pierce the still air, heard the scuffle of neighbors stepping out of their homes to watch the all-consuming orgasm of spark and fire tearing apart the Victorian home.

The flames grew so high Marty couldn't see over them to peer at the basement door. He climbed a large cedar tree on the perimeter of the Simmons' yard and stared at the entryway to the dank, dark room.

Ear-piercing, inhuman screams echoed through the yard, and Marty smiled, imagining the slithering vampires burning. The screams stopped by the time the volunteer fire department arrived.

Content, Marty jumped out of the tree, grabbed his wagon and walked home.

* * *

Marty picked up the Wednesday paper off the porch before his father had time to put on his slippers. He read the front page article with a sense of accomplishment.

Six charred skeletons had been discovered in the rubble of the Simmons' Victorian home following a devastating fire. Arson was suspected. The bodies of Gina Simmons and Spencer McLain had been positively identified. The identities of the other four bodies had yet to be determined. It was believed that all six had perished during the fire.

Marty knew better, but he would never tell.

Some things were better left unsaid.

SUICIDE ANGELS

CHRISTOPHER DWYER

Moonlight explodes into a halo of crimson and sparkles. I bite my tongue, feel the white hot sting of fear career into my brain with the force of a thousand dying horses. It's hard to tell just how hard I'm breathing, how frightened my nerves really are. My heart doesn't pound very fast, in fact, it doesn't pound at all. It's just a useless fistful of crumpled pink flesh hanging behind the ribcage.

My eye only a millimeter away from the keyhole, I'm entranced by the terror before me. Abel was mixing a drink at the bar in the corner of his apartment, and then the boom hit, like a hundred pounds of dynamite curled into a ball and thrown through a plate-glass window. My ears popped, I fell to the floor, and there she was: couldn't have been more than a hundred and ten pounds of pale flesh and hair the color of burnt cinnamon. She smiled once through the rubble of broken pine door and eggshell plaster, and then picked up Abel *without even touching him.* She lifted a single black-painted fingernail and before I could crawl away, Abel's torso dripped with the charcoal goo that typically runs through our veins in lieu of red plasma. His thin blonde hair was replaced with spinning gray smoke, and it took only a few seconds for me to shove my way into his bedroom and slam and lock the door.

She tosses him to the side and looks around, her eyes like two tiny dark mirrors. Two tattoos that resemble stars adorn her slender shoulders. She's wearing a black tank-top and tight leather pants. When she sees my big baby blue in the center of the keyhole, I panic. She smiles again and I curse the night for bringing me to this apartment at three in the morning. I look around the room for an exit and only one is available.

I'm either tossing myself through the window or this destructive little woman is going to tear my limbs off like she just did to one of the only friends I had. I count to ten, hold my breath at the last digit. Loud clicks and the bedroom splints and pops. Bits of wood fly through the darkness and in a matter of seconds I force myself through the bedroom window, eager night caressing my backside as I plunge to the ground. When my body hits the top of whatever vehicle was parked seven stories from the apartment, vision quickly fades in a mess of black and blue, the colors of a floating bruised peach.

* * *

Pulsating waves of static, wind scraping my face with delight. I open my eyes and liquid strands of moonlight greet me with a dewy slap. My arm in the air, fragments of broken windshield stuck in the skin like seashells in beach sand. I shake my head and let the panic escape my lungs with one last giant gasp. I look around me and see the chaos: more broken glass and long slivers of dented aluminum and steel. My head thumps with the recurring alarm, flashes of red shining in the corners of my eyes like a police siren. I can see the fire swimming out of Abel's apartment, the lone representation of destruction in an otherwise perfect apartment complex. When the fire department turns the corner, I push my beaten body off the top of the car and into the bushes at the end of the parking lot.

The last thing I need right now is to be questioned by guys much larger than me, especially after a woman half my size brutally murdered a friend I had known for a decade. There's only one place I can go at this point, and it's Cale's tattoo shop.

* * *

By night, I'm a bouncer at The December Club, a decently-sized bar off of Tremont Street in downtown Boston. The staff there likes me because I never take breaks and I have no problem lifting a drunk off his ass with one hand and tossing him out the front door. I guess another reason they like me so much is that I'm never tired, I never call in sick and I have no problem taking a punch to the face from an unruly patron.

Of course, all of these positive attributes are only part of my makeup because I'm a vampire.

The Ink Station is about a mile and a half from Abel's apartment. It's only when I pass a brightly-lit diner that I pause for a moment and take in what just happened. I saw one of my oldest friends picked up into thin air and destroyed by a beautiful woman who burst through the front door with a vicious eruption. I light a cigarette and watch its rosy tip cut through the night. A long drag and a little halo of smoke dissipates into moonlight. I close my eyes and force myself to keep walking. When I reach the outside of the Ink Station, Cale's lone Hummer is the only vehicle in the tiny parking lot in the back of the studio. I knock on the front door twice, wait for the light hops of clanging guitars and gritty drums to pause before Cale opens the door barely an inch.

"What the hell are you doing here so late?" The tips of his jet black eyebrows touch in intrigue.

I shake my head and push open the door. The familiar scent of new plastic and glycerin washes me immediately. "What a night, what a night."

Cale closes the door and locks it, then scans me up and down. "What the fuck happened? You get jumped or something?"

My head resting gingerly on the back of the studio's comfortable leather sofa, I crack my neck so loud that I imagine the ghosts in the room can hear it. "Abel's dead, Cale."

Cale nods once, and we both remain silent for what feels like hours. "Jesus," he eventually says. "How?"

"I dropped by his apartment and within fifteen minutes, a little chick that looks like she'd come here to get inked exploded through the front door."

"Exploded?"

I grunt. "Yes, Cale, *exploded*. Like, *boom*." The great thing about Cale is that he's not very good at conversation, but I've learned to deal with it. We've been friends since I moved to the city, only a few months after I caught the virus that made me what I am today.

He turns on the faucet in the corner of the studio and scrubs his hands. "You need any meds?"

I roll up my jacket sleeve and examine the slits where the windshield had broken into my skin. Most of the tiny lines of open flesh have healed. "No, I should be fine."

"You're taking this pretty well."

I frown. "Abel's dead, man. He's gone. They tell you when you catch our disease that you'll live forever. What a crock."

Cale's been a vampire much longer than I. "We're not human, but we're not invincible. You know that, Charlie." He turns off the faucet and starts to clean up his corner of the studio. "What did this woman look like?"

"About five-foot two, if that. Pale skin, brownish hair. Tattoos on her shoulders."

Cale stops what he's doing and closes his eyes. "Tattoos?"

"Yeah."

"Were they black stars?"

I stand up. "Yes! How did you know that?"

Cale's face looks like that of a tired ghost. He drops a bundle of packaged needles and immediately locks the deadbolt on the studio's front door. He presses one eye against the keyhole and leaves it there for a full minute. He leaves the door and drops the thick velvet curtains down in the two front windows of the shop. Pacing a few steps back and forth, he turns to me and gives me a look I've never seen on his tanned face.

"What? Tell me, Cale..."

"Sit down." He points to the couch.

I take a seat in the corner of the couch and ignore my instinct to frenetically rub my hands together out of anxiety. A cigarette is what I need. I pull one out and offer it to Cale but he waves it away.

"Charlie, we both need to be careful." He leans back into the couch and pushes his sandy locks out of his face with both hands. "That woman, fuck, I can't even believe this is finally happening."

"*What* is happening?" My words are quick and clear.

Cale takes a deep breath. "We're being hunted, that's what's happening."

"Hunted? Why?"

"I know a lot more about our kind than you think, Charlie. I've been hearing rumors about this for the last two years, little rumblings that something like this would start to happen again."

I'm already on my second cigarette and it's only been two minutes.

Cale crosses his legs, then uncrosses them. "They're called suicide angels. And they're a lot older than you and I, my friend."

I tilt my head in confusion. "Angels…"

"They're almost legendary, Charlie. We've only heard rumors of their kind, like they were some type of mythical creature that only existed in the imaginations of a million diseased creatures." He pauses, then motions for a cigarette. I lit one off the tip of my own and hand it to him. "You ever wonder why our population is dwindling overseas, more so than in the States? Why you never see as many cross the Atlantic to come to the States?"

"I thought it was just an issue of sustenance, you know, the way we need a specific type of blood, maybe the risk of being on a flight without a meal…"

"That's only the beginning of it. Have you been anywhere else since Abel's apartment?"

I twist in my seat. "No, just walked straight here."

"Did she see you?"

"What do you mean, of course she did."

"For how long?"

I slide forward on the couch cushion. "Jesus, Cale, she burst into the goddamn room and in a matter of seconds I was hiding behind the door to Abel's bedroom."

He shakes his head. "Then she's most certainly looking for you now. Neither of us are leaving the shop tonight. You can take the couch. I'll find a blanket somewhere in the back."

"What makes you think we'll be safer in the morning?"

"Suicide angels are averse to daylight," he says. "Or, at least that's what I've heard."

* * *

I dream of a million black clouds above a purple sky. I'm sitting in a pool of dirty puddle rain, mud and sand stuck to the bottom of my jeans. A comet trails across the sky and penetrates the moon with a single glittery blow. Ice and snow sparkle into a fiery sideshow of dust and bright green explosions. Abel stands next to me, binoculars glued to his eyes like they were a part of his skin. He removes them for a second and drops them to the ground. The black plastic shatters into a million tiny piece, little

shards scampering away like an army of imaginary ants. Abel points to the sky and a thick gray ooze slithers out of his eyes.
 "They're coming," he says.

* * *

I wake to the sounds of humming needles and soft whispers, the fuzzy reminders of sleeping somewhere other than home. I jerk upright and quickly realize I'm laying on the couch in Cale's tattoo shop. A woman with hair as black as tar sits across from me reading a newspaper. She's covered in about a gallon of ink, two full sleeves of dragons, koi fish, roses and skulls. She pushes down the paper and smiles at me, nods at the steaming mug in the center of the coffee table.

"Cale poured that for you a couple minutes ago," she says. "Drink up, it'll make you feel better."

I rub the slumber out of my eyes and slowly sniff the contents of the mug. If it's from Cale, it's coffee with milk and whiskey. The first sip is bliss, pure awareness mixed with a quick jolt of sweet amber. I tilt forward, rest the mug back on the coffee table. I've met the girl in front of me at least a dozen times and I can't remember her name. Soon enough, I hear Cale's voice and I know I won't have to involve myself in meaningless conversation.

"How do you feel?" He wipes ink off his light purple latex gloves.

I nod, the caffeine circling through my body. If there are two things that can bring me to life, it's caffeine and blood. "Not bad at all. I think I'm going to head to my place for a while. Not sure if I should work tonight or not."

Cale smiles. "Take this." He hands me a black business card with raised blue lettering. "His name's Davey. An old friend of mine from back in Philly. He called this morning and told me that something similar happened near Citizens Bank Park late last night."

I scan the card, feel the punching touch of his name: Davey Rain.

Cale puts a hand on my shoulder. "He's driving into town right now. He'll be at the club in the afternoon. Make sure you're there."

I shove the card deep into my front jeans pocket. "What did you tell him about me?"

"Only the things that mattered," he says. "He's been around for a *long* time...a long, long time, Charlie. There's news coming out of New York and Philly about this. It's best to stay informed...and safe." His eyes reflect the pale rays of sunlight peeking in from the front shop window.

"News?"

"Suicide angels." He nods, pulls me aside. "Davey told me that at least three others were killed in Atlanta over the weekend. Two more in D.C. And, of course...one in Boston last night."

I sigh for Abel, one of the only true friends I had. "Call me later," I say, pushing the front door open. I pause when the cool winter wind hits my face. I'm being hunted, we're all being hunted. Hundreds of years of living like unknown legends and now the minutes are numbered.

* * *

I was twenty-six years old when it happened. I can even remember the tune playing in the club. What I don't recall is who infected me. Psycho Killer was ringing in the corners of the Roxy, reverberations of twangy guitar and David Byrne's voice fizzing with angsty glee. I stepped outside for a cigarette, mild summer air a pure signal of heaven. The shadow approached within a second and when I felt the bite, the *sting* of new life enter my veins, I dreamt for a full day. It was like a black-and-white celluloid version of my life, the life that would never be again. I woke up in my apartment, limbs numb and lifeless. It took a full hour for the virus to greet me with dead, open arms. The hunger doesn't resemble anything like that for human sustenance. It speaks your name with the voice of a dying child, whispers in the most remote corners of your brain. It consumes you, asks you to do anything for a single goddamn drop.

Here's the thing about being me: it isn't as easy as find, kill and drink. We're not supernatural creatures that lurk in the shadows. Sunlight affects only those who prefer the darkness. The blood in our veins remains, but when it hits the air it reflects a steel gray quality that most people don't even notice in daylight. The only way you'd know I am who I am is if you put an ear to my chest. You'd hear *nothing*, not even a single thump of my heart.

If my heart could beat, it'd be on overdrive. I can remember every inch of her body, the sweet smell of danger and lavender as if it were stuck to my skin like morning dew. Fourteen seconds was all it took for her to destroy Abel's body like it was fluffy doll. Fourteen seconds till pastel beauty blasted through the door. Fourteen seconds of death and destruction.

I take hurried steps along the pavement, careful not to knock over any kind pedestrians on the busy Boston streets. My apartment is two blocks off of Cambridge Street in a part of town that's often crammed with tourists and children. Some would say it's not the perfect place to live for someone like me, but I have no complaints. Two major train stations are only a few minutes away, and the highway is a stone's throw away from my front door. If I wanted to, if I *needed* to, escape is only a moment away. When I reach the apartment, I scan the alley before the door out of habit. There's nothing there except for the dumpster and a few stray beer bottles.

My apartment is warm, immediate waves of comfort as soon I step foot into the living room. I bolt up the three deadlocks behind me and slam the door. I'm not taking any chances, even in the calm light of day. It's been over twelve hours since my last dose and my body is starting to ask for it. The whispers are almost real, as if a dozen ghosts were blowing kisses from inside the walls. I shake them off for a moment and walk into the bedroom. I push the bed a full foot towards the wall and lift up the crimson rug from the wooden floor. It wasn't an easy device to install, but a hidden dorm-sized refrigerator is the only place to store my stash. I plug in the combination and two floating rivers of cool mist escape from the hinges. I thumb through the clear plastic packages. The top layer of blood is all O-positive. The dozen or so packs below it are what I need: AB-positive.

The first conversation I had after I was infected was with Cale in the back of The December Club, a place I'd soon enough call my second home. One of the few fantastic traits is that you can sniff out other similar souls, and Cale did just that while downing whiskey sours at the club's colorful bar. He was my mentor, my guide to this new world, this new life. One of the first things he told me was that just blood wasn't enough to sustain our life; the only blood that would satisfy the hunger deep within our bodies was that of the same grouping system when we were human. Since my blood was of the AB-positive variety, the only blood I could drink with any effect on my system was AB-positive blood. Although any type of blood could quiet the virus for an hour, one of us couldn't live alone on blood that wasn't within our grouping system. As Cale would say, "It's just like a fucking appetizer."

If there was one thing that made me clamor for my previous life, it would be the fact that only 4% of the general population could provide me with the proper nourishment. This proved extremely difficult for an abnormal soul like me. I couldn't walk into the streets in the middle of the night with a 50/50 shot of fully feeding the virus. The ones that ignored this crucial element of their existence are the ones that are weak. They're the ones that are constantly hungry. This is why I learned to keep a deep stash buried in my safe. This is why I developed the trait of hording blood in my apartment. I could never take the risk of running low.

I toss a packet of the O-positive to the side and sigh. I take a moment to think of Abel, his infectious laugh, his soulful eyes. We would droop our legs over the sides of the Tobin Bridge when the rest of the world was sleeping. We'd share beers and stories, words that calmed the hunger of contact deep below the surface of my skin. Some would say I could live forever and never know what love could be. Abel was my brother, a soul that would pour you a drink and relieve the tension in your bones with just a smile.

I fish out a packet of AB-negative and waste no time. I don't need a cup; I just pinch a hole in the corner of the bag and drink. When the blood rushes through my body the whispers turn into silence, every pore of my body dripping with the sweat of satisfaction. I sit back against the wall and let the blood soothe my insides, full nourishment the only thing that a vampire craves more than sex. Sunlight drips into the bedroom window and for a moment I'm alive again, in my head my heart is beating and I'm back with my family. I'm normal again.

It's only when that initial jolt passes that reality kicks in once again. The voices in my belly are quiet for now, but like every one of my kind knows, a pint can only keep them at bay for oh so long.

* * *

The telephone rings and I shove the receiver to my ear with a violent jag. "What?" My voice is crackly, like it's bouncing off the walls of an old and tired radio.

"Charlie, there's a guy here who's looking for you." The other voice is Mickey's, my boss.

"What's he look like?" While it's true that my body is never actually tired, sometimes after a full dose the eyes need to sleep.

Mickey clears his throat. "Older, but you know, he's one of...*us.*"

It must be Davey. "Tell him to sit tight. I'll be there in twenty minutes."

Within moments, I'm in the shower and scrubbing off the bits of Abel's blood that I didn't notice before. I sigh once, remember what is like to have real friends in a world that needed them.

I towel off in the bedroom and grab a pair of broken-in jeans. Black t-shirt, brown leather jacket. And, of course, a nine-millimeter pistol lodged uncomfortably into the back of my jeans.

* * *

The Boston transit system is a lot like the fourth or fifth layer of hell: every soul trapped down here is vague of smiles and warmth. Every passenger looks as if the world could end at any moment and it's something they'd welcome. The train shifts for a second and I balance myself with a hand gripping the dirty steel bar above the row of seats below. I close my eyes and sniff. Traces of urine and sweat and rage. I look around the car and don't see a fellow lifer like myself. Another sniff. No, I'm the only one on this train.

I get off at State Street and walk for a mile or so before the sun dips below the horizon. The December Club's lights echo from a distance, its attractive glow alluring and dangerous. I don't even remember what day it is, but I can tell it must be a weekend because there's at least three or four dozen mini-skirted girls waiting behind the velvet rope. Slowly letting them in is a hulking brute of a Mexican named Johnni.

"Charlie, you working tonight?" He smiles and points to the entrance, letting a girl who's presumably underage into the club.

I pat him on the shoulder. He's all muscle, much stronger than I. Any shifts that I'm not covering, Johnni's usually here. Who can complain? It's good money and you get the chance to knock around people who have even the slightest attitude.

"Not scheduled, but I came into visit…" My words trail off at the sight of a woman with the eyes of a tiger, twisted vines of ink adorning her pale frame. The wind sucks the air out of my lungs for a second and all I can feel is that cold metal keyhole pressed against my face, the eager breeze of death ripping limbs and life. The girl giggles and holds a man's arm, probably her boyfriend. I catch my breath again.

"You okay, buddy?" Johnni puts up a hand to the long line and grips my shoulder.

I nod. "Yeah, just thought I saw someone I knew." I force a grin and motion towards the entrance. "I'll catch up with you later. I gotta talk to Mickey for a bit."

Johnni nods and continues scanning driver's licenses. I clutch my chest, feel the panic swimming alongside the smooth edges of my ribcage. It all seems like fantasy to me; another breed on the hunt for vampires, tasked with hunting us down like fucking rats. I push open the doors, neon rays dissipating into a cloud of cigarette smoke. I scan the bar for an older gentleman but only come across an array of twenty-somethings and Goth burnouts. When I step into the lounge a familiar voice slices through the thick noise overhead.

"My friend." Mickey's holding onto my arm, that golden smile plastered across his face like he was a used car salesman.

"Mickey," I say, eyes continuing to scan the rest of the club like a focused hawk. "What's going on?"

His smile fades into wrinkles. "My office, now."

"I'm looking for…"

"I know." He cuts me off. "He's in my office."

I follow Mickey into his office, loud rock music from the club downstairs lightened into silence. He slams the door shut behind me and motions for me to sit next to a sharply-dress man, pin-striped suit and an aura of prestige. His hair is as gray as dirty snow. The man stands up and offers his hand. I shake it with full force and his fingers are strong and firm.

"Davey Rain," he says, perfect white teeth glimmering in the dark light of the office. "You must be Charlie."

"That'd be me," I say, plopping down into the plush leather guest chair in front of Mickey's desk.

Mickey coughs, then shrugs his shoulders. "Gentlemen, we have a problem on our hands."

"That's putting it lightly, cowboy." Davey crosses his legs, peek of black dress socks marked with white dots. Not many of our kind dress like they're running for office.

Before Mickey can interject I raise my hand, gently let it fall to my lap. "He's right, Mick. I know what's going on. Pretty soon our entire race is going to know what's going on."

Davey nods, lips parted in a frown. "Well, I can tell you for sure that Philly knows what's going on. Dallas found out last week. New York is going through it right now, and well, the whole friggin' east coast is ablaze." He clears his throat and pulls a faded black cigarette from a bronze case. He lights its tip and smoke engulfs the room within a few seconds.

"Is this really a threat?" Mickey leans over the front of the desk.

Davey chuckles. "A threat, sir? You can ask your good friend right here if *threat* is the right word for what's going on."

Mickey looks at me, and I look at Davey. Davey nods. "Tell him what happened last night."

I look to the carpeted floor, try to focus on a rogue patchwork of crimson loops and swirls. "Abel was killed last night. Torn apart by a woman that looked like she could be a dancer here. Short, pale, star tattoos on her shoulders. Didn't even have to break a sweat, picked him clean up off the ground and tore him to pieces." I swallow urgency, let it boil in my throat.

Mickey's mouth stays open. He leans back in his chair and takes a deep breath. "Who did this?"

"They're called suicide angels, or at least that's what the folks down south have been calling them."

"Are you kidding me?" Mickey twists in his chair. He's never been the kind to accept the fantastical, save for the fact that he lives off blood and could probably live forever.

"Listen to him, Mick," I say. I turn to Davey. "Continue."

"They're fallen angels. Eternal souls vaulted from the divine. Angry angels with a path to burn."

Mickey groans. "You believe this shit, Charlie? Fallen angels? Can't be real."

Davey smiles, full grin swooping from his cheeks. "You mean to tell me you can accept your lifestyle, you can accept *our* existence...but you're not open to the possibility that there's something out there even more twisted than our kind? Just think, my friend, of the possibilities." At his last word, his eyes are as wide as tea plates. His voice booms with authority. "The virus that swims in our blood, the virus that controls our every thought, our every action, it had to come from someplace."

"What is this? Retribution?" Mickey's standing up, turned to the open window that looks down into the club. Flashing lights penetrate our reflections.

"There are things that we're never meant to know, gentlemen. If creatures like us can exist, why can't angels?" He reaches into his briefcase and pulls out a slick silver laptop. He props it open and pushes a button below the screen. When the monitor bursts alive with light, he holds a hand up. "Are you guys ready for this?"

Both Mickey and I nod in unison.

"Okay then." Davey fiddles with the laptop for a few seconds and a square box is alive in the center of the screen. He pushes the laptop towards the edge of the desk and motions for us to look at it. "This is thirty seconds of surveillance footage from one of my bars in downtown Philly." He pushes a key and the video comes to life.

The first few seconds are black-and-white motions of at least a dozen men standing, drinking, talking, laughing. The bartender leans over the beer tap and pulls back the handle. As he slides the glass to the man next to the cash register, a rogue burst of smoke explodes from the corner of the screen. Bodies are tossed by an unseen force, a poor patron's scalp is ripped from his skull like it was latex. The smoke clears nearly twenty seconds into the video and we can see her: the black and blonde hair, tattoos on her shoulders like medals of evil. She grabs the bartender with a single hand and in a matter of seconds two little dribbles of white fly from his face. He falls over the edge of the bar, eyeless and lifeless. The angel turns to the camera and smiles. She's not the same one from last night but it really doesn't matter. The video stops and I finally take a breath.

"It's not safe in the city." Davey stands up and points at me. "We need to go. You, too, Mick."

"We're not going anywhere." Mickey's voice booms with anger.

"We don't have a choice, Mick." I stand up with a jolt.

Davey turns off the laptop and slides it back into his briefcase. "Some of my guys are in a hideout on the border of New Hampshire and Maine. So far, they've only hit the most densely populated areas. We might be safe there, together."

Mickey pushes back his thick black hair. "This is fucking ridiculous, guys. We're just supposed to pack up and leave our lives like this? And for how long?"

Davey shakes his head. "I can't answer that. Do you want to die, or do you want to come with us?"

Mickey opens the closet in the corner of the office. He flicks the light switch, reaches on the top shelf, and tosses down a large gray duffel bag. "I need about twenty minutes."

"That's fine," Davey says, shoving his arms into his blazer. "I bet our boy Charlie would like to stop at his place before our ride, don't you?"

I nod, place a hand on Mickey's shoulders. "Mick, be careful."

"I concur," Davey says, and hands Mickey a business card with an address scrawled on its back. "We'll all be there."

* * *

The population hit its benchmark sometimes in the '80s. Some inside sources claimed that we were only outnumbered fifteen-to-one by normal humans. Clans erupted all over the country, some clashing with each other even though the constant threat of being outed hung over our heads like a lingering dark cloud. Although it didn't happen overnight, the numbers dwindled into the '90s. Some, like Mickey, claimed that the scarcity of rarer blood types prohibited a regular feeding cycle for most of the infected. Without that fresh burst of life, our bodies shut down. The virus turns on us, causes our organs to eat themselves in lieu of proper nourishment. Our bodies have the same medical qualities as a dead human if we were shot in the head or hit by a car. Others, well, they're not so lucky to leave something so quaint behind.

When I was a pup, I saw first-hand what the hunger can do to us. A rogue lifer stepped into the December Club one summer afternoon with a gun planted at the sky, lips as tight as bridge cables. He pointed the pistol at one of the bartenders and in a matter of seconds I was on his back, pounding his skull with the bloody edges of my knuckles. We didn't know he was like us until the sixth or seventh hour of keeping him locked up in the walk-in refrigerator in the back of the club. He shuddered in the midst of frost and hunger, his skin melting like cookie-colored candle wax. It took a full hour for the virus to sweep through his body, destroying every last living cell. I watched in awe till all that was left were the burnt edges of bone, a skeletal ghost lain in a pool of orange dust

It's almost as if only the strong survived. Only those who were willing to become monsters stepped outside of the boundaries of decency and planted their teeth into the soft flesh of a human. For some, it was just too hard. Even I found myself sitting in dark days during those years. It was only when I learned to stash, learned to make the right connections did I find myself fed, satisfied, and, until now...*safe*.

Cale was well-connected within the East Coast societies. He knew the leaders of local clans. He knew how to get the right quantities of plasma without causing a stir or raising attention. And, most importantly of all, he hooked me up with Mickey, who kept me well-fed and well-paid with a gig at the December Club.

It's very rare now that I sniff out a fellow infected soul in the public realm. We're an endangered species, whittled down to the smallest number in decades. If you're not like me and you live in the rural areas of the country, I can't imagine you'd be anything but fucked. Only the powerful ones survived the worst, and now the few of us left have to deal with something even more violent than starving the virus.

Everything before this week was perfect. I lived day-to-day with the same routine, the same bittersweet emotion of eternal life. I stay off the radar. My driver's license is under a different name. I don't have credit cards or bank accounts. I deal in cash and blood. I don't have many friends. It's a simple life, but it's a life I've been used to for so long. And now that all seems to be crashing down around me. For once, I'm not worried about my next meal. For once, I'm not worried about finding a woman who I can share my terrible secret with.

Because now, all I'm worried about is *death*.

* * *

Davey switches the radio station with a quick twirl of his perfectly-manicured fingers. Hard rock, jazz, then silence. He can't settle on a station. He finally puts his hand back on the steering wheel and we continue into the night. We reach the Ink Station and Cale's already standing on its doorstep, plum cherry tip of a cigarette dangling from his lips. Davey rolls down the window and smiles. "Two hours and we're not stopping." Cale nods and opens the back door, tosses his duffel bag between mine and Davey's and hops into the truck with a sigh. He looks back at the trail of fog and exhaust, as if the tattoo shop is his home.

I lean against the passenger's side window, cool glass pressing into my cheeks. Before long, I'm dreaming of the life I lived before all of this.

* * *

Night burns into a smoldering trail of haze and moonlight. I wake to Davey's voice. "We're here, partner."

I'm out the truck and surrounded by the woods, far different from the world two hours ago. Cale tosses my duffel bag at me and I catch it with both arms. He looks around and shakes his head. "Thirty years and it comes down to this," he says. "Thirty goddamn years."

I can't do anything but look away, listen to the speckles of rural nature tickle the innermost portions of my mind. It's beautiful up here and dangerous at the same time. Only a few yards from us are the booming echoes of misplaced laughter and other voices. Drips and drabbles of other clans, souls lost and wandered into a place where we all might die. Davey motions for us to follow him up to a bleak and gray building that's oddly out of place up here in the woods.

"This place was once used to store my group's supply," he says, dragging his bag over a hefty shoulder. "For years I'd make trips up here with my guys and fill up. Local government thought it was a waste management facility. Never would have thought we'd have to use this place for a safe haven."

The voices grow louder as we approach the entrance, some of them familiar, most of them new. Davey holds the door open for us and we're greeted with a dozen different sets of fiery eyes. These are the hunted brethren, the fellow lifers that have come here as a last resort. I find my place at a table in the corner of the lobby where I recognize Betty, a black-haired raven that once tended bar at the December Club. Her face lights up when she sees Cale and I, arms outstretched and gripping my shoulders with the force of a burning memory.

"Charlie," she says, lips as red as Christmas. "Long time."

A single peck on the cheek. "I know, Betty. Too long."

Before we can start a conversation, Davey's standing on the counter of the makeshift bar in the corner. His words cut through the thick stench of ammonia and fear.

"My friends. We are not here because we are afraid. We are not here because this is a final stand. We have not come here to die. For the last hundred years, we've lived as we've wanted and along the way there's been bumps. We've seen our share of misfortune. We've seen our share of hardship. And tonight, my friends, is just another hurdle that we have to approach with caution. We've lived this long and tonight is not the last time we'll see each other, you can mark my words."

He hops down from the corner of the bar and greets a group that has just walked into the building. I look around, see a set of doors and I imagine this place is not equipped as a bunker or even as a home.

Cale grabs my arm. "I'm not in the mood to socialize. I can't believe what we're doing here."

"I know, I know. But this is the only way we're going to be safe, or so says Davey. I've seen what they can do, Cale. I'll never forget those moments. I'll never forget what they did to Abel."

Cale looks away, sighs. Davey approaches from the corner, two beers in one hand. "Drink, my friends. I refuse to realize the fear."

I can't help but smile. Long sip of alcohol and my nerves subside with a groan. Ten or so minutes pass and I feel just as Cale did. I set the bottle on the edge of the table and slide away into the opposite side of the room. I open the door next to the bathroom and find a storage room, dozens of large boxes stacked perfectly along the walls. It's cool and dark and perfect. Cale's right behind me.

"Don't feel like socializing?"

"Not tonight."

"Me too." He plants his backside against a stack of boxes and lets out a deep breath. He unscrews the top of his beer and flips the bottle to his mouth.

I sit cross-legged on the cool tiled floor, stomach mixing alcohol and the whispers of the virus. It's hard not it ignore it's siren but there's enough fear careening through my mind to keep it at bay for at least the rest of the night.

Cale finishes his beer and rolls the bottle along the floor. He burps and tilts his head back. "Jesus, Charlie...we really should be at the club, you know? Mickey booming with laughter, tearing through a bottle of scotch with everyone. This just doesn't feel right."

Before I can speak, the familiar rumble of broken glass and bursting explosions echoes from the room outside the door. Cale's eyes widen, black and blue drops that radiate with dread. I stand up and my brain flutters, wonder quickly if I'm dreaming the sounds on the other side of the wall. Before I can turn the knob the door dents and cracks into a million sprinkles of wood and gray paint. One of the group's bodies is bloodied and beaten, tip of his skull scalped around his temple. Mushy squiggles of brain and flesh goop onto the floor and it only takes me three total seconds to grab Cale's arm and jump out of the broken entrance in the storage room door. I push my way through smoke and screams, quick glance of black-and-blonde hair swooshing into the wind. I don't take the time to find Davey or anyone else involved in the slaughter. I can hear Cale's words close behind me. *The truck...the truck...*

In a squeal of seconds I find the open wall that once stood solid before the angel burst her way into the building. Moment of freshness from the cool night air, soon dissipating into a frantic run for Davey's truck. Cale reaches the driver's side and flips open the door. I jump into the passenger's seat and breathe again while he plucks the keys from the visor. Loud roar of the engine and we're off. I take a single second to look behind me, long wispy trail of smoke and fire spinning from the building.

The truck careens along the dirt road, Cale pressing hard on the gas pedal. The speedometer rifles with glee and soon enough I can't hear the disparate voices in my head. He doesn't anticipate the curve at the end of the road and time freezes as we're spun upside down.

Crank of metal and wood, gush of red from the open wound in my forehead.

*   *   *

The stars blush and smile, bits of glitter exploding into long streams of hazy purple liquid. I can't feel my arms or legs and I imagine this is where my soul is trapped. The virus robbed me of my soul and forever I'll be a part of somewhere that has no depth, no air.

I look down and see my boots are level with the sea. I'm walking on water, the glistening edges of violent waves crashing against each other in a fit of winter storm. Snow and ash fall from the sky. When I close my eyes I fall backwards into sand. She's standing above me, hair floating in the wind like a cloud of black snakes.

"The angels form the demons," she says.

I can't speak, can only watch a whisper of smoke escape from my lips. She raises a white-painted fingernail and I'm drawn to the ground, an unseen force pulling me below the sand and into darkness. When I finally shout, my voice is beaten and broken. I hear the murmur now, like a million dead souls singing with their final breaths.

The angels form the demons.

* * *

I wake to the sounds of blood sloshing against my chest. It's wet and painful and I don't know where I am. Blurry vision gives way to an aura of broken light. I wince when Cale's severed head is thrown onto my lap. I'm lying at the side of the truck, steady downpour of rain dousing the goosebumps trailing across my arms and legs. I claw along the ground, fingernails digging against a mix of dirt and grass and mud. It's only when I bring my hands to the air that I can see the two events unfolding before me: the rain is my best friend's blood and the light is coming from the fire in her eyes. A suicide angel, the same one from the beginning of my downfall. Leather pants as tight as latex paint. Pale skin, two tattoos now drenched in the blood of her kill.

She stands above me, the rest of Cale's body floating in the air. On the horizon, the last breaths of night slip into the distance. The trees beyond the fence shudder in the wind. I kick off Cale's lifeless head from my legs, his face locked in a cold, dead stare. My breaths are erratic and as she nears closer to me, every inch of every hidden memory of my life before all of this flashes in the corners of my eyes, each scene and every bit of dialogue muddled by the sparkling cigarette burns popping into view with every drop of my eyelids.

I can't see the sun, but I know it's in the distance. I know it's there. She kneels next to me, traces a finger alongside my arm. Her touch anesthetizes me for a moment, leaves my blood in a standstill. The angel opens her mouth and I can hear her words. They swing past the curves in my brain, past the memories and past the consciousness of my mind. Lost and back again. Lost.

She straddles her wet frame over mine. I can barely feel the weight of her backside. She leans forward, lips that could kill with a single bloody kiss. The thrush of a million blind souls drives my body to slide against the mud. She pushes me back down without moving. A long trail of icy breath slips from my mouth and into the air, caught between the moon and the sun. The center of my shirt splits and the fabric snaps. Her face curls into a smile and I know that it's only a matter of seconds before it's over. She closes her eyes, eyelids as dark as wet mulberry. My body throbs and each jolt from her hands twists my veins until they pop and collapse. Her hand stuck to my bare chest, she slides it down to my pelvis, leaving a path of gashed skin and boiling blood. The virus is frightened and subdued. Even its powerful grip can't stave off execution at the hands of the angel.

The hair dangles in front of her face like charred icicles, her cheeks as white as virgin snow. The other hand digs into the new chasm between my chest and stomach. She pulls out a handful of my insides, steaming hot blanket of angry blood slithering away from the mess. She shows her teeth and in only three seconds does she stand up again. My hands wobble in the mud before the bone erupts from below the skin. She lifts a finger to the air and my body slides along the grass until the sound gives out to a wall of black noise.

The curves and lines of a miscible disk of light penetrate my final visions. My eyes follow the comet trail of red dust dancing above my face as night burns into a cavern of lost echoes, breaths swept away in a muddle of melting static.

ANGELS OF DEATH

ANTHONY GIANGREGORIO

The dark alley in the deepest part of Dorchester, just a mile from Boston, seemed to embrace the shadows of the night like a blanket.

Filled with the detritus of a fallen society, rats scurried amongst the trash, searching for another morsel of rotting food. At the far end of the alley, another shadow stood, blending into the blackness as if part of it.

And in truth the shadow was.

Moonlight crested over the dilapidated rooftops and a spear of illumination cut through the dark to expose the visage of the shadow. At first the male face looked human, but as the man who owned that face smiled, the distinct shape of two fangs could be seen.

The man turned after checking his back trail, then he sprinted to a hidden doorway at the far end of the alley. He knocked three times and waited. He hummed a tune from his youth, the song from the early 1800's. He had never gotten into the newer forms of music, having a sense of nostalgia.

But though in many ways he disliked the twentieth century, he had to admit there were a few perks that had never existed back when he had first been *turned*.

A small metal plate in the door about head height slid open and a pair of black eyes glared at him.

"What the fuck do you want?" a gravelly voice demanded.

"Vlad sent me," the man said, his tone filled with sarcasm. There was no Vlad and there probably never was, but even a vampire could have a sense of humor. He did make sure to flash a smile so his fangs could be seen.

A clacking of deadbolts came to his ears, and a second later the door was opening inward.

No sooner did the door open, then the steady drone of a bass could be heard.

The man strolled inside, flashing his most sincere grin to the doorman. As for the doorman, he merely grunted, his bald pate reflecting what little light was in the small hallway.

The man slid the doorman a twenty and nodded as the door slammed close behind him, for all purposes sounding like a steel grating in a dungeon.

He walked down the hallway, the steady beat of the bass growing. There was another door and another doorman, this one with a slight bulge under his dark sports coat. He nodded to this new bouncer, knowing what that bulge was. Though technically undead, a bullet to the head could kill and one to the body sure as hell didn't tickle.

Most of the myths humans knew of vampires were just that—myths. Vampires were still human in many ways and most just wanted to live their long lives in peace. Take sunlight for instance. In reality, a vampire in the sun would just end up with a great tan. Of course they fed on human blood, but then humans fed on the flesh of animals. How is that any different?

The second doorman looked him up and down, waved a wand over his person to see if any hidden weapons were on him, then nodded, seeing he was clean. Turning, he opened the door he was guarding.

As the door opened, bright light and a blast of music hit the man like a wave and he stepped into *The Underground*, a place where vampires could relax and be themselves.

No sooner did he enter then a shrill voice cried out from a corner. "Adrian, it's about damn time you got here!"

Adrian turned, knowing that voice in an instant. He shook his head as another man jogged over to him, having to weave in and out of the dancing crowd. Adrian had hoped he might get at least a few minutes to get a drink before Carl found him.

As Carl ran up to him, Adrian reached into his mouth and popped the plastic fangs from his teeth.

"You did it again, huh?" Carl asked as he reached Adrian, seeing the plastic vampire teeth in his hand.

Adrian nodded. All around the two men people danced and gyrated, but it was on the edges of the room where the true fun was.

Speaking up to be heard over the music, Adrian said, "Yeah, I just love the way Boris looks at me when I smile at him."

Boris was the first bouncer with the dark eyes that Adrian had passed to enter the underground den.

"He says he doesn't like you," Carl added.

Adrian shrugged. "He just doesn't know me, that's all. Is it my fault he doesn't have a sense of humor?"

Carl shook his head and downed the last of his drink. "You thirsty?"

"Yeah, but not for what's in your glass."

Carl grinned, knowing what Adrian meant. "Then go to booth five, there's a chalice with your name on it."

"Sounds good, I'll catch up to you after I've had a bite to eat."

Carl was going to say more, but Adrian didn't let him. He spun and slid into the crowd, moving through the sea of people. A few familiar faces smiled at him and he did the same, a few women receiving a peck on their cheek in greeting. The entire club was filled with vampires, each having a fun night on the town.

Adrian reached the edge of the dance floor and counted booths that lined the wall until he came to booth five. Sure enough, it was empty, with the exception of the exquisite beauty lying naked on the table. She wore a small gold pendant of a cross on her neck and Adrian chuckled at that. She was a defiant one, then. Though crosses were nothing to vampires, just another harmless myth, every vampire knew what it represented and none enjoyed having the one thing they couldn't have thrust in their face; for to be one of the undead meant Heaven was forever out of reach.

Just before Adrian went to her, his mouth already watering, he caught a snippet of conversation from behind him. Two men were conversing and both sounded troubled.

"So did you hear what happened over on Cambridge Street in Boston?" one asked the other.

"No, spill it," the other replied.

"One of them suicide angels found a flat with us and tore the shit out of some poor bastard. They said when she was through, only dental records were gonna identify the guy."

"Shit, I didn't know they were so close. I heard of something going down in Philly a few weeks ago, but here, too?"

"Think we got to worry?"

"About what? If one of them bitches ever tries for me, I'll cut her fucking angel heart out. They don't scare me a bit."

"Not me, man, I don't wanna deal with them, they're relentless. I hear if they get your scent, they're like bloodhounds."

"Bah, more bullshit. It's all hype. So one of us gets whacked, it happens. These angels are becoming bigger than they are."

"Yeah, hey, I'm empty, wanna get another beer?"

"Sure, then let's get something to eat, too, I'm famished."

The two men moved off and Adrian glanced over his shoulder as they moved across the large room of the nightclub. So there had been another angel attack.

They were becoming more frequent lately.

Though no vampire wanted to admit it, as every one of them felt they were the dominant species on the planet, something new had been added to the equation.

They were being hunted by what had been dubbed suicide Angels.

These *angels* were relentless killing machines who never spoke and wanted nothing more than to kill every vampire they could find.

Whether the vampire race wanted to admit it or not, they were being hunted, and so far no one had escaped alive, and it was only thanks to brief glimpses that any Intel on the angels was known at all.

His stomach rumbled and he could feel the hunger calling, so deciding what had happened in Boston was none of his affair, he crawled into the booth. With a nod to the chalice, he began to feed, the woman writhing below him, slowly coming to an orgasm as a small amount of her life's blood fed him.

Not enough to kill her, in fact, it was more like donating blood to a local hospital.

Chalices were volunteers who wanted nothing more than to become a vampire. True, there were some who simply got off on being with a mythic creature, and some were so into Goth that the vampire scene was the only way to reach *true* fulfillment, but some simply just got off on getting *fanged*, as the saying went.

Of course, fangs were a myth and in reality two small cuts of the flesh on the neck were all that was needed to get the blood out of the chalice without causing serious harm. Adrian had even heard of a few vampires who had taken to getting dentures with fangs in them so they could go the whole Bela Lugosi route.

Hey, one man's disgust is another's fetish and all that.

A small metal poker, looking a lot like a skewer for shish-kabobs, sat next to the woman's head, the tip coated in a thin sheen of her blood from when Adrian had poked her. He leaned back and smiled, relishing the aftertaste on his tongue, as he wiped his mouth with a napkin. Always the gentleman was Adrian, and proper etiquette was a must.

"Damn that's good, aged to perfection. How old are you, darlin'? Twenty? Twenty-one?"

"Twenty," she purred as she rubbed her hands between her legs. Feeding and sex were intertwined to the point the lines had blurred for her. If Adrian was correct, he bet the chalice couldn't orgasm unless she was being fed upon. And like drug addiction, each time she would need to go a little farther to get the same rush. It was possible one day she would be sucked dry. It had happened before, though no one wanted to talk about it; bad for business and all that.

A chalice wouldn't be so excited about volunteering if they knew they might end up being sucked dry till they resembled a withered grape in the sun.

Carl popped up with a beer in each hand and sat down across from Adrian so he had to look over the woman's breasts to see him. The chalice's nipples were rock hard and her eyes were closed as she moaned in pleasure, savoring the last of her orgasm.

"One of those for me?" Adrian asked.

Carl looked at him blankly, then nodded. "Huh? Oh, yeah, here ya go. Thought you might be thirsty."

"Yeah, I am," Adrian said as he took the beer. A few droplets of condensation from the bottle dripped onto the woman's chest. The drops slid into the valley between her breasts and then rolled down her stomach, where she used her hands to rub the water over her warm skin.

Adrian watched her and debated if he should take her home and screw her. All he had to do was ask and she would jump at the chance. But he didn't, maybe for that exact reason. When there was no hunt involved, no pursuit, it sometimes became dull, lackluster.

He turned and gazed into the gloom-filled room, his eyes studying the other patrons. About twenty dancers were on the dance floor at the moment and the hard bass of the juke box blasted from the speakers mounted in every corner. There was an empty stage in the far right corner. On Fridays and Saturday nights a live band would play. They were called the *Bloodsuckers* if you believed it, an inside joke if there ever was one. All four band members were of course, vampires.

But the stage was empty tonight with the exception of a young couple sitting on the corner of it, talking together, their heads pressed forehead to forehead so they could be heard over the music. Adrian let his gaze slide to the booths on either side of him. Chalices were on each table, their naked bodies glistening under the soft lights overhead. Smoke filled the large room like it was a giant fireplace with the flue closed, and the cacophony of music mixed with people yelling and talking was an uproar of horrendous proportions.

In other words, just another night at *The Underground*.

Adrian finished his beer and felt his bladder pushing on his belt. Though technically undead, with a heart that didn't beat anymore, what went in still had to leave sooner or later, so he decided it might as well be sooner.

"I gotta use the head," he said to Carl who was playing with the chalice. He was sucking her right nipple and gently nuzzling the breast with his chin. By the look of it, Carl would be bringing the chalice home tonight. "I'll be right back."

Carl looked up and barely acknowledged Adrian as he moved off to the bathrooms at the rear of the dance floor. When he reached the small hallway leading to the bathrooms, he had to slide between two women who were sniffing cocaine off the back of a man's hand. Adrian knew immediately the man was a vampire, thanks to a sixth sense he and other vampires had for recognizing their own kind. The women were human, and were probably the man's escorts, or perhaps even mates.

Entering the bathroom, he heard the soft sounds of a woman grunting in pleasure. Walking to the stalls, he saw a pair of feet, male by the shoes, and behind those he saw the feminine feet of a woman, both of her feet spread apart so her toes were pointing at right angles. By the sound of it, she was certainly enjoying herself.

Adrian went to the urinal and did his business. He wasn't there for more than five seconds when the woman cried out and there was a scuffle in the stall. The door slammed open and Adrian saw an attractive redhead with dark eyes storm out while adjusting her skirt.

"I said not in the back, I told you that already," she snapped as she left the bathroom. A man came out right behind her, saw Adrian and flashed him a knowing grin. As he did, he was zipping up his fly then chasing after the woman. "Oh, come on, baby, let's talk about this," he pleaded as he chased her back into the nightclub.

Adrian smirked to himself and finished his business.

Flushing, he went to the sink and washed his hands, always the dutiful vampire. He remembered what his mother used to say about cleanliness and doing it for yourself, not for others.

He stared at his face in the mirror, seeing a few dark circles under his eyes. He wasn't getting as much sleep as he should and he made a mental note to correct that. Though immortal, he still needed to take care of himself. It was his choice if he wanted to go through life as an overweight vampire, a rundown one, or a healthy, vibrant one.

Wetting his hands, he ran them through his hair, using his fingers as a comb. Wiping them with a brown, paper towel from the pile on the sink, he turned to head back and join Carl.

It was as he was reaching for the door handle to the bathroom that he froze at the massive sound of something being smashed coming from the dance floor. Immediately, the jukebox cut off and he could hear screams and yells mixed with gunshots.

His hand hovered over the door handle as he listened to what sounded basically like a war was being fought in the nightclub.

His hesitation was no more than a second, but to him it felt like a lifetime.

Then his hand became unfrozen and he reached for the knob, throwing open the door, and charging into the nightclub. As he ran down the small hallway, he could see brief glimpses of chaos as the gloom-filled club was ravaged by something so powerful it was a blur.

Adrian reached the end of the small hallway and his mouth fell open as he stared at the carnage before him.

Every vampire in the room was fighting for their lives as a blur with dark black hair weaved in and out, always avoiding grasping hands, but at the same time dealing death with each blow made.

He watched as the blur grabbed a man by the arms and tore them off like the man was no more than a doll stuffed with straw. The blur spun and began using the arms like bludgeons, smashing people to the floor until the arms were nothing but bits of bone and flesh.

And even then the blur found a use for the arms. Down to the nubs, the blur spun the arms around and used each one as a dagger, plunging the tips into the eyes of two screaming patrons.

A chalice ran screaming past the blur and Adrian could only watch in abject horror as the chalice had her head torn off and tossed aside.

Then Adrian saw Carl, moving up on the blur, a ruthless Bowie knife in his right hand. Adrian remembered the knife well, the two having been hanging out together on Kneeland Street at the Army/Navy store when Carl bought it.

With a throaty yell, Carl leaped at the blur, but as he hung in the air, mouth and eyes wide in attack mode, knife gleaming in the gloom, the blur spun, ripped the knife from his hand and then gutted him with it, all in the blink of an eye.

Carl's insides splashed onto the floor amid a hot sticky puddle of blood and viscera as his body continued its motion to roll and come up against another vampire.

"No!" Adrian screamed but stayed rooted to his spot, not knowing what to do. Meanwhile, the blur wasn't idle, whipping amongst the other vampires and ripping heads off and severing limbs in a cyclone of blows and impacts that seemed to shake the very foundation of the nightclub.

Adrian glanced to his right to see the two bouncers, both bodies now missing their heads and one having no arms. Something came up against his feet and Adrian looked down to see it was the bouncer with the dark eyes, the orbs now glazed over in death. Blood still spurted from the gaping neck where the head had been separated from the torso, a few inches of spine twitching like a dying worm.

Adrian kicked it away with a grunt of disgust and weighed his options.

He could try and fight whatever was destroying his friends. Or he could try to reach the exit and escape. To his right the shattered doorway beckoned, the cool air from the night seeping in.

The blur took off another head and tore the legs from a screaming chalice, the legs becoming large clubs to beat down all that stood in its way.

Adrian tried to get a better look at the blur, to see what it could be that was decimating his fellow vampires, but all he saw was the obsidian hair and a blur of bare shoulders. As the blur paused for a fraction of a second, his eyes picked up the ornate tattoos on the blur's shoulder, both in the shape of stars. But then the blur was in motion again and a spray of blood was left in its wake as it weaved through the dancers of the club like a scythe through wheat.

Adrian had been standing at the edge of the dance floor for no more than a few seconds, and in that time, the blur had killed every single person in the nightclub.

Then, as if in slow motion, the blur paused and finished off the last vampire. This one was a man, tall, with large shoulders and bulging muscles that could have crushed a normal assailant with ease.

The man managed to grab the blur, and for the first time since entering the club and seeing the carnage, Adrian saw what was killing his people.

It was one of them—a suicide angel.

The angel's hair was so black it seemed to absorb any light in the club touching it, sapping it into itself like a sponge to water. The angel was a woman, or more precise, a girl, a waif of one to be exact. Her limbs were thin and seemed like they could be snapped in two easily. The angel wore tight-black leather pants and a halter top, also black, the white skin of her shoulders exposed to the air. The two star tattoos seemed to gleam in the wan light, as if they had a mind of their own.

All in all, the angel looked frail, thin and harmless.

But looks could be deceiving as the larger vampire was about to find out.

Adrian watched in amazement as the angel reached out and grabbed his head, placing her thumbs over his eyes. As the man tried to break the angel's arms, the girl pressed her thumbs deep into his eyes sockets, crushing his orbs to mush and then continuing until her thumbs were so deep in his skull they disappeared. She flashed perfect teeth and her eyes went wide as she squeezed the head in her hands. Like a rotten melon, the man's head seemed to give out, such as a deflated balloon would do when gently released of its air. The skull cracked and brains slid out to spill onto the floor, splashing at the man's feet.

When the angel released her grip, the head was nothing but a mangled mess of bone and brain matter. The hands holding her arms released their grip and she was dropped to the floor where she landed effortlessly, her grace that of a gymnast. The dead vampire swayed on legs that were devoid of control and the body toppled to the floor, crashing like a tree in the forest after a lightning strike.

The angel wiped her bloody hands on her halter top and then spun to face Adrian. Her porcelain skin was streaked with crimson, bloody rivulets dripping off her chin to splatter onto her boots– black of course.

Adrian was still motionless, as only seconds had passed since the large man had grabbed the angel and was killed, and Adrian quickly came to the realization that his time had run out.

As he looked around the club, past the angel, he realized he was the only one still standing.

Everyone else was dead.

In every direction there was nothing but torn and ripped body parts, a charnel house where blood was the currency. Offal and copper filled his senses and he breathed out as he gagged on the stench. Yes, blood he craved, but not like this. Vampires were a civilized race, and wanton carnage was not in their makeup, though myth would say otherwise.

He was about to take a step back, run to the bathroom and bar the door, maybe try and escape through the bathroom window, and pray the angel might not follow–leave him alive–when she crossed the dance floor in a blur that was too fast to see.

One second she was standing over the body of the dead vampire, then she was standing in front of Adrian, her head no higher than his chest. Up close, she looked like she was a teenager, a Goth one at that, with the dark hair, clothes and tattoos, but as those eyes bore into him, he knew what stood before him was not innocent, and was in fact the deadliest creature he had ever had the misfortune to come across.

Remembering the rumors about the suicide angels–for he knew that was what she was–and seeing first hand what she could do, he knew to attempt to battle the angel would be useless after witnessing her power, so Adrian tried one last ditch effort to save himself. He said, "Why? Why are you doing this to us?"

If he expected a reply, he received none, the angel mute to the point of frustration.

As Adrian looked down at her, at her wide orbs, he would have believed if he'd had a chance to think about it, that he would have seen his coming death swirling in her cold eyes. But he didn't.

Faster than his eyes could track, both of the angel's hands snapped out and grabbed his head. He had time for one quick yell of, "No!" before the suicide angel twisted and tore his head clean off his shoulders.

Dark blood shot through the jagged stump of his neck to hit the ceiling and the overhead fluorescent lighting– the ones still intact.

With his severed head in her hands, Adrian looked out through eyes that didn't believe what he were seeing. In the seconds his brain remained active, he saw his decapitated body drop to the floor and lay still, blood still spurting from the neck stump; then he was spinning as his eyes took in the destruction around him for the last time.

But the oxygen in his brain was fleeting, and as he looked out on death in its truest form, his vision began to dim, similar to the battery in a camcorder slowly fading as the power ran out. Then his vision shut down and everything went dark.

A second later, his severed head was tossed into a booth to fall between the legs of the same chalice he'd fed upon only minutes ago. The chalice was very dead, her throat torn out by razor-sharp fingernails, her blood pooling out to drip onto the floor in a steady pattern.

The angel scanned the nightclub, admiring her handiwork, her face impassive; her eyes hard and void of emotion.

Nothing moved with the exception of the shifting of the bodies as they still sputtered blood, as gravity helped them to settle into the pile of corpses now in the center of the dance floor.

A mangled body slid off a table in another booth, and the sounds of splashing– something wet landing in something wetter. Overhead, the light fixtures, the ones still intact, swayed back and forth, casting shadows where none once were as they swung back and forth. One light fixture in the far corner, hanging only by wires, finally broke free and crashed to the floor in a halo of sparks, as electricity hissed and sparked in the ceiling; the smell of ozone joining the redolence of death.

On the left corner wall, even with a picture of the Boston skyline, a security camera was mounted, its dull red light still blinking, recording the entire tableau of death.

Behind the wall the camera was mounted to was an office, and in this office was a small monitor sitting on a table to the right of a desk for the nightclub manager. The manager wouldn't be returning to the office, for his quartered body was laying on the dance floor under a dozen others.

In crystal clear, glorious black and white the monitor showed the destroyed night club, and the single figure standing in the midst of the destroyed bodies, a small VCR to the left of it.

On the monitor, the suicide angel stood covered in blood, the lack of color on the monitor taking away from the horror of what had happened this night.

The angel looked around, her eyes seeming to study each corner of the nightclub, and then she paused as she stared directly at the camera.

The suicide angel flashed into motion and was gone, only to pop up directly in front of the camera lens, her face covered in gore—but without the color of the blood, her face was still beautiful, almost heavenly.

Black hair, deep eyes that seemed to shift in intensity, the angel glared at the camera, her head tilting to the side in curiosity; until she figured out she was being filmed.

In a move too fast for the camera to record, her hand snapped out, and her blood-red palm—seeming gray on the screen thanks to the lack of color—was exposed for a brief second before she grabbed the camera and tore it from the wall.

The monitor went dark.

TRANSMOGRIFY

RICHARD THOMAS

In order to live I have to die.

I close my eyes for a second and her hot mouth is on my nipples, her hands cupping my breasts as our pale limbs writhe on the bed. A shock of air and my eyes flick open. I run my tongue over porcelain teeth, breathing in the crisp November air, and exhaling strawberry frost. Still, the remorse. When will I learn?

Numb to the bone I stand in the empty graveyard as the sun creeps over the horizon, limping home, drenched in a bloodmist that constantly frames my vision. The acid-rain will soon eat through the screeners I've put on. At this time of year AR50 may not be enough. As much as things have changed some traditions stay the same. I come back to the rituals. The burial.

In the distance leaves burn, wet and moldy. A dense cloud of dirty smoke drifts over the skeletal forest that rings the iron fence, chipped and forgotten. I am alone, as expected. The obituary was a formality but I'm a stickler for details. Long slender fingers push deep into the cashmere overcoat abyss that drapes to my knees and hugs my empty shell. The sharp wind rapes me again and again. I play a game in the flayed tresses that flit about my face. They are as black as my heart and I hide from the very surroundings I set out to embrace today.

Footsteps. I glance around, picking up the motion of a lone figure, head down, treading towards me. Dark and tall, it must be Remy. Who else would show? Who else was left? I shiver but not from the cold. I fed last night and am still full of the sustenance of her life force. She had been expecting something akin to a gothic romance but was sorely mistaken.

The evolution didn't happen all at once. It took time. Years. Lifetimes. But I have plenty of time. I have eternity.

I rub the port at the base of my skull, a nasty habit like twirling my hair. I have to see Doc Aught soon. Time for a tune-up. A little nanotech and a full viral upgrade and nobody will be the wiser.

A thousand voices whisper and my eyes shoot to the dead branches. A Starling catapults up into the fading light, fluttering its wings. Panic stricken eyes gaze my way as it drops from the sky, twitching for but a moment, then still. Rigid.

He is closer now. There is nowhere to run. Not that I could have. I miss him. When he finally looks up his eyes go wide and his brow furrows, stopping in his tracks. A heat flushes my skin and for a moment I hesitate. The longing blurs my vision as the heat flows to a million points of skin that weep beneath my clothes.

"Excuse me, miss," he says.

"You must be Remy," I say.

"Um...well, yes, but..." his eyes are on my face like a magnifying glass - inspecting, doubting.

"I'm Cinder. But you can call me Cindy," I offer.

"Oh, right. Wow. Finally we meet. It's just..."

"I know. I look just like her."

"Well, twenty years ago, right...the same blue eyes, uncanny."

"Consider it an homage. I had them dyed to the same Tiffany blue a couple of years ago. Mine had always been such a boring brown."

"Right." He turns to the grave and stares at the headstone. "Old school."

"It's mostly symbolic, you know, with the organ laws and all..."

"Yes. She's not in there. I know."

"You okay, Remy?"

"I didn't think there'd be anybody here, especially not you. I thought you were a myth, something that she talked about at night, a phantom that didn't really exist."

"Long story. Nothing you need to know about. Pedestrian."

"Right."

"I was just leaving anyway, it's getting late. Curfew."

"Yes." He stands close to me, a massive presence, more grey at the temples than I remember.

"Here, Remy, she wanted me to give you this."

I walk over to him, every bit of silk rubbing against my flesh, screaming out. I wrap my arms around him and press my head against his chest. The pounding. His hands are on my back and I find myself turning feline. I purr into his grey woolen coat and rub my face in his musky scent. Wormwood and formaldehyde burn my nostrils as I brush up against his legs. My knees are like a cricket making music as they rub together.

For a second he lets down his guard. Remorse and anguish float to the surface like a bloated corpse wrapped in black trash bags. Against my own wishes I take a sip. Just a bit of him for posterity. A quick inhale and he coughs. I lick my lips, rubbing out a bitter coat of wax that I'd pasted on earlier. Ruby Woo. The casing is new, but the inhabitant, ancient.

I push away and step back. For a moment we are knee deep in snow, the Celtic crosses and cracked stones dusted with powder, as his breath exhales in a cloud, eyes dimming to dull ashes. He staggers, barely able to raise his hands from his sides. A crack over the horizon as the sound barrier breaks. The 6:42 to Los Angeles. Always on time.

"It's okay, baby. Everything is going to be fine."

Remy falls over on his side, glancing up at me, his eyes empty.

"You won't remember this moment, for I've taken it. Forget me. Forget her. We're gone, and won't be back. It's better this way. Consider it a bullet dodged, Remy, and move on with your life. Let it go."

"Okay."

"Down the street from you, that blonde with the synthetics, the skin job on a leash she calls a dog, that one. She's a good catch for you. Don't come here again."

"Okay."

I need to go home and jack in. Now. My hunger has been awakened. He'll be okay. He'll be alive. It's the least I can do for him after all of these years. Samantha is dead now. Long live Cinder. Half of the time I'm gone anyway. It doesn't matter.

I'll always be alone.

* * *

Standing at the grocery checkout, the young girl with the blonde ponytail can't look at me enough. Her face flushes red every fifteen seconds. She scans the bizarre selections that I've grabbed in a frenzy as the ache washes over me in waves. Six blood oranges.

A 24 oz. bottle of Intrigue K-Y Jelly. 1 gallon of compressed nitrogen.

"Are you, like...I mean, do I..." she sputters.

"No."

"Oh, okay."

12 razor blades. A six-pack of Frost Gatorade. 8 cellular protein cutlets.

"Are you sure? I mean, didn't I see..."

"No, sweetheart, you didn't."

12 feet of Tripp Lite U042-036 High-Speed USB 2.0 cable. A tube of black cherry lip balm. A 6.8 oz. Red Currant Votivo candle. A 50-count bottle of Vitamin B12-H_SharkOil.

"I mean, I don't like girls or anything, that's not what I'm trying..."

"Honey, look at me."

The high school cheerleader with the punk rock fantasies pauses for a moment with a can of Vienna Sausages in her left hand, the other wandering up to her shirt collar, fiddling with the tab, running behind her neck to massage the only acceptable exposed flesh.

A flash of light and French doors fly open. An empty bed rests in the middle of the room as pale blue moonlight fills the space with stardust. A cigarette smolders in an ashtray on the nightstand as the dull patter of a shower running seeps from beneath the bathroom door. There is an indentation in the mattress. Lace trim edges the sheets, wrinkled ivory bunched in piles. It is quiet in the room but for the echo of a gasp, the exhale of air, and the sigh of completion.

"You couldn't handle it..." squinting at her name tag, "...Jennifer."

I extend my wrist to the scanner, and run the bar-code over it. BEEP. Cinder Bathory. $426,384. Transaction ok? $1,235.45. Accessing account. APPROVED.

* * *

Welcome to Facebook. Facebook helps you connect and share with the entities in your life.

I try to pry the plastic off of the new USB cable. These damn things are so hard to open. My hair is pulled back and to the side for easy access to my port. My skin is pink and splotchy from the blistering hot shower and the obsidian silk robe clings to my damp body like tape.

My hands shake and drop the package to the floor. The third one I've burnt out this month. Nothing has any depth anymore, nothing satisfies. Everything is manufactured, and that makes it farther from the truth, the core of it all, the purity. Soon the snacking will not be enough.

I pause for a second to gaze around my sparse studio apartment. I live like an eccentric millionaire, eating cans of cat food and fearing my own demise while my checking account stands at $400,000. There is nothing but Glacier water and a hexagrid of hemoglobin cubes in the fridge. The grocery bag stands on the counter, forgotten for the moment. A king-size, four-post bed covered with 1000-thread count sheets fills the room. It was hand carved by Buddhist monks four thousand years ago. A blinking 36" monitor sits next to a hybrid computer that I found in Chinatown. Resting on the beaten Salvation Army desk, it waits for me, the leather desk chair eager for my supplication. It has Intel guts, Mac OS XX_Cheetah, a terabyte of hard drive space, and enough security to route whatever happens back to the very brown coats that might be tracking me.

I should move to the desert and leave it all. I've evolved beyond my needs, and my life is more complicated for it. The itching of the nanodrones is in my head, Doc Aught says. It isn't possible for me to feel them. But I do. They crash around the inside of my veins and the siren songs, the rapture, makes me double over and crash to my knees. I tear open the plastic, slicing my index finger in the process. By the dull glow of the monitor I suck at the broken skin, as my eyes slide into whiteness. My history will be my undoing, but it is not the crimson shot I want tonight. They wait for me, a bunch of addicts, scratching at their scabs, ready to tear them open again. And I'm coming. I'm coming.

I unravel the cord and jam it into the side of the computer. Sliding into the small, leather-bound swivel chair I fumble around at the base of my skull and plug it in. My eyes flutter and a gasp escapes my lips. Fingers fly to the keyboard as I login. I have 432 friends. I have 23 new messages. I've been poked 12 times. I skip it all and head to a special private chat room. There are others like me. Others that think they are like me. But they aren't.

Tomorrow they'll be weak, fatigued, with headaches or migraines, depressed over something they can't quite figure out. Their immune systems will plummet and regardless of the hypodermics they shove into their thighs or the bots they have infiltrating their systems, my tech is better. They plug in just like I do, seeking something to fill the void.

PRIVATE CHAT - Room 2112.0101
```
Bloodrunners
[2] members present
Ashestoashes has entered the room
cureforpain: hey ash, wassup
breakingthebroken: so i didn't think that was
fair, you know?
cureforpain: nk, lb
breakingthebroken: sistersister, where have
you been?
ashestoashes: oh you know, same old stuff,
stupid job, stupid boyfriend, blech
breakingthebroken: we were just talking about
that crap
cureforpain: ask her, she'll tell you
ashestoashes: what?
breakingthebroken: oh, nothing, stupid boy i
think is working me
ashestoashes: what do you mean?
breakingthebroken: i'm just being paranoid
that's all
ashestoashes: what happened
cureforpain: come on, spill it or i will
ashestoashes: you can tell me
breakingthebroken: <sigh> i text him, and it's
always real fast and short, brb, or he won't take
my calls, and when i ask him what he's doing he
```

never tells me, i try to hook up, and can't find
him, you know, stupid shit but then...

I lean back in the chair and close my eyes. The flow is slow but
unmistakable. Fear, bits of anxiety, regret, remorse. Even Cureforpain
is letting it out. He's been trying to get Broken in the real
world for months now. Anger, frustration.

ashestoashes: let just tell you something, and
you just listen, ok?

breakingthebroken: ok

cureforpain: here it comes, preach baby :-)

ashestoashes: if he never returns your calls,
if he never has sex with you, if he blows you off
for his boys, if he's always working late, never
wants to see the movies you do, never wants to
eat the food you like, basically, he just doesn't
care about you, move on...

The rig has been filled and the air tapped out. Leaning forward
I'm blinded by a shroud of white as memories cut in and out.
Mountains and a cabin, AUF WIEDERSEHEN! gunfire and the
pounding of horses hooves thundering by. The cold stone of an
empty hallway lost deep in the bowels of some ancient castle. Snow
and the soft rub of animal fur on my naked flesh.

My fingers fly over the keyboard, lecturing the kids once again.

...if he won't let you look at his phone sadness, frustration, anger, betrayal that means there are calls on there or texts he doesn't
want you to see, numbers, and if his phone rings fury, despair,
failure, remorse, exhaustion, nausea at his apartment and the
voicemail starts to pick up and you hear a female voice, and he
purrs in your ear, hold on a sec, baby, abandonment, suicide,
desperation, failure, anger, anger, anger, stupidity, loss while he
jumps up to answer it and you hear the words nothing or nobody
or later, then he is screwing you over he is using you loneliness,
rage, fury, emptiness, anxiety...

breakingthebroken: omg i'm gonna barf
breakingthebroken has left the room
ashestoashes: too much?
cureforpain: naw, she needed to hear it
ashestoashes: so what's up with you?

The sun peeks under the edge of the velvet drapes. Exhausted, I breathe in and out, my skin heating up, tightening. I've turned back the clock three years tonight. I'm five pounds lighter. Sweat glistens on my exposed throat, and I lean back in the chair as my hand slides down the front of my robe. My eyes close as I embrace this mortal coil.

*　*　*

There are predators and there are prey. Donors and recipients.

I have to move around a lot. I have a Xenon AmTran card. I have five million frequent flier miles. Conway, Arkansas. Rolla, Missouri. Peoria, Illinois. Off the beaten path. The security is too dangerous in the metropolitan factions. You can only nibble on the second shift of the Dell computer parts factory for so long. The Caterpillar assembly line. The AT&T Global telemarketing center. They start to get sick. People stop showing up, and glances dart my way. They think it's sex. When the whispers at the vending machines start, it's time for me to disappear into the night.

The places where emotions are raw and on the surface, that's where I linger. But in time I find that no matter how depressing the job, how dismal the future, how anxious my friends become, it has its limits. People leave, people get a bad vibe about you, and they stop opening up. The funeral homes call the police. The hospitals ask for ID. The AA meetings start questioning your steps. Their hackles go up, and their senses heighten. Online it's easier to sip. And the body of water that I surf with reckless abandon is much larger and better stocked.

I'm tired of writing pablum for the broken-hearted, wrist-slashing nation. I need to reinvent myself. I need a new home.

Doc Aught is coming tonight. A house call. Like he does every hundred years or so. Something has to go in the casket where Samantha should be. They may harvest every organ for the good of the people, every bloodshot eyeball and broken digit. But there is always something left. You'd be surprised how many useless parts we have. The vomeronasal organ, a tiny pit on each side of the septum. A set of cervical ribs left over from our reptilian days. The male uterus. A fifth toe. It isn't pretty.

I need to get ready, prepare myself for the transition.

* * *

Silence has expanded to fill my tiny apartment. A section of candlelight throbs from the window ledge. A pair of forlorn window frames blast the studio with a foul chill. I am rotting from the inside out and have waited much too long. The door hangs open wide, a forlorn shriek that swallows the light. I will not be disturbed for this space does not exist. Not tonight.

My pasty skin is a moonglow in the center of a collapsing star. Eyes closed, my face is buried in the lavender scent of the downy pillows. A thin sheen of icy sweat coats my body as my soul fights to escape. Any other night and my head would be filled with visions of fingertips and razor blades, bloodletting and rope burns, tongues shoved into every eager crevice. There is no room for that tonight. Shoulders twitch, my hands grasping and releasing the bedsheets, and I repeat one word over and over again.

Transmogrify.

I have lost myself again. Torches burn at the river's edge. There is the sharp snapping of canine teeth and the grumbling of angry peasants.

"No...no."

Convulsions and my neck snaps back, eyes rolling up into my skull, my tongue darting for moisture in every corner of my mouth.

Forward, back. Forward, back. Flying sideways, a hard turn to the right, pulled around a corner, and gravity pulls my stomach down, pressure on my face, a great rush of wind.

He's here.

I don't need to see him to picture him clearly. So many times we've done this. My keeper. So many times we've hunted together. My lover. His hand is on my bare back, the size of a stingray. His weight crushes the bed and it cries out in resistance. Not a sound from him, not a word. I can't remember the last thing he said to me. Yes. Yes, I can.

"Go."

A tingle races over the surface of my skin as he runs his massive paw up the small of my back, stopping just short of my port. A sigh escapes my lips as a solitary bloody tear glides down my cheek.

I picture him the way I last saw him, in a back alley of New York City, 1908. A bowler hat atop his bald, gleaming dome. The dark wool suit stretched taut across his broad shoulders, his legs like tree stumps ending in squared-off shoes. His prominent nose crowding out small, gleaming eyes, a fire burning inside, his full lips tight. The clink of a beer glass dropped on cobblestone, and his patience had run out. Just like that.

He leans over me and presses his body against mine, his cold musculature like a marble sculpture. I am slowly being suffocated by a distant god and I don't care. A harp string vibrates and the clasp of a briefcase opens. Plastic unwraps and latex gloves snap on. The slow turning of a lid being removed fills my ears as a hint of birch mixed with sassafras drifts to me.

I am waiting for the cord, the cable, the life. He is not.

One hand is firm at the base of my neck and a device is shoved in the port. A leap drive. I struggle but cannot move. He holds me down with one giant palm as the toxic potion fills my nostrils, burning, and the drive comes to life with a hum.

"There are creatures far worse than you, my love," his baritone rumbles.

I am emptying, spilling, falling from a great height as my eyes gush a river. A soul I thought to be long gone, diseased and broken, breaks. Not a single utterance, only the spinning and whirring of the pod at my neck. Outside my window in the suicide of winter there is a void of life. A crackling of ice as a solitary branch fractures under the weight and shatters on the ground.

THE RED STRETCH

SPENCER WENDLETON

1

The white flag was pointed up at the purple starlit sky, the holder wearing the remains of a tattered coffin dress. The strips waved in the desert breeze, uncovering the withered skin frame beneath the garb. Beside the standing corpse was a female vampire in black latex pants and a loose fitting midriff. In tandem, vampire and zombie raised their flags, indicating to the driver's to rev their engines; the race was about to begin.

2

Two hearses were parked side-by-side on Highway 16, their exhausts belching blue fumes, the engines firing up to decimate the competition. Once the two flags came down, the race transpired in mere lightning fast seconds. After staying neck-to-neck for a quarter of a mile, one car overturned for no apparent reason, the driver losing control. Climaxing at speeds over ninety-miles an hour, the wild hearse crashed into the other, the pin-ball refraction like two boxers taking a punch at the same time. Forced in two different directions, each hearse shed sparks dragging against the road, both vehicles thrown forward and flipping over; hurled so fast that the cars seemed weightless as they bore down to earth again and again. The vehicles eventually stopped rolling after losing momentum, and once the desert silence hit the air and the wreckage settled, one man in the crowd decided to take it upon himself to determine the true winner of the race.

3

Sifting through the mess of steel components now strewn about the highway, spread out for over a quarter mile, Daniel Carpenter never imagined a dispute between the bloodsuckers and the walking dead being settled this way. The competition happened far north in the Red Desert—what many on both sides of the skirmish called The Red Stretch. Being a blood drinker, The Red Stretch was notorious to vampires for stalled cars and flat tires, and ultimately, easy necks to bleed. For the living dead, the stranded drivers and their families were easy feasts of flesh. The sand also provided great hiding places for the corpses, burying themselves a foot deep to come up and attack unsuspecting travelers.

Either side could choose somewhere else for their stomping ground, but in the city and the more populated areas, police could easily squelch their fun; despite popular belief, vampires could die from bullet wounds to the heart, just as zombies could perish by a bullet through the cranium.

Another reason to fight for the highway out in nowhere land was that the blood in humans' veins took on a new form out in the stretch. Fear pulsed stronger in their hearts and bodies, as they were so vulnerable and helpless on the highway; the blood became a fine vintage in result, their hearts pumping so potent an elixir it was worth dying over to preserve. Daniel believed this taste was enhanced for zombies, too, the elevated terror equating to better tasting meats.

This is what ultimately created the popular demand for The Red Stretch, and it left little for both sides in the means of compromise. The corpse bastards had good reason to stay, and so did they. That meant there was only one way to settle the turf dispute, though the hearse race wasn't created until later on when many trespasses were committed by the undead against the creatures of the night.

4

The living dead made their first move to banish the vampires from The Red Stretch a month ago. The strike occurred at Daniel's mansion, secluded from the city, the structure Victorian in architecture and fashion inside and out, but the basement was the main attraction. Daniel had built a reservoir of blood the size of a public pool ten feet deep and surrounded by high dives and a deck for vampires to let the blood dry on their bodies; where lovers and friends invited each other to lick their bodies clean.

The floors outside the reservoir had drains installed in them, the walls tiled and easy to spray clean, especially after the wilder orgy parties. A wet bar and disco floor was stationed opposite the stock tank, mimicking an upper class version of a rave.

The blood pool had attracted three dozen vampires that specific night, dressed down to nothing, making it easier to wade in crimson and sip on cosmopolitans or throw back fingers of spirits. The only problem: the taste of the blood had turned sour. The blood's flavor was smoky and harbored the funk of moldy cheese. And the pool was off-colored by a rainbow swirl of greens and blacks, creating a muddy rainbow. Then the first scream rattled in the crowd, the vampire spilling out of the pool terrified, fleeing in repulsion. The others soon followed until everyone was clamoring to escape the red pit.

Then one-by-one, blackened domes broke the surface of the pool, the domes soon turning into bodies which floated up as corpse buoys. Blood oozed out of their orifices like submerged vehicles dredged from a river bottom. The shock of their unveiling kept the vampires at bay as the eight zombies crawled from the pool and left the party, unapologetic in tainting their supply of blood—what had taken five years to maintain and cultivate.

The blood pool had to be drained the next day, and Daniel remembered the horrible moment when each vampire in the city's limits watched the pool empty in mourning. To this day, he hadn't put another drop in that tank. The orgy parties were finished thanks to the living compost heaps, and soon, other vampire activities would cease to be celebrated until the dispute over The Red Stretch was settled.

5

Daniel kept walking forward in a determined pace. It was an hour from sunrise; barely enough time to select the winner before the sun became a threat—not that the living dead cared. Patrons on both sides of The Red Stretch were growing antsy waiting for the verdict. Would it be vampires or zombies leaving the city tonight? Who would claim The Red Stretch as their own?

He kept a careful eye on the thirty magpie bodies standing to the left of him; their hollow eyes were watching Daniel, their faces stone and blank of emotion. The vampires were a bigger crowd, forty plus strong. They wore their black shrouds and fine suits, dressed for a funeral, though some carried shotguns and handguns just in case the zombies did lose and decided not to own up to their end of the bargain.

Daniel was now yards out from the first hearse upturned on the driver's side, the second hearse ten more feet up the road completely upside down. He drew closer to the initial vehicle, taking an alleviating breath, and prepared himself to officiate the final outcome.

6

After hearing Trina's screams, Daniel snaked up the gutter pipe on the three-story house located in the Carter Heights upper class suburb. Trina was his girlfriend of ten years, a woman with the best blood hook-ups; she knew how to locate the richest, cleanest blood in the city. This was her old neighborhood before he had turned her. This was a comfortable avenue for fresh blood, but for the first time on the hunt, Trina sounded like the victim the way her screams tore into the night. He too was attacked by the same level of fear upon hearing what she expressed and hurried to reach her.

He dove through the open window to find Trina with her back up against a closet door, on her knees, clutching her forearm. A sizeable bite an inch deep bled fervently, her eyes bulbous and staring at the pulsing wound in pure horror.

Then Daniel's eyes shot to the bed, noting that the two home-owners' chests had been carved out, their hearts missing. On the walls spelled out in big finger paint thick words—the words drawn with the hearts themselves—were: ***THE RED STRETCH IS OURS***.

The dead had been following them on their hunts, or they'd been spying on them, and they knew Daniel would strike at this house next. Terrified for Trina and overwhelmed by the dead's tactics, he lowered to her side, cradling her. Her red hair was mussed up with sweat, her pale skin busy with bullets of perspiration.

But vampires didn't sweat. And it wasn't sweat.

Her skin was melting.

The forearm wound was expanding, the flesh sizzling and deteriorating like an Alka-Seltzer dropped in water. Daniel was bent over in shock as the arm in his grasp melted, the skin and bones threading through his fingers and dripping onto the carpet in knotted gobs. By the time her arm snapped from her torso, her neck and half of her face was kicking up smoke, and her features turned into liquid, the pink and white splattering down her chest and oozing onto her black, crinoline dress, until the dress itself was buried in liquid Trina. Her bones collapsed, splashing raucously in the mess that was once his lover.

Vampires called it the 'gangrene death.' A zombie bite had adverse effects on vampires, their saliva baring enzymes and poisons to turn a vampire's body into fluids. That was another reason why the vampires tried to avoid a war with the zombies; their bites and saliva were so deadly.

Weeping and struggling to leave the mansion, he had no choice but to flea the scene minus his lover. Before he jumped out the window, a group of zombies crept out of the closet to devour Trina's soup, five on their knees, lapping the pink into their skeletal faces.

Outraged and outnumbered, Daniel fled home to safety.

7

The hearse's windows were shattered, the front windshield cracked to the point he couldn't see through it. The groups of vampires and zombies came in closer to view Eddie, the vampire's driver. Eddie wore black leather gloves with circular holes cut above the knuckles. He used to be an amateur racecar driver before he was turned by a flock of female groupies after a particularly impressive race, him being winner of the '13th Annual Lark's Beer Amateur 200.' He'd shaved his head to the skin, returning to his human roots. He was unconscious, and without a seatbelt, he was slumped on his side, unmoving.

Daniel shook the man's body, and he wasn't roused. "Eddie, you with us?"

He had a bad feeling about the outcome, though he hadn't seen the zombies' driver yet.

Other vampires and zombie disputes were solved differently. Rivals would meet at a secluded locale and fight each other until few on each side were left to survive their brethren. Others played

Russian roulette. Another staged event happened in New Jersey. A quarter of the city was turned into vampires and zombies, each side building up their numbers until the FBI became involved, namely the MESS Squad (Monster Execution Soldier Squad). MESS slaughtered them all, and nobody rose up victorious in the aftermath. And that was why the zombies were keeping the determination simple.

Eddie, the vampire's driver, had known a zombie in the group before the man had died and returned to life; his name was Carter Hill, and Carter had been a fellow amateur racecar driver. They were both good friends at one time, and it was Carter who had actually given Eddie the declaration of war on a piece of simple paper.

One race. Two people. No staggering deaths. No chance for MESS to execute either side. The vampires couldn't accept this as the truth initially, regardless of the two friends and their history. This was a zombie trap, and they wouldn't fall into it. They refused the offer the first go around, though the offers would keep coming later on in the wake of even more horrible retaliations.

Worried his friend didn't make it, Daniel drew himself from his straying thoughts and stared at Eddie for another minute, and then lost it, shouting, "Eddie, come on, wake up!" He checked his body for wounds, and Eddie came up clean. "What happened, man? They did something to you; those fucking maggot feasts cheated."

Daniel dragged him out by the arms and laid him against the hood of the hearse, unsure of what to do; there was no proof of foul play, though Eddie appeared dead for no obvious reason.

Once the vampires saw Eddie's motionless body, the hopes on their faces were dashed. Many looked onward, imagining themselves flocking out of town to an unknown destination. They would lose The Red Stretch.

The zombies showed no signs of acknowledging Eddie's condition. They kept staring at Daniel, patiently awaiting the real indication that they were the winners.

8

The coffin was a place that offered creature comforts for a vampire if he invested the time. Daniel had rigged his coffin with many lavish amenities. For one, he installed a television in front of the face compartment. Then there was a slot where a long plastic straw could extend, and he could lap up from a blood bag at his leisure for a midnight snack. He also had an internet connection; if he couldn't sleep while the sun was out, he could check his stocks in gold and the interest rates of his off-shore accounts—or gothic porn.

There was a webpage he loved called 'Blood-Spattered Gothic Bitches' where women dressed in corsets and BDSM gear and latex suits; the site featured women who'd either bathed in blood or had it drooling from their lips or crawling down their well-lit bosoms. After Trina's death, the porn was a strange coping mechanism, since she enjoyed fashioning herself after the internet gothic cuties. It was pure nostalgia for him that night, and he celebrated in it.

In that comfortable coffin, everything was as it should be. He planned to sip on blood and stare at female flesh until his alarm clock went off, indicating the sun had gone down. When that alarm finally did go off, he tried to push up on the coffin lid, and it wouldn't budge. He shoved and shoved, though in the coffin, there was little leverage.

Crying out, pissed and scared, the image of the woman on the screen who was spread eagle on a tiger skin rug whose stripes had been dyed pink and white, mocked him in his moment, reminding him of Trina and how she had suffered the gangrene death.

The tacking of hammers came next, elevating his terror.

They were nailing him into his coffin!

There was only one thing to do, he decided. He texted as many of his vampire friends as possible. The hammering continued, and he imagined the various outcomes after the final nail was driven. They could burn him alive; just pour gasoline over the wood and light him up. Or the zombies could transfer his coffin to some-where in broad daylight and open it up and watch his ashes play out across the sky. They could bury him so deep in the dirt, far beyond six feet under, and trap him forever in the earth until he fossilized. That's what it took for a vampire to die if they were to starve to death. Until they were bones, there was sensation in some form, and that style of death would be agony as it would be pitch black.

The hammering had stopped, bringing him out of his toiling thoughts. It was an hour before his friends came to save him; Frankie, his good friend, used a chainsaw to shave off sections at a time, careful not to hurt him. His special coffin was in ruins by the time he was free. Stepping out, he read what had been nailed to the wall, the same declaration to settle The Red Stretch.

They should've settled it then, Daniel believed, but the vampires voted and couldn't gain a majority. They were too afraid to do battle with something that could so easily kill them all. With hindsight, he knew the idea of two hearses racing down a highway was too unbelievable to put stock in, another hindrance against meeting the zombies' demands. But their indecision ended up costing the vampires more suffering.

One more incident occurred before they were forced to reckon with the dead on their unique terms.

9

The second hearse was tipped over on its top, one back door open, the back cab crushed like a flattened tin can. He slowly approached, crunching over triangles of glass wet with green-black blood. There was a set of severed digits scattered about the road, but the remains didn't mean anything; it took more than losing a few fingers for a zombie to be put out of commission.

Eddie was still slumped on the ground behind Daniel, unmoving. A few of his friends surrounded him, their heads cast down in deep concern.

What happened to you, Eddie. Why are you dead? he wondered.

Daniel imagined leaning into the window and a zombie face snaking out and biting into his arm. He'd dissolve just like Trina did.

Watch yourself. This shit isn't over yet.

Daniel braced himself, leaning down to peer into the hearse. The blackened shadows kept the driver hidden under the veil of night, and he had to lean in much closer than he wanted to in order to see inside.

10

The final straw leading up to the hearse race occurred six days ago at The Clinic. The Clinic was an abandoned mental hospital on the edge of town; four stories of padded cells and empty hallways and tiled floors. This is where volunteers, namely humans, offered their veins to the vampires. This situation was created by a human organization to curb human death by giving the vampires what they wanted.

The halls were turned into rough cubicles where hundreds of volunteers came and went during the night hours to serve up their arms for butterfly needle insertion. Blood bags were chilled in foam coolers, hundreds of gallons produced in one night. Richer volunteers dropped off blood in coolers, delivering the red from those too afraid to be in the company of the monsters but still wanting to contribute to the cause.

But that night the donors donated to a different cause. Daniel arrived late that night, and the attack was already over. The cubicles were slathered in blood. Guts and entrails decorated the tiles where mad men once took their meds and screamed at things that didn't exist. So many ripped off arms were left as vestiges with butterfly needles inserted into them, leaking the precious blood onto the floor. Volunteers were chewed up and devoured, their brains smashed and smeared to gray slop on every tile section. The vampires couldn't do a thing to save them, knowing if they came into too close contact, they could get bit and melt to death.

They'd lost over half of their volunteers that night by the undead cannibals, volunteers who wouldn't offer up their crimson ever again in fear of the undead party crashers. Now the vampires had no choice but to take the dead up on their offer to race next week on The Red Stretch.

11

Lying upside down, the zombie driver's face looked like a gargoyle, when the tomato-red eyes suddenly opened, and it drew a Magnum. The shots sounded like two boards crashing together, and Daniel's chest exploded. Thrown back, scraping his palms against the road and landing on his back, he was gushing blood down his middle. His sternum was riddled with hot shrapnel, though his heart was untouched.

Cursing himself for not being extra careful, and damning himself for ever trusting a zombie to own up to their end of the bargain, and for also accepting such a ridiculous idea as drag racing, he dug out the Messingham tucked in his side holster beneath his suit and unloaded the clip into the zombie's face, watching the pottery explosion until the gunner was headless.

Vampires seeing this, unleashed their sawed-offs and Rangefinders and semi-automatic weapons, firing them at the undead who crowded together, shielding themselves. But they weren't shielding themselves. They were drawing guns, too, digging their bony fingers up into their midsections and producing the firearms. And now the battlefield was lit up from both ends, hundreds of rounds shed in thirty seconds.

Daniel had taken another bullet to the ribs, though the wound was only a black hole in his clothing, judging by his quick analysis. His ear was clipped by a rogue shot. A sharp whiz and then a breaking of cartilage, and all he could hear were angry hornets in his eardrum cavity.

Diving down behind the wrecked hearse, he took careful aim to blast through a female puss-mannequin, the bullet popping both of her eyes as it sailed through her head and out the other side, the exit wound erupting and spitting out a gush of cranial diarrhea. He kept spreading death from his barrel, re-loading twice, before he glanced up at the night sky and noticed the silver moon shining in the sky.

12

Without warning, the lantern-yellow eyes of the werewolves closed in from all directions. Their hairy gray backs pulsed and bent with impossible muscular formations, honing in on their easy prey. Vampires were thrown up in the air and easily snapped in half, their pelvises broken off from torsos, the torsos separated from the necks with a wicked crunch, all of it raining down onto the road to be devoured by sloppy-faced snouts. Talons scraped the pavement as the seven foot tall wolves bared down upon the rest of them, tearing the zombies into pieces with the ease of peeling an orange. Under hammer fists, zombie heads were squashed, oozing and spitting their insides out onto the same pavement they had originally fought over.

Helpless to the wolves, the vampires were also outflanked by the rising sun. Daniel's skin was puckering and parting, the blood beneath boiling as his core was heating up. His white flesh was already tinged black, and any moment, he knew he would burst into ashes. The wolves just watched, looking on at all the vampires who'd survived the battle only to be cooked by the sun.

13

Daniel crawled to the shade of the tipped over hearse, buying him precious minutes before the sun would do its final damage. He heard them talk as the wolves morphed back into humans, the fur sneaking back into the skin and smoothing out once the sun blocked the moon. Naked men and women came together to size up the wrecked hearses. One woman picked up a white flag and waved it in the air, chuckling to herself. She talked to a man who stared at Daniel, his wolfish yellow eyes the last thing to fade back to normal, now a hazel brown. "Turf wars, huh?"

The man stole the flag from her hand, his turn to wave it. "Idiots always double cross each other, anyway. And drag racing hearses?" He scoffed, casting his eyes once again to the wrecked hearses. "Oh, well, more meat for us in the end."

He eyed Daniel sharply, giving him a snide smile. "I laced the driver's seat of the hearse with liquid garlic. It took time for it to soak into your driver's skin, but once he sat down long enough, it did the trick. It hits him all at once, the liquid garlic. No wounds. No warnings. His insides were melting when that hearse spun out. That's why he was the first to wreck." The dull pop of a paper bag mixed with a cap gun's crack, as another vampire body went up in a swirl of fire and black dust. "Whoa, up goes another suck-head!"

Completing the cycle of sun-death, Daniel went up next, his soul, his body, his existence, downgraded into an equivalent of a flicked off ash from a giant cigarette. Before his ashes were cast upon the red sands, the burning red embers quickly snuffed out into gray particles, he overheard the woman report to the male, "Maybe instead of hearse racing, they should try bumper cars."

SONG FOR SHADOWS

EDWARD J. RATHKE

It drifts through the ceiling and watches her chest rise and fall through the blanket. The woman sleeps, her sunshine hair draped over the pillow, a tangled sea.

The room dreams, bathed in moonlight fighting shadows. Books and papers and clothes maze the floor. Posters and records checker the walls and jasmine incense fills the cracks.

Her face is a new shore, free of the toll of time's tide. Lips, slightly parted, dune and valley, and her forehead is glass. Life does not yet haunt or wilt her. A youthful freedom that glitters through the blackness.

It floats above, hungry. Descending, it rests upon her stomach and feels the warmth rise like the sea at midnight, the blood dancing just beyond the thin layers. It reaches inside.

The line was too long and the rain was cold, but I needed to get in there until the crows came and eclipsed the sun like great clouds of smoke that birthed nations full of fast food babies sucking on wrenches with the smell of burning tires just down the road from the crematorium where the rotted get disposed in a flame so pure it reaches past Babel to the seat of God whose beard is the ocean and the whiskers are lost among the shipwrecked soldiers who take aim for the nearest shore while they fight pirates and sharks and the brutal sunshine that flakes off their skin in chips of white translucence that falls like snow through the earth where it melts and collects and builds a stream to carry away.

Pulling back, it phantoms to her head where it rests. She shines brightest there and it tastes the heat emanating. Spread on her forehead, it dips once more.

Eight years old and my cousin Molly brings me to her friend Drew's house who's ten and looks like the scarecrow without his front teeth and possibly without his brain, but I never asked and he wasn't the type to bore you with talk because he was a man of action, climbing trees, diving in water, and dancing in the rain, and he'd never tell you that you looked pretty or had a good smile, but he'd hold your hand and that day with Molly was the first time I kissed a boy and I still remember how soft his lips were and how awkwardly liberating it was to kiss him even though we were only kids and it shouldn't have mattered, but it did to me and that's about all there is in the world, but I'm fifteen now and Drew's back, but I call him Andrew and it's been years since we hung out because we kind of lost track of one another somewhere in school because that's just how school was, but we're there in his car and he tells me that he still thinks about me so I ask him why he was never around or called me or whatever and he says that he doesn't like to chase people so I tell him that I wasn't running anywhere besides to him, and he laughs that stupid chuckle with his big grin that wasn't perfect, but it was about as good as...

She stirs and it vanishes in shrouded fragments of dust. Lines tilled in her forehead, she rolls over, her knees tucked and her body curled.

It crawls up the side of her bed and flattens against her back. Each breath is an ocean of noise, particles and atoms racing and colliding and combining. Her ribs and spine tickle it and it sneezes, a flicker of light sparking into her back. She flinches and it is gone.

She rubs her eyes and looks at the clock and touches her back. The kitchen is full of shadowed monsters and she vanquishes them with a flip of the switch. She squints and walks slow to the tap, and fills a glass with water.

She urinates and her eyes adjust and the porcelain is cold. Her room is darker and she crawls into bed and finishes her water and places the empty glass on the bedside table.

It pokes through the wall and slips to the table where it inspects the glass, which is cold and it recoils from the shock of lifeless molecules. Curled up and holding a pillow, her breathing evens, and it returns, crawling under the blanket and grazing the imperceptible hairs of her back. The cells vibrate and it grabs on, follow-

ing their trail from synapse to synapse across the internal landscape.

*Every breath is a year and the calendars are all burning up
and taking the past and future where they will meet and shake
hands and bid one another a farewell like brothers separated by
space, but whose hearts beat together, but opposite in tempo and
rhythm like all those times his hands fell apart on the skin
stretched tight over the bongos so they'd make the right sound
when you hit them just so, but his bones were all wrong for it, too
hard and too sharp, because they were raptors stretching from
his clubbed palms and he laid down in a bunker underground,
afraid it'd happen to his children, so the real world drove on past
to where the church bells rang brighter and holier and the water
didn't taste like the eyes of a child rolling over your teeth and
running down your throat to enter the ballroom with all the other
dancing organs with...*

Pulling back, it wrapped round her and set before her face. The
rapid dream dance of the eyeball in motion beckoned. It felt the
dizzying steps, the kaleidoscopic swirl, and it grabbed each cell and
cut them into molecules, which it reduced to floating atoms. It
swarmed into her, finding each crack between protons and elec-
trons, following each synapse, and disintegrating everything it
touched. The atoms cyclone and fly past like notes in a song, a
symphony it conducts inside her of cindered synapses and soaring
particles. Reaching deep, to her core, through every memory and
splintered nighttime hallucination, it tears into every aspect of her
being, crumbling bridges and cutting wires and burning every
spire. A typhoon rages inside, gutting every cell and swallowing the
hydrogen and carbon and oxygen. The notes all collide and the
crescendo supernovas from her heart to every dilated capillary,
rupturing and erupting.

It floats back and watches her soul splash from her lips and lin-
gers like smoke above her head. The heat drains from her body,
and it is satiated. She fills the room like fog and it flutters through
the ceiling and into the night.

HOLY WATER SMACKDOWN

DAVID H. DONAGHE

We were in *Mexico's*, the best Mexican restaurant in San-Bernardino. I sat across from Roxy, staring at her chest. The woman had perfectly formed breasts. My name is Mike Monroe. I own Monroe's Paranormal Investigations. If it's too weird or strange for the military, they call me.

Roxy and I have worked together for years. Her real name is Roxanne Delaney, but I call her Roxy.

She sat there across from me, rattling on about something, but I only half listened. My eyes took in her pretty face, her high cheekbones and her long blonde hair. She had a slim waist that tapered down to a pair of round hips and muscular tanned legs. Her only fault is her temper. Hot dames have a short fuse. My cell phone rang.

"Don't answer that. You promised me a night on the town," she said.

"I got to take it. It could be a case," I said and then answered the phone. "Monroe's Investigations."

"Mr. Monroe, this is Detective Daniels in Barstow. I have a situation and I was told you might be able to help."

"What exactly do you have?" I asked.

"I am at the scene of a homicide. The body has two puncture wounds on the neck and all of the blood has been drained."

"We're on our way."

"The crime scene is in the parking lot of Paradise Lanes, a local bowling alley."

"We'll find it," I said and then cut the connection.

"What?" Roxy asked.

"We've got a vamp working the high desert. Finish your meal, babe." I motioned to the waiter for the check.

"Great," she said, tossing back her golden locks. I waited while she finished eating. The waiter brought my check and I handed him my credit card. They wouldn't take my card and Roxy had to pay. Boy was she pissed. She stormed out to the car and I followed, admiring her ass.

"Take a picture, pervert!"

A shit-eating grin crossed my face. "I would but I don't have a camera. Let's stop at my place for the gear," I said, opening the passenger door.

"Whatever," she said.

She climbed into the passenger side and slammed the door. I climbed behind the wheel of my black 1984 5.0 Mustang. Firing up the engine, I backed out of the parking lot, turned left on Highland Avenue, and mashed my foot down on the accelerator. We took the 215 freeway north. I pulled off the freeway at Devore, a rural community where most of the people owned horses, and headed down the frontage road to the KOA campground. I am a perpetual camper. Sliding to a stop, I parked next to my RV, jumped out of the car, and ran to my motor home.

Inside my RV, Roxy went into my bedroom to change. She left the door open. When she stripped out of her clothes, I looked up in time to see her standing there in nothing but a pair of blue panties. My heart stopped and my bottom jaw sagged.

"You're such a pervert," she said, cupping her large breast with her hands.

That woman drives me crazy, I thought as she slammed the door.

She came out wearing a pair of cargo pants, a black sweater and a pair of combat boots. Outside, I threw the gear bag into the trunk of the Mustang and we rolled out. Hitting the freeway, we headed north toward the Cajon Pass. After topping out the pass, we rolled through the city of Victorville at over one hundred miles an hour. Thirty-five miles north of Victorville, we pulled into Barstow, the main pit stop on the way to Las Vegas, Nevada.

Taking the L Street exit, I cruised east passing a Chevron station, a Holiday Inn, and a few businesses. The police had the entrance to Paradise Lanes blocked off with crime scene tape. I showed them my ID and they let us through. After parking the Mustang, we jumped out and headed over to where the police were still with the body.

"Which one of you is Daniels?" I asked.

An older man with gray hair looked up. "That's me. You Monroe?"

"Yeah, I'm Mike Monroe. This is my partner, Roxanne Delaney." We squatted down to look at the body.

"You do know what we have here, don't you?" I said to Daniels.

"Yeah. Some nut job that thinks he's a vampire."

"Maybe." I noticed a syringe lying next to the body. The victim had a medical alert bracelet on her wrist. "What's this poor woman's name?" I asked.

"Campbell. Mrs. Catherine Campbell," Daniels said.

"It appears that Mrs. Campbell was a diabetic," I said.

"What of it?"

"Have you had any break-ins where medical supplies were stolen?"

The other detective, a younger man with short blond hair, looked up and said, "We did have that burglary at Croals on William Street last night."

"What did they take?" I asked.

"A lot of syringes and a shit load of insulin."

"What're you thinking? That this murder and that break-in are connected?" Daniels asked.

"Maybe."

"Don't tell me you believe this vampire shit? This is just some shitbird that thinks he's a vampire."

"Maybe, or it could be a sick fucking vampire."

"You don't really believe that do you?"

"You called me, remember?"

Daniels let out a sigh and then lit a cigarette. "We've got the perp on tape. He's a scary son-of-a-bitch," Daniels said and then looked at his partner. "Parker. We're done here. Have the medical people bag her and tag her. Take her to the morgue. I'm going to show Monroe the tape."

"We'll know for sure in twenty-four hours. If Mrs. Campbell doesn't join the ranks of the undead, then you're right. We have a sick, wanna-be-vampire. If not, then we have a whole different ballgame. We'll be ready in either case," I said. Daniels let out another sigh. "Vampires. What next?"

"If Mr. Personality only knew," Roxy said under her breath.

"Don't get your panties in a bunch. He's just doing his job."

"Yeah, but if he only knew what we've seen."

"That's the point. He doesn't know." My mind flashed back to that time in Haiti in the Tombs of the Undead. I've been afraid of tunnels ever since.

Daniels led us into the manager's office.

"Show him the tape," Daniels said to a stocky young man sitting behind a wooden desk. "After that, we'll need the tape as evidence."

"It's your show," I shrugged.

He handed Daniels the security tape and Daniels popped it into a VCR underneath a TV monitor across the room. The image of the parking lot filled the screen. The tape showed a few cars leaving the lot and then Mrs. Campbell walking to her Beamer. A black pickup truck that looked like the only thing holding it together was rust and bailing wire pulled up behind her.

"What's that? A forty-eight or forty-nine Ford?" I asked.

"It looks like a forty-eight. My granddaddy had one like that, only his was in better shape," Roxy said.

A figure stepped out of the truck and my blood turned to ice. He looked like a walking corpse. His skin was pasty white; bits and pieces of flesh had pealed away from his face revealing bloody legions of exposed bone. He wore bib overalls and a wife beater t-shirt. Puss oozed from the open sores covering his face and arms. I saw maggots moving about underneath his skin.

"That dude looks more dead that '*un*', if you know what I mean," I said.

The tall apparition pulled a maggot from the side of his face, tossed it into his mouth and then attacked the woman. Mrs. Campbell must have heard something because she turned at the last minute and threw up her hands. The vamp threw her up against the car, slammed a fist into her face and then lowered his gaping maw to her throat. Mrs. Campbell struggled, slamming her fist against the creature's chest. Her struggles lessened, her feet kicked and then she went limp. The vampire continued to suck.

"Talk about a hicky," I said and Roxy elbowed me to the ribs.

"Have a little respect for the deceased," Daniels said, giving me a dirty look. The vamp threw the woman to the ground, rummaged through her car, took her purse, and then climbed back into his pickup and drove away.

"What do you think?" Daniels asked.

"If we don't catch this guy, this town is in for a world of shit."

"Tell me about it," Daniels replied.

"You won't find this guy in town. He'll be hiding in the outlying areas. Maybe in an abandoned house somewhere. He comes into town to feed."

"That's great. It's a big desert out there. There must be a thousand places he could hide. When you consider the surrounding communities of Hinkley, Daggett and Yermo, there must be hundreds of abandoned houses or trailers."

"My partner and I will start looking in the morning," I said, gesturing to Roxy. "Tomorrow I want to talk to the people at the drug store. Maybe they caught this guy on tape there also."

"You still think that's connected?"

"Maybe. Call it a hunch."

"Do you guys have a good hotel in town? I'm beat," Roxy said and then yawned. Daniels smiled. "I'd go with the Holiday Inn on West Main."

"Are we through here?" I asked Daniels.

"For tonight. Let me give you a police radio." He handed me his business card. "That's got my number at headquarters and my cell phone number."

On the way to the parking lot, Daniels handed me his police radio and showed me which channel to use. I thanked him and Roxy and I climbed into the Mustang and headed east on Main Street. While I drove, I looked at Roxy and rolled my eyes.

"Don't get any ideas, pervert. When we get to the hotel, I intend to get some sleep."

"That's just my luck," I said and laughed.

At the Holiday Inn, we piled out of the Mustang and headed to the hotel lobby. Roxy strutted along in front of me; her boot heals clicking against the blacktop. My eyes dropped to her shapely ass. The sight reminded me of two alley cats fighting in a gunnysack.

I'd like to bite onto one of those honey buns and pray for lockjaw, I thought, following along behind her. I heard the squeal of steel wheels and the sound of railroad cars slamming together. The BNSF rail yard lay north of the hotel.

I hope these rooms are sound proof, I thought.

In the hotel lobby, Roxy strutted up to the counter. "We need a couple of rooms for the night," she said.

"We only have one room available. They're having an off-road race south of town. Everything's booked up," a small Asian woman standing behind the counter said.

"I don't suppose it has two beds?" she asked.

"No, just one queen size," the woman said.

"We could try somewhere else," I suggested.

"No, I'm bushed. You just keep your hands to yourself," Roxy said and then sighed.

"You know me, the original Boy Scout. I'll sleep on the floor if you want."

"No. You need your rest, too," she said, but this time in a much softer tone. She handed me my room key and then headed up to the room and I went back to the car for our gear. After retrieving our gear, I rode the elevator up to the room and let myself in. I heard the shower running. Stripping out of my clothes, I put on a pair of black sweat pants. Roxy came out of the shower wearing a dark blue nightshirt. Her wet hair hung down her back and she smelled of soap. The fabric of her nightshirt clung to her bosom, clearly outlining her hard nipples. God she was a sight.

"Don't get any ideas, lover boy. I'm going to sleep."

I pulled the covers aside. "By all means. Don't let me keep you." She crawled in beside me and I pulled the covers over us and turned off the light. We chatted for a few minutes then I rolled onto my side and touched her left breast. After receiving an elbow to my side for my trouble, I rolled over and went to sleep. Sometime during the wee hours of the morning, she woke up, pressed her body against mine, the nightclothes came off, and we made love.

*　*　*

I woke up the next morning with my arm underneath Roxy's body and my hand on her left breast. Her bottom lay nestled up against me. She opened her eyes, removed my hand, and jumped out of bed. I watched her nude form as she hurried across the floor to the bathroom and disappeared from view. The water in the shower started to run. She came out of the shower a few minutes later with a towel wrapped around her body and another wrapped around her head.

"About last night," I said.

"Don't let it go to your head. Get into the shower. We've got work to do," she said.

I took my turn in the shower and the hot water felt invigorating. Roxy sat on the bed, brushing her hair.

"What do you say to breakfast across the street at Bun Boy?" I asked after stepping out of the shower.

"As long as you're buying."

I got dressed; we rode the elevator down to the lobby, and then crossed the street. After filling up on pancakes, a side of bacon and several cups of coffee, I called Daniels. He said that the security tape from the break in at the drugstore was at the police station, so after breakfast we headed to the police station. After viewing the tape from the break in, there was no doubt.

The vamp reminded me of Uncle Fester from the Adams family.

"What're your plans?" Daniels asked.

"I have some stops to make, but I thought we'd cruise the desert. Maybe we can catch this creep napping."

"We have Sheriff Deputies out there now."

"Like you said, it's a big desert. If they find anything, call me on my cell," I said. We headed to Stator Brothers and I bought a five-pound bag of sugar. From Stators, I headed to the nearest Catholic Church and conned them out of a gallon of holy water. From the church, we crossed town and headed west on old highway 58.

"I got one more stop to make," I said and then pulled through the chain-link gates and into the parking lot of McCoy's Feed store.

"What now?"

"Just something I think we might need," I replied. Back on the road, we headed toward town.

When we reached Maytree Road, I turned left, passed an elementary school, and headed north. Turning left on Burnt Tree Road, we headed out into the desert. We spent most of the day cruising the desert. It was only march, but the weather was already warm and a bit windy. On the high desert of southern California, there are three seasons: summer, winter and wind. The wind blows almost every day, but between the months of April and June, it's like a wind tunnel sometimes.

After cruising the desert but finding no snoozing vampire, we headed east on Interstate-15 and searched the desert near Daggett and Yermo. Roxy made me stop to help a desert tortoise across the road. I warned her that I could face a big fine and do jail time for messing with those turtles, but she just told me to blow it out my backside.

When the sun went down, we headed into Barstow. I bought dinner at the Idle Spurs Steak House. After dining on a juicy steak and a succulent baked potato, we cruised the town waiting for something to happen. I called Daniels to see if any of the Sheriff Deputies had found anything in the desert. I arranged a meeting at Meads Mortuary at midnight. I asked Daniels to contact the owner so we could view Mrs. Campbell's body.

"Is that really necessary?" Daniels asked over the phone.

"We'll find out later tonight. I think that after that, you'll be a believer," I said. Roxy and I headed back to the hotel and I got our gear ready. At eleven-thirty p.m., we rolled out of the Holiday Inn and headed east on Main Street. Turning left on First Street, we passed a doughnut shop and a bar called *Who'z on First.* Crossing a metal bridge that spanned the rail yard and then another bridge that crossed the Mojave River, we turned left on Fort Irwin Road. After stopping at a four-way stop, we continued north toward the outskirts of town. Meads Mortuary was on the left side of the road, across the street from the graveyard. Daniels sat in his unmarked blue sedan when we pulled into the parking lot. He climbed out of his car and lit a cigarette.

"Are you sure we really need to do this?"

"We'll find out in a few minutes," I replied taking a black nylon gym bag from the trunk of the Mustang.

"Let's just get this shit over with," Roxy said while taking my arm.

We ambled across the parking lot to the mortuary. The glass doors opened and a chill went down my spine. I looked into the chalky-white face of a tall man wearing a black suit. I thought it was our vamp. The funeral director was a scary dude who looked like Vincent Price.

"This is highly irregular," the funeral director said.

"Humor us, Mr. Kauffman. We'll be out of your hair in no time," Daniels said. Kauffman shrugged. "Let's get this nonsense over with then." He retreated into the bowels of the mortuary and we followed along behind. He led us down a hallway and through a side door, passing several caskets as we crossed the room. Chills shot down my spine when I passed the coffins. I kept expecting one of them to open. Kauffman led us through a door and down another hallway. He opened a door to a back room and stepped inside. I felt a cold chill, this time, from the cold frigid air. Roxy's nipples pressed against the fabric of her t-shirt. She caught the direction of my glance and gave me *the look.*

"This is our cold storage. We keep the bodies here until we're ready to prepare them for burial." Kauffman crossed the room to a row of metal drawers set in the wall. He slid open a drawer, revealing a body covered with a thin white sheet. The body of Mrs. Campbell lay on the steel slab. I pulled the sheet away to reveal her face. She looked deader than a can of corn beef cabbage.

Pulling a wooden stake and a mallet from the gym bag, I handed them both to Roxy. "Great. I have to do the dirty work?" she said.

"Just hand them to me when I need them," I said and then took out a crucifix. I pulled the sheet away from Mrs. Campbell's chest.

"There's no need to be crude," Kauffman said. Placing the crucifix between Mrs. Campbell's breasts, I watched her skin sizzle and smoke.

"What the hell?" Daniels gasped, stepping back. Mrs. Campbell's eyes shot open and she let out a shriek. She grabbed for my throat and I looked into her dark feral eyes.

"The mallet! Give me the mallet!" I croaked. Mrs. Campbell screamed obscenities and flung the crucifix across the room where it bounced off the wall.

"Do the bitch!" Roxy yelled, tossing me the wooden stake and the mallet. Daniels jumped away from the body. I pushed the late Mrs. Campbell down on the slab and placed the wooden stake between her breasts. She clung to my throat and my vision turned fuzzy. I brought the hammer down on top of the stake, driving it into her heart. Blood shot out of her chest, splattering against my face, and hit the ceiling. Mrs. Campbell screamed and then died, this time for good.

Kauffman stood watching silently.

"It looks like you've seen this kind of thing before," I said to Kauffman.

"Once or twice. I prefer it when the bodies stay dead."

Daniels looked like Casper the Friendly Ghost. "I need a cigarette. Hell. I need a six-pack and a bottle of Jim Beam," he said.

"The first time is always the worst," I said to Daniels.

Leaving Kauffman to clean up the mess, we swaggered out to the parking lot. The radio in Daniels' unmarked sedan squawked.

"This is dispatch to car 34. Come in, Detective Daniels." Daniels opened the door and grabbed the radio's handset.

"This is Daniels."

"There's been another murder. It has the same MO as the one at the bowling alley."

We stepped closer to listen. Roxy crossed her arms underneath her breasts.

"Where at?" Daniels asked.

"At Molly's Pub on Main Street. The perp was last seen heading west on Main Street in a black forty-eight Ford pickup," the voice said through the mic.

"I'll be right there," Daniels said.

"And we'll be right behind you," I said.

Daniels climbed into his sedan and Roxy and I headed to my Mustang. I fired up the engine and followed Daniels out of the parking lot. We headed south on Fort Irwin road, blowing the stop sign at Old Highway 58, and continued south. Daniels had his reds flashing and his siren blaring. I kept the Mustang on his ass. We passed a Mexican restaurant and a low-rent apartment complex as the road curved and intersected with First Street. Daniels tapped his brakes and turned right, heading into town. We were on the metal bridge spanning the rail yard when an old black Ford pickup truck flew passed us heading in the opposite direction.

I had no room to turn around on the metal bridge, but once the Mustang crossed the south side, I flipped it around and mashed my foot down on the accelerator. Daniels did the same thing. Patrons at the Dell Taco on the east side of the street stared out the window, wondering what the commotion was. The pickup had already crossed the bridge and was heading north. The vamp might have been undead, but the engine in his truck was alive and healthy. The Mustang roared and the speedometer shot up to ninety miles an hour.

The vamp slid around the corner onto Fort Irwin Road and we stayed on his ass. He led us back the way we came, passing the mortuary and the graveyard, then slammed on his brakes and turned left on a dirt road heading out to the desert.

I called Daniels on the radio. "Where's he going?"

"He's heading toward an area known as Copper City!"

"What's there?" I asked as we bounced over the dirt road.

"A few people live there! It's mostly abandoned! There's a few abandoned mining claims! Stay on his ass! There're dirt roads and paths leading everywhere! I got back up on the way!"

"Roger that," I said, tossing the radio into Roxy's lap. "Take the wheel." She looked at me like if I was crazy. "Take the wheel!"

She crossed over me and I moved underneath her. At one point, her shapely bottom was in my face. The Mustang hit a bump and she fell into my lap. My hand found her right breast.

"Watch it, buster!" she said, jamming an elbow into my ribcage.

"Sorry," I said and then slid into the passenger seat as the old Ford pulled away. She mashed her foot down on the accelerator, causing the Mustang to lurch forward. Turning around, I pulled a Ruger Mini-14 from my gear bag. I rolled down the window, leaned out, and fired several rounds into the back of the pickup.

"When in doubt, empty the magazine!" I yelled. Dropping out the empty clip, I slapped in a fresh one and fired several more rounds into the back of the pickup truck. The truck swerved back and forth and then took a dirt road heading north. The old Ford slid to a stop in front of a stone cabin. Roxy slammed on the brakes. An apparition jumped from the pickup truck and ran across the desert toward the cabin. Daniels car slid to a stop behind my Mustang. I jumped out of the car with my Ruger in hand and Daniels jumped out of his sedan with a pump action shotgun.

"Hold it, boys! Let the testosterone level drop a notch or two! If we go in there like this, we don't stand a chance," Roxy said while she climbed out of the Mustang.

I heaved a sigh. "She's right. We're dealing with the supernatural. We'll have a better chance at daybreak."

"You want us to sit on our hands until sunrise?" Daniels protested.

"When your people get here, set up a perimeter. Daylight is only a few hours away," I said.

The city police and several Sheriff Deputies arrived a short time later. Roxy and I took a stroll down by the cabin, checking for hidden exits. After the police had the perimeter set up, we headed back to the Mustang and sat inside it.

"Thanks," I said.

"For what?" she asked.

"For not letting me go off half-cocked."

"What are partners for?" she said and then leaned over and kissed me. We sat talking until a purple haze appeared in the east and fingers of sunlight stabbed across the Mojave Desert.

As we exited the vehicle, Daniels swaggered over.

"Are you ready now?" Daniels asked. "I've got SWAT ready to go."

I let out another sigh. "This is what you hired us for. If you go in there like gangbusters, you'll only get a lot of people killed," I said.

"What are we supposed to do? That son of a bitch killed two citizens!"

"Let us go in first. It's what you're paying us for. If we're not back in half an hour, then bring in your boys."

Daniels lit a cigarette. "Those things will kill you," Roxy said.

"Fine, you've got a half hour."

I retrieved our gear, handed Roxy a paint ball gun and took one for myself.

"What good are those things going to do?" Daniels asked as a smirk crossed his face.

"You can't kill these guys with conventional weapons."

"You were damned *conventional* last night with that Mini-14."

I shrugged. "Last night I was shooting at a pickup truck. Today I'm killing a vampire."

Carrying our gear bag, Roxy and I headed toward the stone cabin.

"I'll take point," I said.

"So predictable. Such a macho pig."

"But you love me anyway," I said and then kicked in the door of the stone cabin. The front door banged open. Dirt and beer cans littered the floor and in the center of the room was a pine box. It looked like the kind the county used to bury people in a pauper's grave. Across the room, I saw a wooden door leading to who knows where.

"This boy seems low rent," I said, moving toward the wooden box.

"He's not as sophisticated as some of the ones we've killed," Roxy mused.

I grabbed a wooden stake and the mallet, and then opened the pine box. My heart raced and my breathing came in short little gasp. The lid squeaked open. The undead figure lying in his coffin looked more hideous than he did on the security tape. Maggots crawled in and out of the sores on his face and the putrid smell made me gag when I placed the point of the stake on his chest.

Before I knew what was happening, the vamp shot out of the coffin, knocking me on my ass. He hovered near the ceiling and then descended to the floor. I rose to my feet, grabbing my paint ball gun.

"What are you gonna do? Paint...me to death?" the vamp asked. His voice sounded raspy and his breath came out wheezy,

"Everything's not always as it appears," I said.

"You call yourself a hunter? I smell fear. It...is all over you."

"There's no fear here, pops," I said, even though I felt like I was going to piss my pants. "You don't smell too good yourself."

The vamp moved toward us and we raised our paint ball guns.

"I'll gut you...so you can live...long enough for you to watch me drain your woman's blood. She'll be mine...for eternity," it hissed.

"Eternity hell. Bela Lugosi you're not. What have you got, aids or something?" I asked.

The vamp crept closer.

"Some time ago, I got hold of some bad blood."

"Enough of this. Your breath smells like dog shit," I said.

"I'll kill you slow, then rape your woman before I bleed her."

"Oh, shut up. What're you going to do, Mike? Talk him to death?" Roxy asked.

"What we're about to have here, is a holy water smack down," I said and then we opened up with our paint ball guns. I had drained the paint out of the paint balls earlier and filled them with holy water. When the plastic balls filled with holy water hit the vamp's skin, they burned through to the bone. His skin sizzled and smoke rose from a dozen places.

The smelly vampire bounced around the room like a chimpanzee on crack. He shot up to the ceiling and bounced off the walls, trying to stay out of the line of fire. He let out a hiss and a foul smelling odor filled the room. We stood with our paint ball guns pointed at the creature clinging to the ceiling. The vampire landed on Roxy, knocking her to the floor. He clawed at her shirt, ripping it to shreds. She let out a scream as the vamp lowered his mouth to her throat. I lunged forward and grabbed the vamp by the hair on the back of his head.

"Take this, you shit bag!" I yelled and slammed a crucifix to the side of his neck. The skin under the crucifix sizzled and maggots jumped off his neck. He knocked me over backward and then crashed through the wooden door to the left of the coffin. Roxy stumbled to her feet, oblivious to the fact that her breasts were exposed. Oblivious that is, until she caught me staring.

"God, Mike, you're such a pig."

"Let's go," I said, diverting my eyes. We moved to the wooden door and I flung it open. The door led to what I thought was a cellar, but when we reached the bottom of a set of stone steps, I looked down a long tunnel.

A tunnel. Why does it have to be a tunnel? I thought.

"Are you okay with this?"

I nodded. "Yeah, I'm fine."

Fumbling with my gear bag, I took out a flashlight and tossed it to Roxy.

"Let's get this son of a bitch," I said, taking out another flashlight for myself. When I stepped off into the darkness, a cold breeze blew a foul odor toward us. "He's down here," I said in a low voice.

"I hope this tunnel dead ends soon. If it splits off into different directions, we could lose him," Roxy whispered.

I could tell by the sound of her voice that she was as scared as I was. Her shadow displayed against the sidewall of the tunnel distracted me. Her breast bounced up and down, causing her shadow woman to do the same. Of course, she caught me looking. The tunnel ended two hundred yards in. The vamp lay on a large rock wheezing and coughing. We opened up with the paint ball guns. The vamp let out a shriek, attacking Roxy again. He knocked her over backward and clawed at her throat. I grabbed a horse syringe out of the gym bag and then jumped on the vamp's back. Sticking the needle in his neck, I pushed the plunger. He let out a blood-curdling scream, stumbled to his feet, took a few steps backwards, and then collapsed.

I helped Roxy up and she stood, clinging to my arm.

"What did you give him?" she asked.

"My version of a Beijing cocktail. He's diabetic. I filled that syringe with sugar and holy water," I said.

Bending down, I grabbed the mallet and a wooden stake as the vampire's skin began to smoke.

"So he's in a diabetic coma? How do you think of these things, Mike?"

"It just comes to me, darling. Most of the time it comes down to the basics," I said, placing the wooden stake against the vampire's chest.

"Just do it and let's get out of here."

"Case closed," I said and drove the stake through the vampire's heart.

BORN AGAIN MICHAEL

CALEB ROSS

Michael asks about my scars again. He won't give up. I fend his questions between those from customers, bookending the feeding habits of corn snakes and the signs of pregnancy in guinea pigs with lies, lies, and lies. "War wounds," I've told him, but then he asks "what war?" "Allergic reaction," I've said, but then he offers Benadryl from his front pocket. I shouldn't let a pill-toting, eight year old boy loiter in my store, but then again I know where he gets those pill-toting habits. This store is a better home than he's ever had.

"Thank you," I tell the woman at the counter as she drops change into her purse. History: she drinks too much, sometimes settles for wells sludge just because she has too; kids to feed, and all that. Too often she buys cat food in bulk. Thing is, she owns a dog.

I look down to Michael. He's pulled one of the feeder mice from its cage and tip-toes enroute to the boa against the far wall. I keep the constrictor's aquarium in the center of a wall, otherwise full of cavy and rodent homes. I'm sadistic like that. "Put it back," I tell him, then. "When I was a boy I was attacked by small, white mice." Pointing to my scars. "They look harmless, but watch out."

"I've got band-aids, too," Michael says and pulls a handful from his pocket with his free hand.

History: Michael has crammed the life of a forty year old into his eight year frame. His mother lactated ketamine, drowned his corn flakes in bourbon, and where other mothers christened kindergarten lunchbox napkins with *I Love Yous*, Michael's sent reminders to lift cigarettes from the 7-11 on his way home from school.

"Let me feed him one," Michael says, pinching the feeder mouse by its tail.

"He already ate," I say.

"Half then," the boy says and separates the feeder's head from its body with nonchalant ease, as though he were sharing a candy bar.

"Christ," I say and move quick to dodge the erupting blood. I usher Michael quick behind the counter to keep the blood from the eyes of customers. The halved mouse is a feeder, yes, but unprovoked killing doesn't keep my cash register full. Already customers have left the store, leaving horrified gasps and a few gagging fits in their wake. "Come back," I plea. "The baby snakes can only eat half an adult mouse anyway." But they are already gone, and the bell above my door has already calmed.

One man remains, a tall, pale specimen who approaches the counter with all attention rapt by the spewing blood, flowing over the floor from behind the counter. As the man sets a bag of Timothy hay and a ten-dollar bill on the counter, I hand a wad of paper towels down to Michael. "Kids," I say to the man, and shrug my shoulders like we've all been there, we've all beheaded a mouse with our bare hands. The pump from the feeder's still-beating heart matches my own heightened pulse.

"Blood doesn't bother me," the man says, his voice unnaturally monotone, like a flat-lined ECG. "In fact, I sorta enjoy seeing it flow. It's like a memento mori, you know?"

I do. Very much. Twenty years ago I was a boy who couldn't stand the sight of blood. That kid who wins science fairs and faints when forced in front of crowds, that was me. Nineteen years ago, a neighbor sliced his wrists with a canned corn lid. I walked in just as he cut. He spun around, painting his walls and floor and my face in red. I tasted the rust and copper of his blood, imbibed the panic in his eyes. Now, new blood literally means life to me.

This man, I search for a wink, any sort of knowing gesture. But I come away with nothing atypical. History: he's a simple man who speaks in riddles. Born middle class. Will likely die middle class. His Bela Lugosi appearance serves as the only spike in an otherwise average life.

"Not sure I follow, sir." I give him his change and receipt with my free hand. With the other, I hold the feeder body below the counter and let the blood pool in my palm, careful to retain as much as possible in my hand.

"Just keeps me thinking about life when I see other things die, is all." He thanks me and steps out onto the cool evening air.

I turn back to Michael. He's abandoned cleaning the mess in favor of dragging designs through it with the towel. "It's the ocean," he says, gesturing toward three hieroglyphic waves rubbed into the blood.

I give him a bottle of Virex TB from behind the counter and tell him to clean everything before the stain sets. "I'm going to grab a bag from the back. Don't leave." I don't need this last command. He won't leave. History: when he's home, his mother throws needles at him like darts.

I step into the back of the store, the mouse body now floating in a palm full of its own blood. As soon as the door shuts, I have the body over my mouth, wringing it like a sponge. It's like drain cleaner, the way everything just dissolves and washes away. Truly everything, I forget my own name for a moment with each swallow. There's heaven in ignorance like that.

History: those nineteen years ago, when I interrupted my suicidal neighbor, the moment I tasted his blood, I was changed. Seriously changed. Like seeing-tits-for-the-first-time changed. I don't use the 'V' word, but really what am I? I've never seen a pair of fangs, the sun doesn't cook me, I can't fly, but I do crave. The best I can understand is that when violence meets the taste of blood, synapses reroute. It's nicotine, really. Alcohol. I drink like anyone drinks; to forget. When my need to forget compounds, I'm left with an addiction.

What's to forget? Since tasting the suicide, I've been in touch with a hidden world perspective. Christian fanatics call it compassion. Social theorists would call it a form of collective consciousness. Hippies would call it 'free love' or some shit. I call it mild torture. When I meet a person, I *know* their history. When I taste them, I feel their history.

Therein lays the conflict. Naturally, not everyone has a history worth feeling. For the first few years, I started fights on the schoolyard playground. Most of the empathy that came with those cuts and abrasions was standard grade school fare. I felt the history of kids beaten at home, a few kids molested, but mostly I tasted what I already had: a fear of teachers and cooties.

In high school I part-timed at a nursing home and skimmed from blood tests. During my short three years time, I imbibed Hell. I learned that between drinks, I could purge the crippling empathy with a journal. This was an old Junior High trick my school counselor taught me when I sought his guidance during a devastating few weeks in which I *felt* that 1) my neighbor beat-off through binoculars aimed at my mother; 2) his son beat off to pictures of his own mother; and 3) my mother knew both of these things, and imagined them when she...you know. The counselor referred to my desire for blood as a "childhood phase." He blamed the *Blade* trilogy. "Get your feelings out on paper; you'll feel better," he told me. It worked for a while.

19 July
This depression-era, black lunged racist named Edgar had me help with his diabetes testing today. One taste I took. One. Racist for a reason really, back in some hometown of his he tries to forget, a group of Mexican dealers fucked his sister, tied him to a tree and forced his eyes open with dinner forks. Kept yelling, something in Spanish, real hate in these faces. He cried when they did it. Punishment was all it was. Turns out, Edgar did nothing. Wrong guy. His sister didn't live through the hospital stay. Lucky I say. Feels good to get this out.

25 July
We got this transfer case named Aggie come in today, swollen and rocking like a damn waterbed. I hadn't drank anything since the Mexican history, so this lady, harmless looking enough, gets wheeled in and my mouth waters. Don't know what she had, if anything, but I tell her "routine blood test" and fill two needles. This poor fucker needs to pray for death. My own ass hurts after feeling what she lived through. Rape yes, but with dicks and objects; sometimes simultaneously. From her father, her uncle, a neighbor; sometimes simultaneously. They took bets on the number of beer cans they could hide. Told her they'd stand her on her head and use her as a koozie. I never drank the second needle.

But I decided to downgrade to mice. Animal instinct is much easier to swallow than human emotion. Morally neutral animal blood doesn't have the lasting effect that human blood does, with its subtle complexities and nuances and—listen to me; I'm a fucking wine snob. Water vs. beer, really. One keeps you going. The other keeps you going in a much more satisfying way. But even though animal solace is temporary, it's still solace. So chin up and let the drug have its way with me.

"What are you doing?" Michael stands in the doorway.

"Christ, kid," I say, and shift the feeder quickly to my side, feigning nonchalance, like eating nothing more than a candy bar. "Ease up on the surprises." If I didn't know better, I'd say he, with this fucking Hollywood movie stealth, was the _ampire.

"Do you need this?" he says, holding out the Virex TB. He points to my chin.

"No," I say, and lick my lips. I drop the feeder into a bucket on the floor.

"What were you doing?" he asks again.

I wipe the remaining blood from my mouth with the back of my hand. "Let me show you something," I say, and lead Michael back out to the sales floor. When he isn't looking, I lick the blood from my hand.

Two new customers have wandered in, a mother and daughter with matching enormous bee sting lips. They engage a sleeping puppy locked in a kennel. History: truly happy, these two. These are humans I could bleed without the adverse effects. "Can I eat you?" I ask them, quickly recover with "help you," but they are already out the door.

I usher Michael to a glass cage along the wall opposite the snakes. Inside, a Chilean rose tarantula cowers in the corner. "This is Maurice," I say.

"I know Maurice," Michael says. He smiles and taps the glass.

"Maurice doesn't eat food like you and m—...like you. Instead, he drinks the insides."

Michael nods, never pulling his eyes from the spider.

"Like apple juice. A person can either eat an apple or squeeze it to drink the juice inside. Let me show you." I open a drawer beneath the enclosure and pull out a single cricket. I drop the cricket into Maurice's pen. "Watch," I say to Michael.

Maurice immediately senses the meal and skitters to the front of the enclosure. Within seconds, he bites. Michael watches. "What's he doing?"

"He's doing what I was doing when you saw me with the mouse. Sometimes, the best part of something is the inside." I could turn this into an after school special, sell it for real blood money. *Skin color doesn't matter, little boy; we're all red on the inside.*

Michael watches Maurice slurp the cricket to a hollow carcass. "So," he says, stepping back from the glass, "you're a spider?"

I look up, the evening has turned to night. Traffic has slowed to a sporadic headlight. "Pretty much," I say and pull him away from the enclosure. "Get your jacket. I'm driving you home."

"I don't know. Last time my mom didn't like it."

"I know. But I'm not going to let you walk home in the dark. I'll talk to your mom if she gets upset."

History: Michael has reason to fear his mother. I pray, for the entire ride to Michael's house, that his mother isn't home. I pray that she's, at least, passed out. The engine revs to Michael's anxious pulse as we near the home, enter the street, and idle into the driveway, headlights off. "You can just drop me off. I think she's asleep, anyway."

"Let's make sure she is," I say and unlock our doors.

We're tiptoeing through the living room, our hearts calming, when the light comes on. For a second we're caught in this guerilla delivery. She's been waiting for us. Another myth destroyed: _ampire's can't see in the dark; or perhaps just not my species. The *Scaredus Shitlessi.* Known natural enemies: boogey-men and vice-addicted mothers.

Adrenaline makes me thirsty.

"Where the fuck have you been?" she says to Michael, a drink in her hand. Something stained red with tomato juice, maybe too much grenadine. The drink sways at the end of a frail arm, thinned to bone with divots pocked throughout the flesh. Needle divots, fist divots, scarred mouth-sized divots. She disregards me.

"Ted's store," he mutters.

"Later…" she begins, a finger waving in his face, but the thought drops as she looks to me and steers her finger to my face. "He's home safe and sound. You can get going now." She takes a sip from her drink.

I look down to Michael. He's pissed himself.

"I'll stay around for a while," I say and push aside a stack of magazines on an oak end table. I sit. "Michael hangs around my store a lot. Maybe you and I should get to know each other."

Michael's mother takes another sip. Condensation drips from her glass, colored red by the liquid inside. I cough and pull my attention away from the blood with thoughts of baseball and nude grandmothers.

"I'm open to getting to know one another," she says, sliding next to me. Her thin frame finds plenty of room on the table next to me, despite my subverted attempt to take up as much space as possible. "I'm Mary." She licks her lips. The veins under her tongue pulse to the rhythm of my own beating organs. This close up, I can see a soft peppering of white powder under her nose.

"About Michael," I say, leaning back as she advances. "Since he and I are around each other quite often…"

Maybe it's the gravity but the final capillary levy somewhere in her head breaks free and blood pours. She's sipping from her drink and doesn't notice the beautiful cocktail being mixed, literally right under her nose. "Let me get you a drink," she says. She takes a large gulp of her own, "and a new one for me." She sets her glass, the cubes stained crimson, between my legs on the table.

"Go get a change of pants and a toothbrush," I say to Michael, who hasn't moved since we arrived. "Go out back and meet me at my car."

He's gone when his mother comes back. "Where's the kid?" she says.

"Bathroom," I say.

"Toast," she says and hands me a glass, fumes so thick the air around it moves.

"I've got my own," I say and hold up her discarded *Bloody Mary.*

I shouldn't. I know this woman. I don't need to *feel* her. But addicts, we don't live on logic; we live on sustenance. Her blood feels like sex.

I pull the glass from my lips, muscles numb from my mouth down my throat through to my fingertips and toes. I hold the glass by its rim and rattle the ice cubes. "I could go for another," I say.

She smiles, says, "Me too," and turns toward the kitchen. Once she's out of sight, I run through the front door, out to my car, and meet Michael.

"Get in," I say.

It's not until his house dips below the rearview horizon that Michael asks where we are going. "Crazy," I tell him, and smile until he does.

These are beautiful moments. Fresh with drink, the world succumbs to my perceptions. The road guides me, the radio harmonizes with my pulse, the darkness outside doesn't hinder; it protects from traumas unseen. I've been high before. This is high*er*.

"You'll be okay," I tell Michael. "You're going to stay with me tonight, all right?" I search my gums for residual blood.

"Did my mom say it was okay?"

"I didn't ask."

"Take me back," he says. "She's going to be really mad."

"I can't," I say and already, too early, the mother's history begins to swell. The road throws me, the radio emits dissonant static, the darkness hides cruel purpose. I'm a young Mary, cornered...

"Really," Michael says. "She doesn't like it when I'm gone."

...Cornered and crying. My gut writhes, turning against itself, starved, reduced to tear away at its own tissue. "You're not going back tonight." I'm coughing the words and straining to keep the black road in front of me.

"What are you going to tell her?" Michael says. "She doesn't like being alone."

And I know why. Why she fights to keep her son close. Why it means beating him, to keep him scared to leave. Why it means cutting him if it's the last option she sees. The boy, he's a blanket, a shelter. He's a dog on a chain, bred and beaten to keep its owner secure.

"I'll tell her…I'll tell her something."

Michael continues to beg retreat. His cries die to murmurs at the back of my skull. I can feel him listening for the voice of his mother hidden in the radio static, the wind outside the car, the throttled engine translated as her slurred demands. He's afraid of his mother's wrath. He's afraid of a life without it.

I think of her, alone for months. Parents gone. I can read the evening's journal purge already…

October 12th

Michael's mother lost her parents to a car wreck when she was young, too young to know that death meant fending for herself. Family was a reclusive group, country home, distant neighbors, and an extinguished farm light. She tried praying, but even God didn't know she was alone. No friends came. No friends existed. She ate crumbs, but those lasted only days. Body breaks down after too long with no food. It eats itself, first digesting expendable tissues, then muscle, and finally, when you're an abandoned little girl with no family or friends, no one that even knows you exist, your body steals nutrition from the brain. The first lobe to go: the moral center. Cannibalism. Self. Nerves are dead so she can't feel the flesh tear from her arm. She takes the sight of her blood like spilled juice…

As we roll to a stop in front of my building, I'm still itching, but they are controlled urges. I have to carry Michael up the stairs, practically tie him to the couch. But eventually, he calms.

I, on the other hand, continue to vibrate.

…The boy split her malnourished frame, even those years later, after medication, hospitalization, therapy, she stayed frail. The boy came suddenly, unplanned, an unprovoked attack from a guy she smiled at in a grocery store cereal aisle. She tried to get rid of him. Alcohol. Needles. Basement set-ups where guys with coat hangers traded elbow grease for a few grams. But he came. He tore through his mother. Mary bled.

Michael, he's settled, though floating on couch cushions saturated by his sweat and urine. I'll clean them in the morning. Until then, he needs to know that a night of sleep doesn't have to be met with a morning of iodine and band-aids. I turn back to the journal.

"What are you writing?"

"Christ." He's over my shoulder. I close the journal and fend his question with bullshit. "Recipes."

"I can't sleep," he says.

"Probably because you're standing," I say, but shake away the joke and ask, likely the first sincere concern he's ever heard. "Why?"

He shrugs. "I think I'll die if I fall asleep."

The words flow too smoothly. A boy his age shouldn't know how to piece together such a statement. "That's not true."

"But I want to," he says. "I want to fall asleep forever."

Nineteen years ago, when I walked in on my neighbor, when he sliced his wrist and bathed me with his blood, I was, myself, a beaten bag of frayed nerves and short circuits. That's how I knew my neighbor. Eight year-old me and this middle-aged product of divorce, jail time, court cases, bankruptcy, all the shit that muddles an otherwise promising head, we happened upon kindred depression one day when I brought his dead dog to his door. I had seen them walking together in the mornings. Then I saw the missing dog posters. When I found the animal, days later, flies already feasting, I brought the dog to him. Said I was sad for him. We became friends by communal misery. I wasn't friend enough to keep him from suicide, though. But his blood, I tasted it, and fell into its relief. I found my drug.

"You don't want to do that Michael."

"Yes, I do."

_ampires are just suicidals who have found their drug. Some people succumb to the burdens of the world, never knowing that imbibing the history of someone else may be all the fix they need.

My neighbor, if only he'd tasted blood, may never have taken his life.

"I'll sleep on the floor next to you for tonight," I say. "If you feel the same way in the morning, we'll talk about it."

He nods. I walk him back to the couch, cocoon him within blankets, and tell him, "I'll put some water on the end table for you. There's a lamp if you need it."

He's already fighting the pull of his eyelids.

I set a glass of feeder blood along with the open journal on the table next to him, inviting him to read. Violence and the taste of blood. It's this or suicide, and Michael has too much potential to waste it on death.

DEVIL CHILDREN UNITE

NIK KORPON

A wooden stake in his hand. Drops of blood fell like hesitant tears. The crowd screamed, threw out their arms like receiving the sacrament. Teenage angst and packaged rebellion, exorcised through changing vocal cords. Sweat, cigarettes, spilled beer and mold hung in the air like algae. Emerson swam in the moment, driving the kids into a frenzy where we thought they'd cover the floor in foam. Pendulum hips, shirtless with blood and sweat slicked over xylophone ribs. The quiet drone of feedback like a train entering the far end of a tunnel.

A beating heart, Jon kept time with his bass drum. One hand poured beer down his throat, the other dried his forehead with a hand towel. He tossed the bottle to the side, nodded toward Emerson—now swinging the mic cord around his head like a lasso—shook his head, laughing to himself. He did this every night. Gerry with a G leaned against the side of the stage, his purple-tinted John Lennon glasses bobbing out of sync with his ponytail. Bajet clapped his hands, bass hanging crooked at his waist, and baited the crowd to follow. Only a hundred bodies in the club but I could barely hear the drum beat over them. People held up their lighters, Freebird-style. It made me nauseous.

My stomach growled, now acclimated to regular eating over the last year. Used to be, we could only eat once a week and try to conserve our energy in the dry days. This band never would've made it then.

Emerson sauntered to the right side of the stage tossing garlic to the crowd and rested one leg on the speaker. Leather pants stretching, he gave them a fair shot of his crotch. Jon and me, we could've been Ramones. Bajet would get lost in an elevator of anorexic lumberjacks, but there was always something off about him. But Emerson; motherfucker's an undead Mick Jagger. He took the rock-n-roll vampire thing a little too seriously.

I started building the riff that ended our last song, "Original Sin as a Bedtime Story," and he surveyed the crowd, looking for the lucky fan. His gaze paused too long on her. Cropped black hair, light make-up, piercings that sparkled in the light, tattoo covering her chest. She'd followed us down from Boston, last six or seven shows. We didn't know her, but fuck if we knew she was trouble. Even if Emerson played blind man to it. Jon led in with his high-hat and snare, Bajet weaving through the backbeat with single notes. I edged closer and nudged Emerson with the head of my guitar, a blast of feedback as I muted the strings for a second. He spun around, eyes blazing. A thin line from the corner of his mouth that glinted different from sweat. Saliva. I opened my eyes wide, gave him a *What the fuck?* look. He narrowed his eyes, ran his tongue over his teeth and smiled. I whipped my guitar around but he leaned back before I could hit him. He held his hand towards the crowd—still staring at me—two down from the girl but close enough, and brought a kid onto stage. The kid's friend started freaking, looking at everyone around him for acknowledgment, a celebrity by association. Poor kid had no idea.

Standing in the cross drawn on the middle of the stage, face agog at sharing our space, at participating in the spectacle, Emerson circled him like a shark. We picked up the volume, pushing to the brink then pulling back then pushing, leading the crowd along the razor edge of aural orgasm. They screamed, flagellated themselves. The kid had obviously been to one of our shows before and fell to his knees as Bajet and I drew closer. He bent his body back, face flipping between excited teenager and deity so quickly it could trigger epileptic seizures, outstretched arms and neck already bared. Emerson stood in front of him, chest dripping, rising, falling. He licked his lips and wrapped the mic cord around his neck like a noose. The crowd screamed so loud they turned white noise. Emerson nodded to us and with a cymbal crash, we shoved the crowd over the razor edge as Emerson sunk his teeth into the kid's neck. His eyes shuddered, glassed over the look of recognition that no, you're not part of the show, you're not a gimmick, you're not a prop for theatrics.

You're dead.

Screams so loud they disappear bathed us as Bajet and I fell to our knees and bit his arms. My chin was sticky, cheek rubbing against his forearm as I readjusted. Underneath the shrieking feedback, the beat fell apart for a second as Jon craned over his drums, staring at us like an oasis. He hurried through the drum roll finale, giving the crowd something to cheer about, then tossed his sticks into the club and waved. Geezer the Roadie dropped the curtain and Jon vaulted his drum set, pushing Emerson to the side.

"Don't take it all," his voice muffled into the kid's neck.

Emerson leaned back and lit a cigarette. I looked up a mouthful later and he was a ghost.

Backstage on a couch with springs poking through the fabric. I sipped a beer and toweled blood from my face. Burped and tasted copper. Tossing the rag to the side, I strummed a Tom Waits song, sung to myself.

Bajet sat cross-legged in the corner, a pile of dead matches in front of his knees. Another match flared and he watched the flame until it licked his fingertips. Spoon, rubber tubing and needle in his lap, thread of blood on his forearm.

Jon and Gerry with a G on the other couch, hunched over papers on the case of an amp. Gerry with a G glanced up at Bajet, then Jon. Jon told him not to worry about it, then started with residuals and merch royalties. He'd always been good with numbers.

Our band worked on the same principles as horror movies: take a base primal fear and make it tangible. Engage the viewer, allow them to be a willing participant and taste the bile of adrenaline in their throat. We went a bit over the top with it for appearance's sake but I figured if no one said boo about Iggy Pop, then fuck it. You were safe watching a horror movie, because they were controlled. You were safe watching our show, because there was no actual danger. In theory, anyway. And the types of clubs we played, no one would notice if we left another body in the alley. Drop one of Bajet's needles a few feet away and homicide would've probably actually thanked us for making their job easier.

A flare-up in the corner. The smell of burnt hair. I poured beer on it, threw Bajet's book of matches into an ass-sized hole in the far wall. He pulled another from his pocket. Jon didn't even look up. Gerry with a G rubbed his hands together, talked about marketability.

Way back, I never would've allowed myself to dream this. Years fell like leaves and fear had eroded into disgust, morbid curiosity, maybe, like the way you'd poke a dead bird to see if you could make its wings move again. We were the same, but different. The type of thing that Lincoln, MLK and Ghandi understood. They had charisma, though. With them, people could identify and empathize, they could look past preconceptions and see the person behind it. Us, we needed a better mouthpiece. All that Hollywood bullshit didn't help, either.

The door opened like a breath and Emerson swaggered in, unbuttoned shirt billowing behind him like a cape the color of sex. Gerry with a G started to stand until Jon laid a hand on his shoulder. Emerson looked at me, flashed a grin as if he was about to spit razors.

"Guys," he said. "This is Sparrow."

In walked the girl, piercings flashing, face flushed. She smelled of body fluids. "Hi," she chirped.

Jon gave a curt wave. Gerry with a G tried to stand again. Bajet watched his fingers burn.

I downed my beer. "What the fuck kind of name is Sparrow?"

Emerson edged forward, shielding her almost.

"Don't worry about him," he laughed.

"He's got daddy issues." Sparrow chirped, held his arm.

"Yeah," I said. "He was burned at the stake."

Sparrow's giggle caught in her throat, eyes darting left and right. Gerry with a G coughed into his fist. A cloud of sulphur in the corner and Jon just smiled.

"You guys are really good," Sparrow finally said. "I saw you in Boston…"

"And the seven nights since. Yes, we know." I opened another bottle of beer.

"Thanks for coming to the show," Jon said. "We appreciate our fans."

Gerry with a G piped up. "And you're getting in on the ground floor. Devil Children are going to be huge!" He rubbed his hands as if to start a fire, a terrible turquoise ring on his knuckle.

Sparrow nodded, eager to show how happy she was for us. Emerson looked at me from the edge of his eyes, mouth moving like he was licking his teeth. He laid a hand on the small of her back, rubbed in small circles.

Geezer appeared in the doorway, held up an eyeball-sized bag and nodded to the corner. Jon called Bajet's name. He looked up, looked through Geezer. A smile formed like a developing picture. He stood, walked across the room. His bones might've been made of toothpicks balanced on end. Jon smirked, a triangle of white flashing over his lip, and patted Gerry with a G's shoulder.

"Your costumes are," Sparrow paused, gauged my reaction to her, "authentic."

"Right." I killed my beer, stood. "Sparrow, real nice of you to come out and all. Can you excuse us for a minute?"

Emerson tried to glare a hole through my forehead. She hesitated back a step, knuckles pale holding his arm, as if my breath would blow her away. She rubbed the toe of her ballerina shoe on her calf. Jon gathered the papers, asked if Gerry with a G wanted a drink. Emerson patted her hand and she followed them out the door.

So angry, he was vibrating. The room, too small to hold us.

"What the fuck is your problem?" Emerson said.

"Her," I said. "You."

"No. You. You are the problem. She did nothing."

"You did. You brought her around here. You're going to ruin this for us." I sipped my beer to calm down.

He snorted when he laughed, shook his head. "You have no idea what you're talking about."

"You fucking idiot. Look around us. It's money, it's easy living. They're handing it to us. And you're going to ruin it."

"You worry too much. She doesn't know anything."

"That's not the point. This is about us."

He took a cigarette from Jon's pack, lit a match and held it in front of my face.

"Fuck you." I smacked it away. "You remember how we had to hide? Remember that goddamn ache? You want that again? This is a constant food supply."

"Whatever." He started to turn and I grabbed his shoulders, spun him around and crumpled his shirt in my fists and brought them against his neck. He smirked.

"Don't do it." My breath, hot, rushing from my mouth with flecks of spit. Words scraped their way up my throat. "Don't do it to that girl. I see it when you look at her, and you won't go all the way."

He swallowed, Adam's apple bobbing against my knuckles. "What if I love her?"

I exhaled, closed my eyes, laughed. As much to myself as to him, I said, "You don't love her. You're just bored."

"And if I do?" He wasn't smirking anymore. I hadn't seen him look at someone like that since we were ankle-biters and Poe was lamenting Lenore.

"Then leave her alone." I relaxed my fists, stepped back. He tried to smooth the wrinkles from his shirt. I handed him a cigarette.

"Look, I'm sorry. I really am." I gave him a bottle of beer. "But there's no compromise in this. Either stay a virgin, or have the abortion."

* * *

Halfway through *Draw an Ink Heart with my Dagger*, at our Welcome Home show in Baltimore, Emerson tried to light me on fire.

He staggered across the stage like a drunken rooster, grabbing a girl in the front row and licking her face then dousing the group in liquor. A bottle in one hand, a wooden stake in the other. He carved an "S" into his chest and tipped the bottle over it. The lights over the stage made his body a bloody kaleidoscope. Jon shot me a worried glance. I shrugged. Then Emerson turned to me, stuck a Zippo in my face. Guitar half-cocked and ready to decapitate, he spat at me. I wiped vodka from my eyes and he shouted into the mic, "Like father, like son," then went into the chorus.

Four songs passed in a blur, random images flash-frozen in my memory. Emerson writhing on the floor, holding the hand of the inevitable Sparrow. Bajet humping his bass at some kid's open mouth. Gerry with a G hiding in the wings, clapping like a wind-up monkey with cymbals for hands. The smell of burnt flesh, so strong I could see it.

Motherfucker tried to set me on fire.

The razor-edge build-up of "Original Sin." Jon and the beating heart. Emerson stood on a stack of speakers, looking for the lucky fan, our meal. I edged towards the speakers. Jon threw a drumstick at me, shook his head like a seizure. The speakers wobbled as Emerson pumped his hips. Jon threw another drumstick at me. I just smiled.

I kicked the bottom one, bringing the whole thing down like a headshot. Two speakers fell into the crowd, a shower of sparks when they hit the floor. Faster than a spider, Emerson had already jumped off, grabbed a kid and brought him on stage. The crowd screamed, rabid. Just another part of the show.

Kid on his knees, arms outstretched with Bajet and Emerson surrounding him, I dropped my guitar to the floor.

I shirked away when Jon grabbed my arm, said, "I'm not hungry," and walked backstage.

Three empty bottles strewn at my feet. Bajet on the nod in the corner. Geezer and Gerry with a G had gone to the bar next-door. Jon adjusted the head of his snare, tentative glances up at me. I contemplated the label of the bottle.

I sighed, leaned my head against the wall. "I can't do this anymore."

"Yes you can," he said. "You're pissed, it'll pass."

Downing my beer, I said, "He tried to set me on fire. I think that's a little out of line."

Jon smiled to himself, shrugged. "You tried to drown him in speakers. I'd say you're even."

"I dunno." I opened another bottle, flipped my guitar over. Fractures like lightning bolts snaked up the neck. "It's different now. He's gone over or something. Almost like it's sport-hunting to him."

Sharp cracks as Jon tuned his drum. He paused, started to speak and took a cigarette from Bajet's lap instead. Bajet lifted his head, said, "Fate," and nodded off again. A jet of smoke from Jon's lips, like exhaling a soul. He looked at the fake security camera in the corner.

"It is what it is." Taking a drag, he said, "And we are what we are," and he turned his head to me. "Nothing ever changes."

The door opened, the stink of sweaty bodies mixing with the musty air of the band room.

"Don't come near me," I said to Emerson. Jon turned, cocked his head. Sparrow lilted through the doorway, so high she was almost preserved. The popped collar of her denim jacket seemed to be the only thing holding up her head.

I blinked for years. "What do you want?"

"She's hanging out tonight," Emerson said, stepping into the room. "No big deal." He guided her to the couch, set her down as if she was a crystalline egg and nestled himself next to her.

"You idiot," I said. "It's bad enough we have to travel with one pincushion, and now you bring another?"

He shrugged. "It's cool." He whispered to Sparrow, brushing hair away from her forehead the way you'd touch fine silk. A smile ebbed over her face like a changing tide. Eyes unfocused. The corner of her lip twitching. Her hand like a porcelain leaf falling into his lap.

Behind them, Jon set down his snare. I imagined squeezing the bottle until it broke, shiny triangles jutting from my palm like emerald teeth.

"Emerson," I said. "We need to talk."

More whispering, then over his shoulder, "Yeah, sure."

"Now, I mean."

He shrugged. She breathed ragged as if she was trying to giggle, and her head dipped to his. Brown dots on her collar. Two holes in the side of her neck.

"You selfish prick." I stood. "What did you do?"

He turned to me. "Mind your own fucking business."

"You are a bastard."

"I said shut the fuck up." He sprung to his feet, stood inches from my face. Her blood in the cracks at the corner of his mouth. Copper riding on his breath.

"Hey, guys, chill out."

Emerson said, "Stay out of this," and as he pointed at Jon, I rabbit-punched the side of his neck. He gasped, stepped back with his hand over his throat. I lunged towards him and caught my foot in a cable. Spider-like, he sidestepped me, dug his hand into my head and threw me to the ground. Straddled over me, fist raised, he paused for a flash. A vein pulsed in the side of his neck. And an anvil dropped on my mouth. Warm gushing over my face. A white triangle stuck in his knuckle. Cold air where my tooth had been and the anvil dropped again, a streak across my cheek so hot with pain I could see it. And again. And again.

His fist dripping onto my chest. Jon shouted something, grabbed Emerson by the arm and pulled him backwards. They grappled like a bug on its back trying to right itself. I wiped my face, lifted myself on my elbows. Sparrow, still in the same position. Each blink five seconds long. Fading from existence. From one world to another, like a tunnel lined with dripping water and shadows that tore at your skin, emptying into a void haunted by insatiable hungers and loneliness so profound it numbed your fingertips.

I grabbed my guitar, staggered to my feet as if I was made of pipe cleaners and thread.

"Hey."

They paused, arms knotted together like flesh yarn.

And I brought the guitar down on Jon's forehead, the wood shattering, body attached only by the strings. His eyes rolled back before his head touched the ground. Emerson, shocked frozen. Eyes darting, hands still holding Jon's.

"What the..."

And I fell to my knees, pushing the neck of the guitar into his shoulder. His mouth opened to scream but could only gasp. A pop, like a carrot snapping, and Jon's finger jutted at an obscene angle.

Hands and knees, I crawled to the couch. Emerson wheezing, Jon coughing. I dragged myself up next to Sparrow. Her eyelids cracked open, languid brown irises rolling towards me. I stroked the back of her hand. It felt like the inside of an oyster shell. As if I was handling a newborn, I folded down the collar of her jacket, leaned her head to expose the virgin side of her neck. Out of respect.

A metal vice on my ankle. Emerson's hand. His face flecked red and brown. Watery colors in the corner of his eyes. "Please," he whispered. "Please."

Her irises lightened, began to turn gold before me. Top lip twitched, something inside her mouth growing.

"Please," Emerson whispered. His hand on my ankle weakening. "Please."

Two fingers on the underside of her jaw, concentrating to feel a pulse, I lowered my head and kissed her neck, whispered you're welcome. I opened my mouth and tasted copper, then felt her pulse whimper. Fade. Fade.

Fate.

THE IN CROWD

ROB X ROMÁN

The pain was excruciating. She could feel its teeth tearing into her neck. It didn't stop with one bite. Its sharp fangs mercilessly tore at her throat. She felt them shred flesh and muscle, digging deeper and deeper as if trying to bite through her. She felt the warm splash of blood against her chest and shoulder as it tore open her jugular. This must have been what the creature wanted because the violent snapping at her neck stopped and the sickening slurping began.

She tried to see what was happening, but it held her head firm in one clawed…was it a hand? She couldn't understand why death hadn't taken her. Surely she had lost enough blood by now, but her brain stubbornly held onto consciousness and her heart refused to stop pumping the life that was now coursing into the thing's maw.

If the sudden loss of blood wasn't killing her, she hoped that the lack of air would send her into sweet oblivion as the thing all but crushed her airway with its other *hand.*

The smell of the thing was disgusting. It smelled of excrement and puke and other putrid scents she had never smelled before, causing the bile to rise up into her throat, but the vise-like grip wouldn't allow her to vomit.

Why can't I just drown then? she pleaded to no one in particular as she felt another set of claws digging deeper into her breasts, white hot pain searing every nerve. The weight of the thing sitting on her chest also made it harder to breathe, much less move.

"You're so damned stubborn," said her fiancé in disgust. "Why can't you, just for once, entertain the possibility that I could be right?"

It had been the argument they'd had since they first started dating. She refused to take any man at his word, much less her fiancé. *She* had gone to college and earned a degree. *He* barely passed his GED tests. There could never be a question of who was smarter because, obviously, she was. Even now she started taking night courses to further her education while he worked as a bouncer at a nightclub with no prospects of getting a higher education or a better job.

It was he who had told her to take a cab home after class.

"The streets are too dangerous over there at night," he'd said.

"Are you saying I can't take care of myself?" she'd asked.

"By yourself, if somebody jumps you in a dark alley? No!"

That was all she needed to hear to do exactly the opposite of what he suggested.

Knowing the defiant look on her face, he'd softened.

"Look," he'd started, "if the cab fare is too much, I'll pay you back for it. Just *please* don't walk home alone at night."

His plea fell on deaf ears. She couldn't wait to walk back to the apartment that night to prove how wrong he was. When he got home, she would laugh at his ignorance and mock him by repeating, "Just *please* don't walk home alone at night," over and over again.

She finally realized, as life started to leave her, that he was right. The alley she so defiantly chose to take as a shortcut would become her final resting place. Feeling her weaken, the creature loosened its grip on her throat, allowing only one word to escape her lips.

"Please."

The creature had gorged itself. Though the human body held a great deal of life giving blood, it knew it would only be a short time until the pangs of ravenous hunger would strike again and it would have to brave the dangerous world once more to slake its thirst.

It sat back on its haunches atop the woman's chest, licking the final dregs of blood from its face and arms with its serpentine tongue. It would suck the blood that had soaked into its clothing once it returned to its shelter to rest.

It recalled the word *please*. While it was familiar with the tones of speech humans made, it could not decipher most of the language. It usually heard the *please* word much louder just as it was attacking, but never afterward and never in such a soft murmur.

It heard the crash of garbage at the end of the narrow alley. It could have been one of the small, common night creatures it sometimes fed on, but it wasn't taking any chances. The world of man was dangerous and caution was the beast's only ally. It pulled its toe claws out of the woman's chest and used its short, powerful legs to spring onto a downspout. Its long powerful arms quickly pulled it up the length of the pipe and onto the roof. If someone had seen it, they would have described it as a half-dressed, tailless monkey using the city's apartments as its playground.

As the creature made its way back to its shelter, bounding from rooftop to rooftop, its mind traveled back to so very long ago, before the human world became the bright, dirty and noisy place it was now.

It remembered living in large broods in the cold mountain ranges of its home. It remembered the abundant numbers of large beasts they used to feed on.

It then recalled the first coming of man and how the numbers of their livestock had dwindled almost overnight. It winced at the memory of threatening starvation and the need of an unprecedented migration to find more food. Everywhere they went, the human infestation was soon to follow until man had become an unavoidable fixture upon the landscape. The world had changed. The creature and its kind would either have to adapt or disappear into extinction.

They began by raiding the enclosures man had built to keep their beasts from roaming. The number of successful attacks dwindled quickly as the men trained their pets to stand guard. Sometimes the men themselves would keep watch. It was from one of these guardsmen that the brood would learn of the rich taste of human blood. Unfortunately, the discovery of this new food source would also lead to the discovery and extermination of the creature's kind in large numbers.

They moved from place to place in droves, feeding on lone humans when they could, but the outcome was always the same—they were discovered and either slaughtered or driven out.

It recalled finding refuge deep in the bowels of a ship that cut across the oceans to a new land, others of its kind with it. Though the craft was filled with men, they dared not reveal themselves for fear of death at the men's hands. The creatures subsisted on the small rodents that infested the craft.

When they finally arrived, the creatures chose to wait until nightfall to make their escape. Once safely on land, they decided to split their meager numbers and travel in various directions to assure their survival. Traveling alone reduced the risk of detection.

Sorrow filled the creature as it recalled the seemingly endless time it had spent alone, away from its kind. It had successfully avoided human contact, other than to feed. It had learned the use of man's garments to clothe itself, so it could lie in the shadows of night undetected. Many men had confused it for human refuse and had gently tossed shiny discs at it. What purpose they served, it had no idea, but they certainly had no nutritional value.

Over time, the creature grew tired of moving from shelter to shelter in order to avoid man's notice. It found a home, a perfect home, where no one ever suspected it was even there.

*　*　*

The Aquarian Theater was a wonder to behold from the day it opened its doors in 1910. It was a place where the elite went to be seen. It was a Mecca for silent film and its stars alike who often addressed their admirers from the stage built before the screen. It was once said of the theater, "If you haven't seen it at the Aquarian, you haven't seen it at all."

When *The Jazz Singer* was released in 1927, the Aquarian heralded the birth of the talkie with a star-studded extravaganza that makes the Academy Awards look like a rainy day at the park.

Even through the depression, business for the Aquarian did not falter. Many a hopeless soul found salvation in the flickering images that helped them escape the reality of a miserable world.

With the growing popularity of television, the silver screen magic of the Aquarian had finally begun to lose its luster. In a last ditch effort to save the building in the 1970's, the Aquarian became a grindhouse for all sorts of cinematic sleaze. The clientele these exploitation films brought in did much to vandalize the once beautiful interior.

Before the city planners could knock down this once majestic building of a bygone era, the steel mill had closed down, killing the heart of the town. In a few months time, the town was abandoned, frozen in time.

Now, the Aquarian is the favored hangout of a few high school students from the neighboring town of Wychester, about an hour away.

Peggy Brant, high school senior with a hard-earned free ride to film school, excitedly drove her '67 Mustang Coupe to the Aquarian. The car looked better than it ran, but she was slowly restoring it with every dime she could scrimp and save. Her father's enthusiasm in working on it with her also helped in acquiring certain parts when her pockets were empty.

"I can't believe you guys are actually interested in seeing *Nosferatu*," she beamed.

"Yeah, whatever." Her sister, Angela, a sophomore, sat in the passenger's seat, trying to project as much disinterest as possible. Peggy understood it was a Goth phase because, though Angie took to wearing as much black as possible at all times, she still had color in her closet, which meant she wasn't ready to completely buy into the macabre lifestyle just yet.

Peggy's excitement sprang from the idea that she would have the chance to expose her sister and her friends to the other subject she loved more than vintage automobiles–classic horror movies.

Though she understood and even enjoyed some of the directions modern horror film had gone in, there was nothing offered in today's cinema that could take the place of Max Schreck, Lionel Atwill or Boris Karloff, just to name a few.

"Look," Peggy said while holding up the DVD of *Nosferatu*, "I even brought the version with Type O Negative playing the soundtrack so your sensitive ears wouldn't bleed listening to classical music."

It killed her not to play the version with the 1922 score, but she had to remind herself it took baby steps to introduce the uninitiated to vintage horror.

"Who's Type O Negative?" Angie asked.

Peggy almost took out a street lamp. If her sister didn't know who Type O Negative was, there was no way she was even *close* to being Goth.

"How can you be Goth and not know who they are?" Peggy asked, still in shock. "That's like being a nerd and not knowing who Captain Kirk is!"

"I'm not Goth," Angie said, matter-of-factly.

"You're not..." Peggy was confused. "If you're not Goth, then what are you?"

Angie smiled a wry, close-mouthed smile. "You'll see," she said.

With that, they pulled in front of the Aquarian behind a black Prius. Angie got out carrying two camping lanterns and portable speakers, while Peggy carried her DVD projector, the DVD, and a small cooler of sodas.

"Who do you know owns a Prius?" Peggy asked.

"Jason."

"Jason? Jason owns a Prius?" Peggy stifled a giggle.

"Is something wrong with that?" Angie asked, a hint of irritation almost cracking the facade of her feigned disinterest.

"No! No, not at all," Peggy blurted, the humor of the situation getting the best of her. "How environmentally conscious of him."

Angie's eyes narrowed to slits in annoyance before she quickly turned and headed toward the theater's broken side entrance.

"How environmentally conscious... and girly," Peggy muttered to herself as a giggle escaped her lips.

Peggy walked into the Aquarian, which was illuminated by the soft glow of what must have been a hundred candles. While truly an impressive sight to behold, she imagined herself finally getting the opportunity to yell, "Fire!" in a theater. Making herself aware that the path was clear to the fire exit, she'd just entered from, Peggy followed the glow of the camp lanterns her sister carried to the middle of the center aisle of seats. That was where she would set up the projector.

"Have you seen the guys?" Peggy asked Angie.

"We are...here," came a disembodied voice from the front of the theater.

Peggy turned to see two bodies cast in silhouette by the candlelight. It was obvious the larger silhouette was Derek, the below average jock, obviously making the other one Jason.

"What's with the mystery, fellas?" Peggy asked nonchalantly as she went about setting up the DVD projector and speakers on some old crates she carefully placed on the seats. "Are you hiding your identities so no one knows you came here in a Prius?"

"Is something wrong with that?" Jason asked her classmate.

"No, no," Peggy reassured him. "It's totally butch."

"Just ignore her, guys," Angie said as she made her way toward them holding a soda for each boy. She handed a can to Jason, but before she could hand over the other, Derek, her boyfriend, swept her up in a kiss.

"Greetings, my beloved," Derek oozed in what Peggy could only describe as soap opera speak.

"Hey, uh, beloved Derek," Peggy called out, "did you remember to bring the beloved genny?"

Annoyed, Derek shouted back, "It's in the aisle on your left!" Then he went back to his melodrama with Angie.

Peggy looked to her left and found nothing. She then walked over to her right where she found the generator complete with extension cord.

"I got it, Valentino," she said, "it was on my other left. Thanks!"

With the generator started and the DVD loaded, Peggy was ready to start the show.

"Okay, boys and girls," Peggy announced, clearly excited to be screening a movie in the historic Aquarian, "get ready for the silent vampire that launched a thousand screams!"

* * *

It watched from the safety of its shelter as the ghostly images appeared on the broad, silver surface below. It could not remember the last time images like this appeared. This had been its home for a very, very long time.

It remembered back when the place was filled with humans who stared in the same wonder and amazement at the images as it did. It was here it had learned much of the human language and their intended meanings through the tones in which they were used. The meanings of words like *damn* and *I love you* were not lost on it. Often times it found itself mimicking the sounds almost perfectly.

The set of images playing before it were bereft of speech. Though it did hear voices and music, it knew enough to realize the intonations were not coming from the human phantoms moving across the silver expanse. It had witnessed, long ago, similar mismatched intonations with narrow-eyed humans and creatures much larger than itself.

As the presentation unfolded before its eyes, it felt its heart race. It was looking at a being that shared its features! The legs were much too long and the arms were far too short, but the face, the face belonged to that of its brood!

The hairless head, the wide, staring eyes, the pointed ears and the long, sharp teeth that sat at the front of its mouth like the small, long-tailed animals its kind were forced to subsist on during their ocean voyage.

There had been many times it saw images in this place of humans with features and appetites similar to its own, but their teeth were too far apart and small where its were close and menacingly long. They were beautiful and perfect where it was ugly and mis-shapen. It had missed its brood mates so much that it would even welcome the company of those distant cousins, but it never found them out in the world, only here as ghostly images where they often met a cruel demise. Maybe they were hiding, too, and hiding well.

Now it was seeing what must have been another relative, but much closer than the others. Though the creature did not behave as its brood did and managed some fantastic feats, it still felt a kinship with the image and its loneliness became almost unbear-able.

For an instant, it keened uncontrollably.

Peggy hit the pause button.

"Hey!" Derek yelled, forgetting his more dramatic persona. "What's going on?"

"Did you..." Peggy paused, listening to the silence. "Did you guys hear that?"

The creature, realizing what it had done, covered its mouth with a claw, hoping not to be discovered and forced to move from its home after so much time.

"Hear what?" Angie asked, clearly annoyed.

"It almost sounded like a cat yowling," Peggy answered. "What do you think that was?"

"Gee, I don't know, Peggy," Derek shouted sarcastically. "Maybe it was–*a cat!*"

"As much as I would hate to detract from this most interesting repartee, can we please continue with the film?" Jason asked.

Finding Jason's choice of words odd for the guy who only spoke in grunts in the eleventh grade, Peggy turned the movie back on, but kept an ear out for her phantom cat.

* * *

"So," Peggy said as she made her way to the front of the theater, carrying both camp lanterns. "What did you folks think of *Nosfer*... whoa!"

Sitting in the front row before Peggy were Jason, Angie and Derek, all dressed in black. Each one of them was wearing make-up that made them look pale and gaunt. Jason was wearing white contact lenses. There was a long silence before anyone spoke.

"So," Angie said with a satisfied look. "What do you think?"

"I think Jason wins the Marilyn Manson look-alike contest," Peggy said flatly.

"Peggy!" shouted Angie in frustration.

"What? I'm sorry, but you guys look ridiculous," Peggy giggled.

"Damn it, Peggy!" Angie sprang from her seat, but before she could get any closer to her sister, Jason lifted a halting hand.

"It's okay, Angie," Jason said under a smirk. "Your sister has yet to understand...us."

Jason slowly rose from his seat and walked toward Peggy who leaned back against the old Aquarian stage. She folded her arms, waiting for anything they had to throw at her. Jason simply turned and leaned against the stage to her left. Derek joined them at the stage, but flanked her. Angie rested against his large chest as he wrapped his arms around her.

"What...have I yet...to understand...Jason?" Peggy stammered, mockingly. "That you...are taking...acting classes from...William Shatner?"

Jason threw his head back and laughed. For the first time, Peggy noticed his teeth, particularly his incisors; they were fangs.

"No, foolish one," Jason mocked. "We're vampires."

With that, they all smiled, revealing sharp incisors.

Vampires!

The creature heard the word clearly. That's what man called its kind–vampires! Were there vampires here now? It stole a furtive glance from where it hid. It saw three of them surrounding the human girl, but they resembled the human-like variety.

They *did* exist! It had found others like itself at last!

But what were they doing with the human girl? Why were they not devouring her? Was this some sort of ritual of theirs? The ghostly images of the past did seem to court their victims for a time before drinking their blood. Maybe if it watched, it would learn their ways and find it easier to fit in. At long last, its loneliness was coming to an end.

It was Peggy's turn to laugh. She laughed long and loud. There was a moment there she thought she would pass out from lack of oxygen, but she regained her composure and then laughed some more.

"Peggy!" Angie yelled. "You're being a real jerk!"

"Let her...laugh, Lucrezia," Jason soothed. "As I said before, she simply does not...understand."

"Wait a minute, wait a minute, wait a minute," Peggy said with an outstretched hand, holding up a finger as she bent over to catch her breath. "Lucrezia?"

"Yes," Angie said, "Lucrezia's my vampire name."

"As in Lucrezia Borgia?" Peggy asked, impressed that they just might know who she was.

"Who?" Derek asked.

Peggy ceased to be impressed.

Jason slowly bent at the waist, bowing for effect.

"You may call me Udo and our dear Derek here is Radu."

"Okay, if you guys tell me you don't know who Udo Kerr and Radu Tepes are, either you're lying or you've used up all your coincidences for this lifetime," Peggy said, flustered.

"I have been known to bend the spine of a book or two, my dear," Jason grinned.

"Bend the spine of a book or two," Peggy said thoughtfully. "Wait a minute! You guys have been reading that tweenie crap, *Borne Unto Night*, haven't you? Okay, maybe *Udo* and *Lucrezia* have, but I bet the Big Ragu here has been watching the movies."

"That's Radu," Derek corrected.

"She knows, she's simply trying to... get your ire up," Jason said.

"So is this what all the kids do for attention?" Peggy mocked. "Is everyone wearing novelty teeth and *outing* themselves as vampires these days?"

"Hey, being a vampire is not a gay thing!" Derek said nervously.

"I'll give you points for knowing what *outing* means, Ragu," Peggy said, patting his shoulder.

"So," she continued, "why is it you're all vampires all of a sudden?"

"It's not all of a sudden," Angie insisted. "Vampires are who we are! Vampires are what we've always been!"

Peggy had finally had it. What she had taken as a joke was obviously something they had taken far too seriously. It was something they needed to snap out of. Being Goth was one thing, it was real, it was true, but being a fictitious entity was another thing entirely.

"You're not vampires," Peggy seethed, "you're losers!"

Losers! The sound rang through the creature's head. It had heard that word before in that intonation with that inflection. It meant something was worthless. Why were its fellow vampires allowing this human to vocalize that way?

Peggy laid into them. "Derek, you're such a muscle head that even the other jocks find you too stupid to hang out with. Jason, you've been socially awkward for so long it's a wonder you even know how to speak, much less string together words that aren't monosyllabic. And my little sister, Angie. You've been trying to please everyone else your entire life. In trying so hard to fit in with everybody, you've made yourself an outcast! Do you realize mom loves reading that *Borne Unto Night* crap, too? She also loves Donny Osmond. Donny Osmond! You're creating a make-believe life around a series that attracts middle-aged women and Donny Osmond fans! How sad is that?"

Silence hung heavy in the Aquarian. Peggy couldn't believe the verbal onslaught she had just unleashed. She knew what it was like to be an outsider. Being a motor head and a horror freak set her apart from most, but in staying true to herself, she eventually won like-minded friends, true friends. Unfortunately, her outburst did nothing to smooth the way for that message.

As she tried to come up with a way to soothe their hurt feelings, Peggy could hear her sister quietly begin to sob. As she looked at Angie, she caught the welling of tears in Derek's eyes as they glinted in the candlelight. Jason was quietly brooding to himself.

"Guys," Peggy said.

"Don't you think you've done enough damage, Peggy?" Jason asked, his voice wavering.

"Sure," he continued, "vampires aren't real, but is it a crime to want to feel unique? To feel different?"

As gently as she could, Peggy answered. "How can you feel unique when everyone else is posing as vampires because of these trashy, tweenie romance novels?"

"I think you should go," Jason said.

"At least act like *real* vampires like Count Yorga or Blacula," Peggy offered.

"I said I think you should go," Jason insisted.

With that, knowing she had lost them, Peggy collected her things, except for the lanterns, and was about to walk out when she stopped to talk to her sister.

"Angie, I..." Peggy said, barely above a whisper.

"I'll get a ride home with Jason," Angie choked under a veil of tears.

Peggy went home alone.

Angie sobbed. She wasn't crying because her sister had so viciously torn down her illusion, she was crying because Peggy was right. She couldn't remember the last time she dressed in an outfit she had picked out herself. She was always dressing in some clique's uniform just so they'd accept her. Even now she dressed the part of a vampire because it pleased Jason and Derek. In a world of pleasing everyone else, she had ended up alone.

Derek tried to comfort her. "Don't let what your sister said bug you. She has no idea what she's talking about."

"But that's the thing, Derek," Angie said. "She *does* know what she's talking about. She knows *exactly* what she's talking about."

"Not about me she doesn't," Jason said.

"She's right about *all* of us, Jason," Angie insisted. "We're all losers. We're all lonely."

Lonely.

The creature heard the vocalization of *lonely* and the sound of despair. It was confused about why they would let a meal of human blood get away from them so easily, but it understood *lonely*.

This was its chance to reconnect with its kind. Admittedly, not exactly like its brood mates, but it had been so long that it didn't matter. Whatever their differences, they would find common ground with each other and none of them would have to be lonely anymore.

It vaulted from the balcony and landed in the aisle with a faint thud.

Angie noticed the sound.

"Did you guys hear that?" she asked.

"Was it your sister's cat?" Derek asked sarcastically.

"No, she's right," Jason said and pointed into the aisle. "Something landed over there."

"Guys, something's coming this way," Angie said, frightened.

A short shadow with long arms waddled down the aisle toward them.

Derek hopped up onto the stage and lifted one of the lanterns. Jason joined him and lifted the other.

"You'd better stop right where you are," Derek threatened, "or I'll tear your friggin' head off!"

The figure leapt onto the backs of the first row of seats and then bounded onto the stage, landing in front of Jason.

Before Angie could get a clear view of the creature that had joined them, she turned, gagging from the horrid stench. Derek and Jason could do nothing but stare at the horror that had sprung from the shadows to face them.

It couldn't have stood taller than five feet, its incredibly short legs making up only a small fraction of its height. The claws on its feet, looking like the talons of a raptor, softly clicked against the floor of the stage with each tiny step it took. Its long, thin arms ended in massive hands that easily touched the floor, each finger tipped with a claw as dangerous as the ones on its toes. It wore blood soaked clothing, a sweater and slacks, tattered from constant wear and poor attempts to make them fit correctly over a figure they could never be tailored to. The exposed forearms and head revealed pale flesh, almost gray, marbled with blood and grime. The face was unbelievably familiar. It was practically identical to the vampire they had seen only moments ago.

If it not for the impossible proportions of the creature's body, the boys would have thought this was a prank. Even Derek wasn't dumb enough to think this creature could possibly be a classmate in disguise.

As the creature had seen so many humans do, and since these distant brood mates looked and acted so human, it reached out a claw in friendship in hopes they would understand the gesture. It knew their loneliness all too well. Soon, it would belong again, belong to a new brood.

Strangely, the two human vampires it faced slowly backed away. Not understanding the ritual, it slowly advanced toward them. The large one dropped the glowing object it carried and tried to scurry away, but gained no traction. The other one swung the glowing object, hitting the creature across the face.

Stunned, it stepped back on its short legs. Taking a moment to feel its face, it looked down at its claw to find it was bleeding.

Angie, overcoming her nausea from the fowl odor, jumped onto the stage, ran past the creature, and stood behind Jason.

"Jason, what is it?" Angie desperately asked.

"I have no idea," Jason said, scared out of his mind.

Confused, the creature reached a bloody hand out to the one that had struck him.

"Lonely," it intoned.

"Did...did it just say..." Angie began.

"Die, you freak!" Derek yelled as he found his courage, and his footing, and kicked it into the front row seats.

The creature was no longer confused. It understood the intention of the word *die* and the physical attacks were no longer seen as strange rituals. These human vampires meant to do it harm. Its instinct for survival took over.

It found purchase on a seat back and launched itself at Derek. It landed firmly with both clawed feet digging into the boy's chest. Derek fell on his back, hard.

Derek yelled in agony as he felt the creature's claws dig into the pecs he had worked so hard to shape and build. Determined to give as good as he got, Derek put all his strength into a backhand that connected with the creature's head. The blow dislodged his attacker from its fleshy perch. Torn chunks of flesh and muscle remained in the creature's claws as Derek wailed in agony.

The creature bounced across the stage, its head ringing from the blow. It quickly scrambled to its feet, slipping a bit on the gory mess that was still caught in its claws.

The creature could smell the heady aroma of human blood as it poured forth freely from the wounds on Derek. The blood revealed Derek's true nature.

There was no possible way these vampires could be anything but true humans, humans posing as brood mates. This was the ultimate deception, the ultimate disappointment. Now only rage burned in the creature's heart. These humans were nothing more than food now.

Derek, his anger over his ruined chest overriding the intense pain he felt, launched himself at the creature. His arms wrapped around its torso as they slid across the worn wooden stage. Splinters dug deep into Derek's forearms and the creature's legs.

Derek desperately tried to squeeze the life out of the thing while it lashed out at him with all it had. Its legs scraped and clawed against Derek's tattered chest and stomach. Its long arms raked deep, red furrows along his back, tearing his shirt as ribbons of flayed flesh splattered the stage. Its mouth bit and chewed at Derek's head. In a flash, most of the boy's ear was gone. In another flash, pieces of his scalp and hair were torn violently from his skull.

Jason and Angie didn't know what to do. Frozen in fear, they watched as their friend was torn to bits. Blood and ragged pieces of flesh spattered them.

Derek's screams reached a fever pitch, the pain becoming far too much to bear. He loosened his grip for only a moment. It was all the creature needed.

The monster hoisted Derek's pain-wracked body up onto its powerful legs and hurled him into the theater seats. A sickening crack echoed through the theater, signaling the snapping of

Derek's spine. Still alive, Derek was thankful for the sudden numbness that enveloped his body.

The large human was no longer a threat to the creature. Derek would live only long enough to slake the creature's thirst later. Right now, it was still furious and much needed to be done to assuage it.

It turned to the remaining humans. In the ghost images it had seen in the past, it had watched as horrendous things were done to the frailer of the species and took note of what lengths the males would go to protect them. It would make them both suffer.

Jason tried to slowly back away from the creature with Angie shuffling close behind him. Jason knew there was nowhere to go, but somehow he felt as long as he kept an eye on the creature, they could dodge any attack thrown at them.

Jason was wrong.

In an instant, the creature used its long arms and launched itself at Jason. Its powerful legs made contact with Jason's knees, crushing his kneecaps and sending his splintered shinbones tearing through the backs of his legs. The naked ends of each femur clacked against the stage as Jason landed hard. The stage splintered beneath him. Broken wood bit into bone, acting as a prop that kept him upright.

The shock to his system was instantaneous. Though still conscious, Jason was surprised at how little pain he felt. The creature was a hair's breadth away from his face; standing on Jason's destroyed and severed shins. It reached a long arm behind him and quickly shuffled back, dragging a whimpering Angie with it.

"Leave her alone!" Jason shouted. "Leave her alone!"

The creature kept a steady eye on Jason as its claws played gently across Angie's face.

"Jason," she sobbed. "Help me, Jason."

When her eyes were plucked from her skull, Angie cried out.

"Stop it!" Jason screamed. "Leave her alone!"

Jason could only watch in agonizingly helpless horror as more pieces of her face were flayed away with the simple pull and twist of the creature's claws. After what seemed like hours, the unconscious face of the girl he once knew was nothing but a macabre display of exposed and torn muscle.

Just as he was thanking the heavens for granting her unconsciousness, the creature reached down to her belly and slowly tore a ragged gash across her abdomen. The same pain that had caused her to slip into oblivion now brought her back to the waking nightmare. If she still had her eyes, she would have seen the creature pulling out her intestines, designing a sick display for its captive audience. Her screams faded again as she slipped back into unconsciousness.

The creature marveled at the resilience of these humans. Though her life force was weak, the frail one still lived, but it would have to feed on her, and soon before she died and her blood spoiled.

The creature's anger had past, spent from the battle with Derek and the slow torture of the female. All it had left was hunger, sorrowful disappointment, and one last human.

Slowly it crept toward Jason.

Jason's legs were ruined. He knew he wasn't going anywhere, but his need for survival was still strong. He had one thing to try; one idea that he had hoped would save him. It was the only common ground he imagined he shared with this creature as it was the only word it had uttered. Maybe mutual misery and understanding would save his life.

As the pain from his ruined legs slowly became an agonizing reality, Jason raised a wavering hand toward the creature.

Curious, it stopped, wondering what gesture this man might be making.

"Lonely," Jason muttered.

The creature stepped nose to nose with Jason.

"*Loser*," it hissed.

Jason screamed long into the night.

EXTREME HELSING

G. R. MOSCA

It was believed that the last of the Carpathian Vampires had secreted themselves somewhere on the Gerlach Peak in Slovakia. The television network hoped that we would climb the peak, find the lair of these nocturnal devils, and provide them and the public with one hell of a reality program. If the footage from our helmet cams and our cameraman were any good, they would look into spinning the show into a full season.

What they needed was a 'catch', something that would capture the imagination of the general public. Something that would make them want to watch this program. In the eyes of certain network executives, I was the thing that would rivet millions of viewers to their television screens when our story was aired.

My name is Stephan Helsing and my great, great, great grandfather was the infamous vampire hunter. I'm more of the surfer-type and extreme mountain climber but when the 'rubber hits the road' it's all in the name.

New York City
The ten of us settled into a boardroom of XBC Television Corporation, subsidiary of yadda, yadda, and yadda. We really didn't care much who owned what, we were concerned about the fact that they had booze and we wanted the drinks to keep coming. It's really amazing how naive youth can be.

We were a real assortment of yahoos. There was myself, Mike D—a famous snowboarding champion who made his bones in the North American Extreme Games, and James Franklin—a world-renowned freestyle climber. Along with James was his older brother Randall Franklin; also a world-class climber, Brian Johanson; an Olympic Silver Medal winner for downhill racing, and our cameraman. The cameraman was a quiet but out-of-shape guy named Daniel Breckman who wasn't really sure why he would be hanging with the rest of us. He was a family guy and he felt more than a little uncomfortable around us. He already looked like he missed his family and we were only in New York.

As we were getting pleasantly buzzed, some 'Suit' started giving us the gist of the assignment. We had all heard of vampires, but nobody really took it too seriously. Sure, we were aware of them, but not really too worried. Hell, there aren't that many suckheads in Aspen, Colorado at any time of the year.

The 'Suit' puts on a little slide show. The first bunches of slides were your typical artist rendering of a vamp. We're not even watching. But then a few slides later, this picture comes up on the screen and I think we all just about lost our breath. Everything became very quiet in the room and that 'Suit' knew he had us.

"Gentlemen, may I call your attention to your destination. Gerlach Peak in the High Tatras, part of the Carpathian Mountain chain. Note the sheer faces and the bowl-shaped peak. This mountain at one time was called Cauldron Mountain. The peak or near to it will be your destination. We feel this is the best area to locate and capture any photographic and video evidence of vampires. We strongly advise the group to summit up this face and arrive during daylight hours. Any vampires located will be docile and unable to defend themselves. We can't be sure how many there may be or exactly where they may be located, and this will be your challenge. With the help of Stephan, we are certain you will be successful."

The room immediately exploded into whoops, glad-handing, backslapping and cheers with many fists waving and clinking of glasses.

"Any questions, gentlemen?"

Village of Gerlach

We arrived in the village of Gerlach safely and a little jet-lagged. A small man who was assigned by the network to be our translator met us at the airfield. The guys and I wanted to work off some steam after sitting in a private jet for hours, so we immediately headed for the nearest Beer Hall. Gerlach is a picturesque village, a place my great, great grandfather might have felt at home in visiting. There are no apartment buildings or office skyscrapers, everything is on the 'down-low'. Meaning: village square, wooden-shingled houses with carved figures, little signposts telling you where everything is, except we can't read Slovakian.

The Beer Hall is hard to miss; it's lit up like a Christmas tree and there is a gigantic beer stein on the front of the building.

We entered through the heavy, oak doors and forty heads of local villagers turned in our direction. The room got really quiet, it started to feel a bit uncomfortable. This lasted for about ten seconds when suddenly someone started chanting, "Mike D., Mike D., Mike D."

Before we knew what was happening, the entire hall was moving towards us, patting us on the back, asking for autographs. I noticed some trays of beer steins already heading in our direction. It turns out that Mike D. is a bit of a celebrity in Eastern Europe and we got treated pretty well.

During the evening we drank hard, but at one point our translator brought this little fellow over to my table. He turned out to be Heinrich Gerlach, the Mayor and—from his name—one of the founding residents of the village. He had been notified about our visit and what we intended to accomplish. I think this had to be cleared with a village official just to satisfy the network lawyers. Heinrich looked like a sad little man—long face and tired eyes. He began to talk to me about incidents that had taken place over the years.

I was amused, then shocked at his recounting of cattle mutilations; not one or two but hundreds of them over the course of decades. Then there were the missing animals—everything from pet cats and dogs to goats and sheep. There was vandalism to the village church that could not have been attributed to any of the townsfolk. Urine and feces smeared on the altar, vestments ripped apart, and stained glass windows broken. Other cases were minor in comparison but disturbing nonetheless. These included the doors of village elders being sprayed with a liquid that stained and scented doorways in a horrible manner and killed any vegetation it came into contact with. Then with a heavy voice he told me of the missing children. There had been more than a few but it was beginning to occur with more frequency.

It started with a little girl about ten years ago. She never came back home from the fields. A search was mounted to no avail. Her parents were grief-stricken and the town was shocked. A few months later a teenage couple who had been at a Harvest Dance left later that evening for their parent's home and were never seen again. There had been more since then.

I thanked the Mayor for sharing these concerns with me and shook his hand. He looked me in the eye, took my hand in his, and said something in Slovakian. I couldn't understand what was said but our translator told me that the Mayor was quite taken with us and had offered me his personal blessing of protection.

Mike D. came over and I repeated some of the stories I had just heard from Mayor Sterlach. Mike D. seemed genuinely interested in them, then he told me that he had been talking with some of the young village lads and they had related the strangest story to him. It seems that on random nights throughout the year, strange lights appear on the peak of Mount Gerlach. This may not be odd except for the fact that the peak is about 2700 feet high and nearly vertical, making it dangerous to climb in the daytime, let alone in the evening. They told him that these lights appear to dance around the peak, defying anything a mere human could accomplish.

When we left, we were all pretty toasted and we literally stumbled out of the beer hall and into the cool mountain air. James and his brother Randall were arm and arm, supporting each other while Mike D. and I followed our translator towards the inn where we would be staying.

Near the Town Square, I couldn't hold it in anymore and fell behind to relieve myself beside a wrought iron fence. As I pissed into the snow, I blearily realized that I was melting the snow from a bronze plaque. On this plaque was the figure of a bat with outstretched wings, large ears and piercing beady eyes. As the rest of the plaque became visible from beneath the snow, I could make out the text in Slovakian. As I have said, I do not speak or read Slovakian, but when I was finished, there were three words that I understood very clearly. On the plaque, with the picture of a bat, was my ancestor's name.

Abraham van Helsing.

Gerlach Peak – Day One

We arrived at the foot of Gerlach Peak for our first view of the mountain. As promised, it was not the tallest rock but its sheer, vertical face would offer a slow and challenging climb. We were all experienced climbers but Mike D. and Brian excelled in other winter sports. None of us thought there would be any problem summiting Gerlach. It looked pretty gnarly but we were up for the challenge. Hindsight is always 20/20 but if I had thought about why we were climbing this mountain, I would have asked somebody just what the hell were we supposed to do once we got up there.

We checked our equipment. Everyone was outfitted with a harness, ropes, cams, nuts, caribiners, the best climbing shoes, climbing gloves, personal GPS trackers and a Cam-gun. The Cam-gun was new and it shot a post into the rock at a high-velocity. We could then rope into the post and feel secure in having a good anchor for the rope line. We all had these and were testing them for the manufacturer. We had helmet-cams and wrist-mounted walkies for communication with base camp and Mike D. carried a snowboard strapped to his back. Each of us also had an odd package that contained a cross, a small stake, a wooden hammer and a vial of holy water. We couldn't help but scratch our heads at that one.

Daniel, our cameraman, would take footage of our summit from the ground and join us by helicopter the following day. We had it all figured out, it was going to be that easy.

* * *

We stood at the base of Gerlach staring up at the summit while the peak glared back at us, at least that's how it felt. The skies were clear with a light breeze and moderate temperatures. We started our attack of Gerlach Peak with a small crowd of well wishers from the village to cheer us on. With good conditions I estimated that we would summit in two days with a half day to explore, then a two-day return or we could opt for helicopter retrieval, weather permitting. It was impressed on us that we had to summit in the daytime just in case there were suckheads waiting for us on top. I think we shook our heads in agreement but had a good laugh about it later that day.

At the moment, I was planning on summiting by the morning of the third day but only because it is more difficult to climb at night.

*   *   *

We had a good day of climbing with a bit of friendly competitive show of skills between the five of us. James being an excellent freestyle climber took more chances and relied less on being roped in than the rest of us. At the end of the day, we all did really well and made it almost halfway up the mountain. Just before sunset, we stopped to make camp for the evening. Using the Cam-guns, we shot posts into the cliff wall and hung our mummy bags onto the posts. We would sleep suspended on the vertical rock face, over 1000 feet in the air with nothing between us and the ground except a sheet of nylon and our dreams. There is nothing else in the world like it.

Gerlach Peak – Day Two

We awoke on the rock wall with a beautiful morning sun illuminating the world around us. We poked our heads out of the mummy bags to take in the new day. Amazing!

*   *   *

Something is very wrong. Brian is missing. We were spaced apart about ten feet away from one another but Brian and his sleeping bag are gone and there are torn pieces of his mummy bag still attached to the posts. Randall thinks he can see a blood stain on the rock face where his bag had been, but he can't be sure. Everyone is up now. We pack in a hurry and try to figure out what to do next.

We radio base camp and they assure us that Brian did not climb down during the night, nor do they have any report of a body being found at the mountain base. They check his GPS, we all carry personal GPS locators as a precaution, and it shows that he has summited already. We are pretty floored by that news flash. I ask again for base camp to repeat. It comes back on the walkie, "Looks like Brian made you guys look like a bunch of douche's. He is already on the top. Repeat. He is already on the peak."

We're floored. We now believe that Brian probably made it look like his bag got ripped and he is already at the top having a good laugh at our expense. Nothing left to do but to get cracking.

* * *

We continued to climb up the rock face. Winds began picking up and I could feel the temperature dropping significantly as we ascended higher. We're still under cloud cover and looking up, we can see that a beard of clouds now obscures the peak. We'll probably finish the climb in fog until we break through past the cloud cover.

* * *

We're another hundred feet above last evening's encampment and James shouted that he's found Brian's sleeping bag stuffed into a shallow crevasse. We pulled it out and the bag was soaked with a sticky, dark liquid. We're pretty stumped as to what he might have spilled in his bag but we figure this to be another part of an elaborate prank he's playing on all of us. We're going to pound that guy senseless when we see him. Disgusted, we just stuff the bag back into the crevasse. Another climber's souvenir left on the mountain.

* * *

Storm clouds moved in quickly from the west. Even though were close to the summit, we needed to hunker down. This looked like a bad snow storm and base camp was advising us to either seek shelter or anchor ourselves into the rock face and get ready for a bumpy afternoon.

* * *

The storm is over for the most part. It dropped a lot of powder on the rock face and we'll need to use snow poles to figure out where the voids and crevasses are so we can safely anchor into the rock face and complete the climb. Earlier in the day, we had to chow down and sleep through the storm. Now the sun is setting but we're determined to complete the last leg and reach the summit by this evening.

Once on the peak, we can do a little exploring with our lanterns and flashlights, and celebrate with some drinks around a fire. There's nothing like partying at 2700 feet.

* * *

We were completing the last hundred feet of the climb. James was point, testing snowdrifts for voids and clearing them to expose the rock face. He came to a crevasse and stuck his pole in to gauge the depth of the snow. It happened so quickly, we hardly had time to register the screams. James stuck his pole into a drift, and it went in pretty deep. Before he could pull the pole out and test another spot, two powerful arms emerged from the drift and grabbed either side of his head. We heard his screams and saw a face emerge from the drift. It reminded me of the face of the bat on the plaque I had seen in town. Its skin was dark and mottled and stretched over its skull, its eye sockets were deep, and set within them were tiny red pinpoints of light that shone like laser beams in the dark. It looked past James for a moment and acknowledged the three of us below, then it smiled; if you can call it a smile. My blood ran cold, as Randall started to shout for his brother and all I could hear Mike D. say was, "This isn't happening," over and over again.

The vampire took James' head and twisted it off his neck, causing a fountain of blood to spout into the air. It casually dropped the head over the crevasse and leaned its mouth onto the spouting neck, sucking in James' vital fluids.

We freaked out, big time. Randall screamed, Mike D. cursed and I looked around for a way out. The thing took its time draining James but when it was done, rather than throwing James' limp body aside, it lifted the body and grabbed the rope line that we were all still attached to. We were suddenly being pulled slowly up the mountainside towards this thing.

As the moon appeared and the last glimmer of daylight died in the west, the vampire opened its mouth and its fangs seemed to shimmer in the glow of the rising moon.

We were screaming, beside ourselves with fear. We were still being pulled up slowly. I was now first on the line, followed by Randall and lastly, Mike D. It's funny, I imagined that this was how a fish felt, caught on a line and being reeled in by a weekend sportsman. I vowed never to fish again. We realized that we were all drenched in James' blood, it stank horribly and Randall puked onto the mountainside. We were moments away from a similar fate when I decided to do the only thing that I could think of– I took my knife out.

I think Randall knew what I was going to do because his eyes grew wide with panic as I cut the rope. We were suddenly tumbling through darkness.

Moments later I felt my body being jerked to a sudden stop. I crashed into the side of the rock face, hard, and I could sense that I was suddenly once again suspended in the air.

I looked above me and saw Randall, then Mike D.

Mike D. had used the Cam-gun to shoot another anchor into the cliff and he had quickly tied us to it using his end of the rope that had bound us together. I looked past Mike D. and saw that the vampire was enraged. It screamed in Slovakian, something gut-tural and obscene. This vampire was old, and feral, almost animal-like. It was naked against the elements and the sinews of its arms and legs strained against the rock. Then it slowly started to inch onto the rock face. Without ropes or equipment, this thing adhered to the mountainside like an insect crawling along a wall.

I spotted a crevasse just below us and motioned to my compan-ions. We quickly climbed down and unhooked ourselves from the rope. The three of us now stood on a narrow ledge in front of the entrance to a mountain cave. There was little time to think as we ran into the cave with moments to spare.

The cave was pitch-black, and with only the illumination from a small flashlight, we raced through the tunnels, running blindly, not knowing where we were going or where the tunnels would lead us. The tunnel led into a larger chamber where we stopped, not knowing what this space was or what might be waiting for us. All of us now had our lights out and shone them against the cave walls. It was warmer in here than outside, but as far as we could tell, we were alone. Randall shone his light on the cave floor and I felt his arm nudge mine. I shone my light as well, followed by Mike D.

In the middle of the cave floor were scores of bodies, all drained of blood. Many were small children whom had been abducted from the village. The clothing spanned a variety of styles and probably as many decades. We even glimpsed what looked like a mountain climber from the 1920's. Our morbid curiosity was mixed with a growing fear as we realized that we had underestimated the danger of our expedition. It was also sinking in very quickly that this mountain was death. The realization was overwhelming.

Footsteps from the tunnel behind brought us back to our senses and we needed to fight or flee. We checked for weapons and really couldn't think of anything handy. Next we tried to spy an exit. There seemed to be a light coming from across the chamber but it would take us some time to reach it. Since neither of our first options seemed viable, I pointed to the chamber floor and motioned for us to try and hide beneath the heap of stacked corpses. As horrific as this sounded, it was the best alternative at the time. We found a place to hide and turned our lights off, praying that we wouldn't be discovered. Shortly, the sounds of many feet echoed through the chamber, then stopped. We heard some guttural utterances pass between the vampires, but we didn't know how many there were or their disposition.

Just as suddenly, they turned and were gone. From what we could guess, they went back down the tunnel but perhaps took a fork to another part of the cave. We quietly crawled out of our hideaway and slowly stood up. It seems that we were alone for the moment. Mike D. looked at us and motioned towards the distant exit we had spotted earlier. He whispered to me that he was going for it and wished us luck. He took the snowboard that he carried like a backpack and headed off. I hoped I would see him again. He had always been a good friend.

Randall and I stood in the chamber for a few minutes, letting our eyes adjust to the gloom. Our plan was to find another way out without running into any suckheads. I was really starting to hate those guys.

We quietly moved towards the mouth of the cave tunnel. From the inky blackness of the tunnel mouth in front of us, there suddenly appeared two red dots hovering six feet off the ground. We froze. The vampire stepped out of the tunnel entrance into the gloom of the chamber. It was the same one who had killed James and it had a smile on its face as it slowly approached us. Blood still dripped from its chin and it flicked its tongue over its fangs. We stood there in fear and awe, not knowing what to do.

As if remembering, Randall grabbed the small package we had all received and pulled out a vial of holy water. Unscrewing the cap, he threw it at the vampire. The open bottle struck it and then fell to the ground, breaking into hundreds of frozen pieces. The vampire looked at the shattered bottle and then back at us, muttered something in Slovakian, and laughed. The laugh was deep, but hollow as it resounded through the chamber.

In a panic, Randall pulled a cross from the package and held it in front of him to ward off the vampire. The vampire returned Randall's gaze and crossed itself in the manner of the Catholic tradition. It looked at me now with a quizzical expression as if to say, what have you got?

I drew my Cam-gun and shot a stake right at it, the stake hitting it in the shoulder. The vampire screamed as it fell backwards from the force.

We ran past the vampire as fast as we could, and back into the tunnel. Blindly taking turns, and running down tunnels, it felt as if we were descending, then ascending through the interior of the mountain. We turned a corner and there was a cave mouth facing the night sky. As we moved closer, we could feel the rush of mountain air on our faces. We stepped to the edge and saw that below us was a sheer drop of 2700 feet, but about twenty feet across from us was a rock wall. We decided that the rock wall offered a way out and we needed to do something quickly. Even now we could hear footfalls behind us.

I attached a rope line to the post and shot the Cam-gun to the opposite wall. I then attached the other end of the rope to another post and shot it into the wall beside the cave opening. Once I had closed my caribiner over the rope line, I stepped off the ledge and began to move hand-over-hand on the line to the opposite wall. I was nearing the middle of the line with Randall preparing to follow when our vampire pursuer suddenly reappeared. It wasn't in good humor. The post I had shot into it still protruded from its shoulder and a thin trickle of fluid slowly seeped from around the stake. It grabbed Randall by the throat with a bloody, clawed hand. Then it saw me dangling helplessly on the line and once again smiled.

We faced each other, me holding on to the rope with both hands for dear life and the vampire staring at me while holding Randall in a vise-like grip.

I yelled at the thing, telling it to let Randall go, then I asked it to leave us alone and finally pleaded with it for mercy. The anger and frustration I felt overwhelmed me and I felt powerless to do anything to help Randall or myself. The vampire took no action but merely stood there as Randall whimpered and tears ran down his face. Then without warning, it grabbed Randall's right arm and violently wrenched it out of its socket. Randall screamed and fainted as his right arm hung limp from his side. The vampire looked at me again. It took Randall's right arm again, and twisting it, tore it from his torso. Randall's eyes flew open for a moment and he let out one shriek of agony, but then he passed out again. The vampire delicately licked the blood seeping from Randall's shoulder and laughed.

I screamed at the horror I was witnessing and grabbed my walkie. I punched the button and screamed for someone to help me. The vampire felt secure that I wouldn't be leaving the mountain. It now took Randall's left arm in its hand, and in one violent motion, tore it from Randall's torso. The vampire threw Randall's arm at me and missed, but by only a few inches. My grip was becoming less certain on the rope and I started to lose hope. If it had to be, I would rather throw myself down into the inky blackness below than suffer the torture that Randall was being subjected to.

The vampire again regarded me and raised its eyebrows playfully. It was tearing Randall apart like a child might pull the wings from an insect, it had so little regard for us. The vampire grabbed Randall's right leg and twisted it until I could hear the bones cracking. Randall's leg separated from his torso like a drumstick being pulled off a turkey at Thanksgiving dinner. I threw up into the void, still not knowing how I maintained my grip on the rope. By this time I hoped Randall was dead so he wouldn't be subjected to any more pain.

As if hearing my thoughts, the vampire threw what was left of Randall's broken body over the edge and into the void. We now stared at one another and I knew it was my turn. The vampire stepped over to the rope line and gingerly grasped it, testing the tension. It then took the rope with both hands and began to pull it towards him. Its intention was to pull the rope and stake out of the cliff wall and reel me in like a fish once more. I could feel the incredible strength it possessed and in fear of what was to happen, I closed both of my eyes.

As I felt it tug on the rope, a thundering sound filled my ears, increasing in volume. I thought it was some new and diabolical trick the vampire was using to instill an even greater sense of panic in me. But then the rock face was filled with a blinding light. I stupidly thought I had died and gone to a better place but it was our helicopter. It crested over the peak, dropping gingerly to hover almost parallel to where I was suspended. I heard Daniel yell for me to jump. I swung my body towards the opened door of the helicopter and again felt myself take flight into the air. Strong arms caught me and pulled me into the interior of the helicopter as it accelerated upwards to safety.

I looked down at the vampire, whose silhouette became a speck on the mountainside. I could hear it scream and curse at my good fortune. I hugged Daniel and then quickly told him to locate Mike D. using the GPS tracker. The locator put him further down the mountain, approaching the tree line. With that the helicopter banked sharply and we headed off to find him.

It didn't take long to locate Mike D. He was moving down the slope at breakneck speed while being chased by a small group of vampires. They were incredibly fast but Mike D. was maneuvering brilliantly. He completed flips and *Ollies* and *Nollies* and spins and every other move that he knew to confuse and elude his pursuers. Whenever the suckheads were closing in on Mike D., he would back flip over them and turn in another direction. They couldn't catch him, and as Mike D. neared the tree line, the vampires melted into the darkness and were gone.

All the while, Dennis shot video of this incredible chase and softly responded to a front flip or *Poptart* with a "gnarly" or "whoa, cool."

New York – Two Weeks Later
Needless to say, when we finally came home, the network was very unhappy with me. I was slapped with a lawsuit for breach of contract and the families of James, Randall and Brian sued me for negligence and wrongful death, and I developed a serious drinking problem as well as a pretty messed up head. Mike D. however got his own extreme sports show on ESPN and the footage Daniel had shot made both of them viral video stars. I on the other hand, was screwed.

Los Angeles
It's been two years since the incident that took place on Gerlach Peak. I still wake up in a cold sweat, screaming, and after one of my panic attacks it takes a lot of booze to calm down.

Last night, I went to one of my favorite watering holes for a good buzz. I find it helps me to sleep better at night. It's a big club with a lot of people drinking and dancing; even on a weeknight. I prefer these kinds of spots. I don't like being alone anymore.

I was sitting at the bar minding my own business when I noticed someone looking at me from across the room. I turned and saw to my amazement that it was Brian. The last time I had seen him was right before he disappeared off the side of the mountain that first night. We thought he had been pulling a prank on us and now here he was in the club. I wasn't sure if I wanted to talk to him or walk over and punch his lights out. He was staring at me pretty intensely and I returned his stare, raising my bottle of beer and giving him a nod. He raised his hand in the air and gave me a surfer hang ten sign.

I couldn't help but smile.

Then he smiled, and that's when I saw the fangs and noticed the pale color of his face. I started to feel dizzy and closed my eyes for a second. When I opened them again, Brian was gone.

As I sat at the bar, I cried for the longest time, remembering what had happened on that mountain. I wonder what Brian must have gone through, and in a funny way, I feel more sorry for him than anyone else. I haven't seen him since and pray to God before going to sleep every night that I never will.

ABOUT THE WRITERS

Chris Deal writes from Huntersville, NC. He has been published in *Word Riot, Rotten Leaves, the Dead Mule School of Southern Literature*, and *Colored Chalk*, among others. His debut, *Cienfuegos*, will be published in early 2010 by Brown Paper Publishing.

David H. Donaghe lives and works in the high desert of southern California. He has three passions in life: reading, writing and riding his motorcycle. When not delving into a good book or putting his face in the wind on his motorcycle, he's writing short stories and novels. With 2 two short stories published so far, he is currently enjoying life and working on his next novel. Check out his other story in Dead Worlds Volume 5.

Christopher J. Dwyer is a writer from Boston, MA. His work has appeared in such publications as *Gold Dust Magazine, Red Fez, Twisted Tongue Magazine, Sex and Murder, Dogmatika, Colored Chalk* and various fiction anthologies. He is the co-editor of *Rotten Leaves* magazine. He can be reached through his official website: www.christopherdwyer.com or for free dark fiction go to www. rottenleaves.com

Anthony Giangregorio is the author and editor of more than 35 novels, almost all of them about zombies. His work has appeared in *Dead Science* by Coscomentertainment, *Dead Worlds: Undead Stories Volumes 1-5, Wolves of War* by LOTLD press. He also has stories in *End of Days: An Apocalyptic Anthology Volumes 1 & 2*, and 2 anthologies with Pill Hill Press. Check out his website at www.undeadpress.com.

Kelly M. Hudson grew up in the great Commonwealth of Kentucky and currently resides in California. He's written a lot of stuff, and if you're interested in seeing more, check out www.kellymhudson.com. His work has graciously appeared in *Dead Worlds, vol. 1-4, Book of the Dead, End of Days 1 and 2, Christmas Is Dead, The Death Panel*, and *The Bitter End*. Kelly thanks you for taking the time to read his story and really hopes you have a fine, fine day.

Nik Korpon is from Baltimore, MD. He likes to bang on the keyboard until something intelligible comes out, or his head hurts, whichever comes first. His stories have appeared in *3:AM, Out of the Gutter, Cause and Effect and TripleQuick* from Featherproof Books. He is a contributor for the Outsider Writer Collective and a Fiction Editor for ROTTEN LEAVES Magazine. He is writing his second novel. Visit him at www.nikkorpon.com

G.R. Mosca was born in Birmingham, England and is a graduate of Bard College. He currently resides in Thomasville, Pennsylvania with his companion Annalisa and their five cats. If you wish to contact G.R. Mosca, you can send an email to: grmosca@aol.com.

Edward J. Rathke lives in Minnesota where he is finishing his degree in behavioral neuroscience.

Jessy Marie Roberts lives in a "haunted" house in Western Nebraska with her husband and two dogs, Tucker and Snags. She grew up in Morgan Hill, California. She has several small stories published in small press venues, including Living Dead Press, with several more forthcoming. Her favorite "fictional" monster is the vampire and she enjoyed writing this tribute to the macabre genre.

Rob X Román (a.k.a. Doc Monster) is a published writer, artist and editor for books, comics, magazines and websites. He also moonlights as an animator. Check out his work at www.docmonster.com.

Caleb J Ross has been published widely and is the author of the story collection, *Charactered Pieces* (OW Press). He lives just outside Kansas City. He loves conversation. Visit his website and drop him a line: www.calebjross.com.

Tony Schaab is a 31-year-old fledgling writer, currently living in Indianapolis with his wife and dog. In addition to having short stories published in vampire and apocalyptic anthologies, Tony has a special affinity for the shambling undead: he runs a zombie-centric review blog, "Slight of the Living Dead," and is currently working on his first full-length novel, *"Zombies Can't Dance."* Visit him at http://tonyschaab.wordpress.com.

Axel Hassen Taiari is a French writer, born and raised in Paris. His work has appeared in various literary magazines around the world, and he is the creator and co-editor of *Rotten Leaves* magazine. He is currently finishing a noir science-fiction novel. Read more at www.axeltaiari.com and www.rottenleaves.com

Richard Thomas was the winner of the ChiZine Publications 2009 *"Enter the World of Filaria"* contest. His short story *"Maker of Flight"* was chosen by Filaria author Brent Hayward and Bram Stoker Award-Winning editor Brett Alexander Savory. Publishing credits include *Cemetery Dance* (Shivers VI, early 2010), *3:AM Magazine, Word Riot, Dogmatika, Troubadour 21, The Oddville Press, Colored Chalk, Cause and Effect, Gold Dust, Vain, Nefarious Muse* and *Opium.* He is a member of the Horror Writer's Association. Visit http://www.whatdoesnotkillme.com for more stories.

Spencer Wendleton is the author of *The Body Cartel,* a novel written under his penname Alan Spencer. He has also completed a number of other projects about zombies, super vampires, grave diggers from hell, psychologists helming deadly machines, and b-horror movies come to life. The author welcomes e-mails at alanspencer26@hotmail.com.

Simon West-Bulford lives in Essex England earning his keep as a Clinical Trials scientist. He is currently working on his fourth novel - *"The Soul Consortium"* www.simonwb.com.

DEAD RAGE
by Anthony Giangregorio
Book 2 in the Rage virus series!

An unknown virus spreads across the globe, turning ordinary people into bloodthirsty, ravenous killers.

Only a small percentage of the population is immune and soon become prey to the infected.

Amongst the infected comes a man, stricken by the virus, yet still retaining his grasp on reality. His need to destroy the *normals* becomes an obsession and he raises an army of killers to seek out and kill all who aren't *changed* like himself. A few survivors gather together on the outskirts of Chicago and find themselves running for their lives as the specter of death looms over all.

The Dead Rage virus will find you, no matter where you hide.

CHRISTMAS IS DEAD: A ZOMBIE ANTHOLOGY
Edited by Anthony Giangregorio

Twas the night before Christmas and all through the house, not a creature was stirring, not even a. . . zombie?

That's right; this anthology explores what would happen at Christmas time if there was a full blown zombie outbreak. Reanimated turkeys, zombie Santas, and demon reindeers that turn people into flesh-eating ghouls are just some of the tales you will find in this merry undead book. So curl up under the Christmas tree with a cup of hot chocolate, and as the fireplace crackles with warmth, get ready to have your heart filled with holiday cheer. But of course, then it will be ripped from your heaving chest and fed upon by blood-thirsty elves with a craving for human flesh! For you see, Christmas is Dead!

And you will never look at the holiday season the same way again.

BLOOD RAGE
(The Prequel to DEAD RAGE)
by Anthony Giangregorio

The madness descended before anyone knew what was happening. Perfectly normal people suddenly became rage-fueled killers, tearing and slicing their way across the city. Within hours, Chicago was a battlefield, the dead strewn in the streets like trash.

Stacy, Chad and a few others are just a few of the immune, unaffected by the virus but not to the violence surrounding them. The *changed* are ravenous, sweeping across Chicago and perhaps the world, destroying any *normals* they come across. Fire, slaughter, and blood rule the land, and the few survivors are now an endangered species.

This is the story of the first days of the Dead Rage virus and the brave souls who struggle to live just one more day.

When the smoke clears, and the *changed* have maimed and killed all who stand in their way, only the strong will remain.

The rest will be left to rot in the sun.

The Zombie in the Basement
by Anthony Giangregorio
Illustrated by Andrew Dawe-Collins

The spooky house at the end of the street was the one all the kids avoided. With its overgrown shrubs and weeds, the place was a modern day haunted house. Especially at night. So when Ricky sneaks into the yard to retrieve his favorite ball, he comes across something he'd only seen in movies and bad dreams. He sees a zombie in the basement window of the old house, but when he tells his friends, no one believes him. Ricky knows what he saw, that something lurks in the old house, something that isn't supposed to exist.

With his best friend Eric by his side, Ricky will find out the truth and prove to everyone that zombies are real. And when the night is done, everyone will know about the zombie in the basement.

Note: This book is for young adults and for those who are young at heart.

DEADFREEZE
by Anthony Giangregorio
THIS IS WHAT HELL WOULD BE LIKE IF IT FROZE OVER!

When an experimental serum for hypothermia goes horribly wrong, a small research station in the middle of Antarctica becomes overrun with an army of the frozen dead.

Now a small group of survivors must battle the arctic weather and a horde of frozen zombies as they make their way across the frozen plains of Antarctica to a neighboring research station.

What they don't realize is that they are being hunted by an entity whose sole reason for existing is vengeance; and it will find them wherever they run.

VISIONS OF THE DEAD
A ZOMBIE STORY
by Anthony & Joseph Giangregorio

Jake Roberts felt like he was the luckiest man alive.

He had a great family, a beautiful girlfriend, who was soon to be his wife, and a job, that might not have been the best, but it paid the bills.

At least until the dead began to walk.

Now Jake is fighting to survive in a dead world while searching for his lost love, Melissa, knowing she's out there somewhere.

But the past isn't dead, and as he struggles for an uncertain future, the past threatens to consume him. With the present a constant battle between the living and the dead, Jake finds himself slipping in and out of the past, the visions of how it all happened haunting him. But Jake knows Melissa is out there somewhere and he'll find her or die trying.

In a world of the living dead, you can never escape your past.

DEAD MOURNING: A ZOMBIE HORROR STORY
by Anthony Giangregorio

Carl Jenkins was having a run of bad luck. Fresh out of jail, his probation tenuous, he'd lost every job he'd taken since being released. So now was his last chance, only one more job to prevent him from going back to prison. Assigned to work in a funeral home, he accidentally loses a shipment of embalming fluid. With nothing to lose, he substitutes it with a batch of chemicals from a nearby factory.

The results don't go as planned, though. While his screw-up goes unnoticed, his machinations revive the cadavers in the funeral home, unleashing an evil on the world that it has not seen before. Not wanting to become a snack for the rampaging dead, he flees the city, joining up with other survivors. An old, dilapidated zoo becomes their haven, while the dead wait outside the walls, hungry and patient.

But Carl is optimistic, after all, he's still alive, right? Perhaps his luck has changed and help will arrive to save them all?

Unfortunately, unknown to him and the other survivors, a serial killer has fallen into their group, trapped inside the zoo with them.

With the undead army clamoring outside the walls and a murderer within, it'll be a miracle if any of them live to see the next sunrise.

On second thought, maybe Carl would've been better off if he'd just gone back to jail.

ROAD KILL: A ZOMBIE TALE
by Anthony Giangregorio
ORDER UP!

In the summer of 2008, a rogue comet entered earth's orbit for 72 hours. During this time, a strange amber glow suffused the sky.

But something else happened; something in the comet's tail had an adverse affect on dead tissue and the result was the reanimation of every dead animal carcass on the planet.

A handful of survivors hole up in a diner in the backwoods of New Hampshire while the undead creatures of the night hunt for human prey.

There's a new blue plate special at DJ's Diner and Truck Stop, and it's you!

DEAD WORLDS: Undead Stories
A Zombie Anthology Volume 2
Edited by Anthony Giangregorio

Welcome to a world where the dead walk and want nothing more than to feast on the living. The stories contained in this, the second volume of the Dead Worlds series, are filled with action, gore, and buckets and buckets of blood; plus a heaping side of entrails for those with a little extra hunger.

The stories contained within this volume are scribed by both the desiccated cadavers of seasoned veterans to the genre as well as fresh-faced corpses, each printed here for the first time; and all of them ready to dig in and please the most discerning reader.

So slap on a bib and prepare to get bloody, because you're about to read the best zombie stories this side of Hell!

THE DARK

by Anthony Giangregorio

DARKNESS FALLS

The darkness came without warning.

First New York, then the rest of United States, and then the world became enveloped in a perpetual night without end.

With no sunlight, eventually the planet will wither and die, bringing on a new Ice Age. But that isn't problem for the human race, for humanity will be dead long before that happens.

There is something in the dark, creatures only seen in nightmares, and they are on the prowl. Evolution has changed and man is no longer the dominant species. When we are children, we're told not to fear the dark, that what we believe to exist in the shadows is false.

Unfortunately, that is no longer true.

SOULEATER

by Anthony Giangregorio

Twenty years ago, Jason Lawson witnessed the brutal death of his father by something only seen in nightmares, something so horrible he'd blocked it from his mind.

Now twenty years later the creature is back, this time for his son.

Jason won't let that happen.

He'll travel to the demon's world, struggling every second to rescue his son from its clutches.

But what he doesn't know is that the portal will only be open for a finite time and if he doesn't return with his son before it closes, then he'll be trapped in the demon's dimension forever.

SEE HOW IT ALL BEGAN IN THE NEW DOUBLE-SIZED 460 PAGE SPECIAL EDITION!

DEADWATER: EXPANDED EDITION

by Anthony Giangregorio

Through a series of tragic mishaps, a small town's water supply is contaminated with a deadly bacterium that transforms the town's population into flesh eating ghouls.

Without warning, Henry Watson finds himself thrown into a living hell where the living dead walk and want nothing more than to feed on the living.

Now Henry's trying to escape the undead town before he becomes the next victim.

With the military on one side, shooting civilians on sight, and a horde of bloodthirsty zombies on the other, Henry must try to battle his way to freedom.

With a small group of survivors, including a beautiful secretary and a wise-cracking janitor to aid him, the ragtag group will do their best to stay alive and escape the city codenamed: **Deadwater**.

DEAD END: A ZOMBIE NOVEL
by Anthony Giangregorio
THE DEAD WALK!

Newspapers everywhere proclaim the dead have returned to feast on the living!

A small group of survivors hole up in a cellar, afraid to brave the masses of animated corpses, but when food runs out, they have no choice but to venture out into a world gone mad.

What they will discover, however, is that the fall of civilization has brought out the worst in their fellow man.

Cannibals, psychotic preachers and rapists are just some of the atrocities they must face.

In a world turned upside down, it is life that has hit a Dead End.

BOOK OF THE DEAD 2: NOT DEAD YET
A ZOMBIE ANTHOLOGY
Edited by Anthony Giangregorio

Out of the ashes of death and decay, comes the second volume filled with the walking dead.

In this tomb, there are only slow, shambling monstrosities that were once human.

No one knows why the dead walk; only that they do, and that they are hungry for human flesh.

But these aren't your neighbors, your co-workers, or your family.
Now they are the living dead, and they will tear your throat out at a moment's notice.

So be warned as you delve into the pages of this book; the dead will find you, no matter where you hide.

THE MONSTER UNDER THE BED
by Anthony Giangregorio

Rupert was just one of many monsters that inhabit the human world, scaring children before bed. Only Rupert wanted to play with the children he was forced to scare.

When Rupert meets Timmy, an instant friendship is born. Running away from his abusive step-father, Timmy leaves home, embarking on a journey that leads him to New York City.

On his way, Timmy will realize that the true monsters are other adults who are just waiting to take advantage of a small boy, all alone in the big city.

Can Rupert save him?
Or will Timmy just become another statistic.

The Lazarus Culture

by Pasquale J. Morrone

Secret Service Agent Christopher Kearns had no idea what he was up against. Assigned on a temporary basis to the Center for Disease Control, he only knew that somehow it was connected to the lives of those the agency protected...namely, the President of the United States. If there were possible terrorist activities in the making, he could only guess it was at a red alert basis.

When Kearns meets and befriends Doctor Marlene Peterson of the Breezy Point Medical Center in Maryland, he soon finds that science fiction can indeed become a reality. In a solitary room walked a man with no vital signs: dead. The explanation he received came from Doctor Lee Fret, a man assigned to the case from the CDC. Something was attached to the brain stem. Something alive that was quickly spreading rapidly through Maryland and other states.

Kearns and his ragtag army of agents and medical personnel soon find themselves in a world of meaningless slaughter and mayhem. The armies of the walking dead were far more than mere zombies. Some began to change into whatever it was they ate. The government had found a way to reanimate the dead by implanting a parasite found on the tongue of the Red Snapper to the human brain.

It looked good on paper, but it was a project straight from Hell.

The dead now walked, but it wasn't a mystery.

It was The Lazarus Culture.

END OF DAYS: AN APOCALYPTIC ANTHOLOGY VOLUMES 1 & 2

Our world is a fragile place.

Meteors, famine, floods, nuclear war, solar flares, and hundreds of other calamities can plunge our small blue planet into turmoil in an instant.

What would you do if tomorrow the sun went super nova or the world was swallowed by water, submerging the world into the cold darkness of the ocean? This anthology explores some of those scenarios and plunges you into total annihilation.

But remember, it's only a book, and tomorrow will come as it always does. Or will it?

DEADFALL

by Anthony Giangregorio

It's Halloween in the small suburban town of Wakefield, Mass.

While parents take their children trick or treating and others throw costume parties, a swarm of meteorites enter the earth's atmosphere and crash to earth.

Inside are small parasitic worms, no larger than maggots.

The worms quickly infect the corpses at a local cemetery and so begins the rise of the undead.

The walking dead soon get the upper hand, with no one believing the truth. That the dead now walk.

Will a small group of survivors live through the zombie apocalypse?

Or will they, too, succumb to the Deadfall.

THE WAR AGAINST THEM: A ZOMBIE NOVEL
by Jose Alfredo Alfredo Vazquez

Mankind wasn't prepared for the onslaught.

An ancient organism is reanimating the dead bodies of its victims, creating worldwide chaos and panic as the disease spreads to every corner of the globe. As governments struggle to contain the disease, courageous individuals across the planet learn what it truly means to make choices as they struggle to survive.

Geopolitics meet technology in a race to save mankind from the worst threat it has ever faced. Doctors, military and soldiers from all walks of life battle to find a cure. For the dead walk, and if not stopped, they will wipe out all life on Earth. Humanity is fighting a war they cannot win, for who can overcome Death itself? Man versus the walking dead with the winner ruling the planet. Welcome to *The War Against Them*.

BOOK OF THE DEAD
A ZOMBIE ANTHOLOGY VOL 1
ISBN 978-1-935458-25-8
Edited by Anthony Giangregorio

This is the most faithful, truest zombie anthology ever written, and we invite you along for the ride. Every single story in this book is filled with slack-jawed, eyes glazed, slow moving, shambling zombies set in a world where the dead have risen and only want to eat the flesh of the living. In these pages, the rules are sacrosanct. There is no deviation from what a zombie should be or how they came about. The Dead Walk.

There is no reason, though rumors and suppositions fill the radio and television stations. But the only thing that is fact is that the walking dead are here and they will not go away. So prepare yourself for the ultimate homage to the master of zombie legend. And remember... Aim for the head!

ANOTHER EXCITING ADVENTURE IN THE DEADWATER SERIES!
DEAD SALVATION
BOOK 9
by Anthony Giangregorio
HANGMAN'S NOOSE!

After one of the group is hurt, the need for transportation is solved by a roving cannie convoy. Attacking the camp, the companions save a man who invites them back to his home.

Cement City it's called and at first the group is welcomed with thanks for saving one of their own. But when a bar fight goes wrong, the companions find themselves awaiting the hangman's noose.

Their only salvation is a suicide mission into a raider camp to save captured townspeople. Though the odds are long, it's a chance, and Henry knows in the land of the walking dead, sometimes a chance is all you can hope for.

In the world of the dead, life is a struggle, where the only victor is death.

REVOLUTION OF THE DEAD
by Anthony Giangregorio
THE DEAD SHALL RISE AGAIN!

Five years ago, a deadly plague wiped out 97% of the world's population, America suffering tragically. Bodies were everywhere, far too many to bury or burn. But then, through a miracle of medical science, a way is found to reanimate the dead.

With the manpower of the United States depleted, and the remaining survivors not wanting to give up their internet and fast food restaurants, the undead are conscripted as slave labor.

Now they cut the grass, pick up the trash, and walk the dogs of the surviving humans.

But whether alive or dead, no race wants to be controlled, and sooner or later the dead will fight back, wanting the freedom they enjoyed in life.

The revolution has begun!

And when it's over, the dead will rule the land, and the remaining humans will become the slaves...or worse.

KINGDOM OF THE DEAD
by Anthony Giangregorio
THE DEAD HAVE RISEN!

In the dead city of Pittsburgh, two small enclaves struggle to survive, eking out an existence of hand to mouth.

But instead of working together, both groups battle for the last remaining fuel and supplies of a city filled with the living dead.

Six months after the initial outbreak, a lone helicopter arrives bearing two more survivors and a newborn baby. One enclave welcomes them, while the other schemes to steal their helicopter and escape the decaying city.

With no police, fire, or social services existing, the two will battle for dominance in the steel city of the walking dead. But when the dust settles, the question is: will the remaining humans be the winners, or the losers?

When the dead walk, the line between Heaven and Hell is so twisted and bent there is no line at all.

RISE OF THE DEAD
by Anthony Giangregorio
DEATH IS ONLY THE BEGINNING!

In less than forty-eight hours, more than half the globe was infected.
In another forty-eight, the rest would be enveloped.
The reason?
A science experiment gone horribly wrong which enabled the dead to walk, their flesh rotting on their bones even as they seek human prey.
Jeremy was an ordinary nineteen year old slacker. He partied too much and had done poorly in high school. After a night of drinking and drugs, he awoke to find the world a very different place from the one he'd left the night before.

The dead were walking and feeding on the living, and as Jeremy stepped out into a world gone mad, the dead spotting him alone and unarmed in the middle of the street, he had to wonder if he would live long enough to see his twentieth birthday.

ANOTHER EXCITING ADVENTURE IN THE DEADWATER SERIES!
DEAD SALVATION
BOOK 9
by Anthony Giangregorio
HANGMAN'S NOOSE!

After one of the group is hurt, the need for transportation is solved by a roving cannie convoy. Attacking the camp, the companions save a man who invites them back to his home.

Cement City it's called and at first the group is welcomed with thanks for saving one of their own. But when a bar fight goes wrong, the companions find themselves awaiting the hangman's noose.

Their only salvation is a suicide mission into a raider camp to save captured townspeople.

Though the odds are long, it's a chance, and Henry knows in the land of the walking dead, sometimes a chance is all you can hope for.

In the world of the dead, life is a struggle, where the only victor is death.

THE CHRONICLES OF JACK PRIMUS
BOOK ONE
by Michael D. Griffiths

Beneath the world of normalcy we all live in lies another world, one where supernatural beings exist.

These creatures of the night hunt us; want to feed on our very souls, though only a few know of their existence.

One such man is Jack Primus, who accidentally pierces the veil between this world and the next. With no other choice if he wants to live, he finds himself on the run, hunted by beings called the Xemmoni, an ancient race that sees humans as nothing but cattle.   They want his soul, to feed on his very essence, and they will kill all who stand in their way.   But if they thought Jack would just lie down and accept his fate, they were sorely mistaken.

He didn't ask for this battle, but he knew he would fight them with everything at his disposal, for to lose is a fate worse than death.

He would win this war, and he would take down anyone who got in his way.

LOVE IS DEAD: A ZOMBIE ANTHOLOGY
Edited by Anthony Giangregorio
THE DEATH OF LOVE

Valentine's Day is a day when young love is fulfilled.

Where hopeful young men bring candy and flowers to their sweethearts, in hopes of a kiss...or perhaps more. But not in this anthology.

For you see, LOVE IS DEAD, and in this tome, the dead walk, wanting to feed on those same hearts that once pumped in chests, bursting with love.

So toss aside that heart-shaped box of candy and throw away those red roses, you won't need them any longer. Instead, strap on a handgun, or pick up a shotgun and defend yourself from the ravenous undead.

Because in a world where the dead walk, even love isn't safe.

Now Available From Pill Hill Press

Coming Soon From Pill Hill Press

Visit Pill Hill Press online at
www.pillhillpress.com